Praise for the Cronus Chronicles Book One
The Shadow Thieves:

"[G]enuinely creates excitement not only about itself but
about what might follow."
—*Chicago Tribune*

"[A] flashy debut . . . Ursu draws her characters with broad,
nimble-witted strokes."
—*Kirkus Reviews*

"Ursu tantalizingly tells her tale."
—*Publishers Weekly*

"A fast-paced action adventure . . .
this Greek-themed frolic is set apart."
—*Horn Book*

"[E]xtraordinary."
—*School Library Journal*

"[The Shadow Thieves] unwinds with
unabashed cheerfulness and gusto."
— *Booklist*

"[A] humorous and slightly creepy adventure. . . .
Readers will anxiously await the promised sequels."
—*Bulletin of the Center for Children's Books*

D0970982

THE SHADOW THIEVES

THE CRONUS CHRONICLES • BOOK ONE

Anne Ursu

SCHOLASTIC INC.
New York Toronto London Auckland Sydney
Mexico City New Delhi Hong Kong Buenos Aires

No part of this publication may be reproduced, stored in a retrieval system,
or transmitted in any form or by any means, electronic, mechanical, photocopying,
recording, or otherwise, without written permission of the publisher. For information
regarding permission, write to Aladdin Paperbacks, Simon & Schuster Children's
Publishing Division, 1230 Avenue of the Americas, New York, NY 10020.

ISBN-13: 978-0-545-04296-3
ISBN-10: 0-545-04296-8

Text copyright © 2006 by Anne Ursu
Illustrations copyright © 2006 by Eric Fortune
All rights reserved. Published by Scholastic Inc., 557 Broadway, New York, NY 10012,
by arrangement with Aladdin Paperbacks, Simon & Schuster Children's Publishing Division.
SCHOLASTIC and associated logos are trademarks and/or registered trademarks
of Scholastic Inc. Lexile is a registered trademark of MetaMetrics, Inc.

12 11 10 9 8 7 6 5 4 3 2 1   7 8 9 10 11 12/0

Printed in the U.S.A.   40

First Scholastic printing, November 2007

Designed by Ann Zeak
The text of this book was set in Hoefler Text.

For my HUSBAND
who tells me stories

Contents

PART FOUR: The Beginning of the End

PART ONE

We Begin in the Middle

CHAPTER I

Charlotte

Pay attention. Watch carefully, now. Look at the sidewalk, there. See that girl—the one with the bright red hair, overstuffed backpack, and aura of grumpiness? That's Charlotte Mielswetzski. (Say it with me: Meals-wet-ski. Got it? If not, say it again: *Meals. Wet. Ski.* There. You thought your name was bad?) And something extraordinary is about to happen to her.

No, the extraordinary event will not be related to that man watching her behind the oak tree . . . that oddly pale, strangely thin, freakishly tall, yellow-eyed, bald-headed man in the tuxedo. (And while we're at it, why on Earth would anyone be wearing a tuxedo at four o'clock on an unseasonably warm October afternoon? And if you are going to wear such an outfit at such a time on such a day, surely it is not because you are going to hide behind oak trees to spy on small, pale, freckled thirteen-year-old redheaded girls with bulging back-packs, is it? Because that would be really strange.) But regardless, it's not about him, not yet. He will come later. Forget him. Focus on Charlotte. Charlotte is walk-ing home from school, and she is in a very bad mood.

Of course, this has all already happened, there is nothing we can do about any of it now, alas—so if we're to be accurate, we should say: Charlotte *was* walking home from school in a very bad mood while the four-o'clock sun cast long shadows over the sidewalk, entirely unaware of the white-skinned, yellow-eyed man in the tuxedo watching her from behind the oak tree.

And no, the bad mood was not, in itself, extra-ordinary. At the time you could often find Charlotte with a black cloud hanging over her head—though a purely metaphorical one—what with the new school year and the piles of homework and the creepy new English teacher and the tremendously banal class-mates, and today her mood was even worse than usual, given that the cast list for the school play had been posted and her name was distinctly not on it and she hadn't been planning on trying out for the stupid thing because she knew she wouldn't get cast and then she did try out, and see? So if Charlotte seemed extremely grumpy—if she was, in fact, muttering to herself darkly—you would have to forgive her. As for the dark mutterings, they would have been hard to decipher if you had been, say, hiding behind a tree spying on her, but we know they went something like this:

"Once upon a time there was a girl named Charlotte who suffered from a terrible curse. She didn't know how or why she'd been cursed, but she did know that nothing good ever, ever, ever happened to her."

You get the point. So anyway, there she was, walking along in an ordinary way, muttering to herself about curses, with her bursting backpack and her metaphorical black cloud and her ordinary bad mood—when something extraordinary happened.

A kitten appeared in front of her.

Not—*poof!*—not like that. Nothing magical at all. Quite ordinary, in fact. A normal chain of events, just what you would expect with a sudden appearance of a kitten. There was this high-pitched squeaking from the bushes and then this flurry of motion, and just as Charlotte was processing these events, suddenly there—directly in her path, right in her shadow, in fact—stood a blue-eyed gray and white kitten.

Charlotte stopped. The kitten stared at Charlotte. Charlotte stared at the kitten. The kitten cocked its head.

"Hi!" said Charlotte, her green eyes softening.

"Meow," said the kitten.

And Charlotte, being of sound mind, reached down and petted the kitten. She scratched it under its chin, then behind the ears for good measure, and then she started on her way home.

"Bye, kitty," called Charlotte.

"Meow!" said the kitten. And the next thing Charlotte knew, the kitten was standing in front of her again, blocking her path and meowing rather insistently.

"Now, kitty," said Charlotte, "I have to go home. Do you have any idea how much homework I have? You should go home too."

The kitten looked at her blankly. Charlotte began to walk on, but once again the kitten ran up and stood in front of her. Charlotte tilted her head and considered. The kitten was awfully skinny.

"Do you have a home?" asked Charlotte uncertainly.

"Meow," said the kitten.

That seemed like a no. Charlotte regarded the kitten frankly. The kitten, in turn, regarded her. There seemed to be only one thing to do.

"Would you like to come home with me?" asked Charlotte.

"Meow," said the kitten.

So that was that. Charlotte picked up the blue-eyed gray and white kitten, tucked it under her thin, pale, freckly arm, and headed home, suddenly feeling that the world was perhaps not so tiresome, if you only looked hard enough.

Now, stray kittens are not, in themselves, an extraordinary phenomenon. And given events that were to follow, finding one would seem positively mundane. But if you were Charlotte, and you had been feeling that life was some cosmic joke that had no punch line, and in the space of a moment you had gone from being Charlotte-without-a-kitten to being Charlotte-with-a-kitten, you too would have found it nothing short of remarkable. (Even if you did not notice that as soon as you picked up the kitten, the man in the inappropriate tuxedo shook his head slowly and skulked off into the shadows.)

When Charlotte arrived home, she found her parents seated in the kitchen, talking. This was not unusual; Charlotte's father taught at the high school and was often home when she got there, and her mother worked from an office on the second floor of the Mielswetzski house for half of the week. Charlotte's mother was a child psychologist who wrote books on adolescence and was very concerned with Charlotte's well-being. This was not always as advantageous as it sounds.

For instance, just last week Charlotte had come home from school to find her mother perched all too casually in the kitchen, pretending she was not, in fact, waiting for Charlotte. But she totally was. Charlotte knew the signs; her mother was not casual about *anything.*

That day the topic of conversation was, not surprisingly, Charlotte and her attitude. Said topic was a particular favorite of Charlotte's mom's; no one in the history of the world ever liked to talk about anything as much as Charlotte's mom liked to talk about Charlotte's attitude. Charlotte thought her mother should be given some kind of plaque or something, or maybe there should be a statue—except the statue would probably want to talk about Charlotte's attitude too.

So anyway, when Charlotte got home from school that day, her mother just happened to be sitting in the kitchen reading, and the kitchen was not really that comfortable a place to be reading, but that's beside the point. And when her mother offered to make her a snack, Charlotte thought for a moment about pretending she had somewhere else to be, but she knew the best thing to do would be to let her make the snack and get this over with.

"So, Char . . . ," her mother said casually, unscrewing the peanut butter lid. "I hear the school play auditions are coming up. . . ."

How did she possibly hear that? Charlotte wondered. One thing about her mother is she has way too many friends.

"Are you thinking of auditioning?" she asked, opening the box of crackers.

Charlotte raised an eyebrow. Hi, Mom, have we met?

"Because I thought maybe you should," she said, spreading the peanut butter on the crackers. "You used to love acting when you were little." She smiled and brought Charlotte the plate.

Charlotte shrugged. "Aw, Mom, I'd never get in."

"Char, honey, how would you know unless you tried?" she said, sitting down opposite her daughter. "You should try!"

"I just know, Mom," she grumbled, tossing her long hair. It was true. In elementary school Charlotte had loved drama class, had loved being in the school plays, and had even gone to a summer day camp where they learned some of the songs from *Annie*. And then she got to middle school and auditioned for the play and the choir and tried out for the softball and gymnastics teams and didn't get in any of them. That was enough of that. Charlotte could see very quickly where the bread was buttered; she might be a loser, but she was no idiot. The world gave you enough disappointment without actually going out and *asking* for it.

"I know you're upset about not getting in before," her mom continued, "but you were a sixth grader then, and they rarely cast sixth graders. You're in eighth grade now. You should try. What's the harm in trying?"

Charlotte shrugged.

"Honey"—Mrs. Mielswetzski leaned in and grabbed Charlotte's hands—"if only you could see what I see! You're so bright and talented. You can do whatever you set your mind on doing. The whole world is your oyster."

Charlotte sighed inwardly. She knew her mother was serious when she started referring to shellfish. What did that mean, anyway? What's so great about the world being your oyster? Does that mean it's really hard to open, and when you do, you have something slimy and gross on the inside?

"Char, I just wish, sometimes . . . that you'd try a little harder. In everything. I feel like you're always running away from things. I wish you'd live your life, really go out there and live it. All your teachers say you have so much potential. If you'd just . . . use it."

Charlotte had to restrain herself from rolling her eyes. Teachers loved to say people had potential; that's what teachers did to keep themselves from getting canned. What were they supposed to say—*I'm sorry, your kid has no promise whatsoever? She's utterly mediocre in every way?*

"It would be fun to be in a play, wouldn't it?" Mrs. Mielswetzski continued. "You could meet some new people."

Charlotte grimaced. Meeting new people had been another one of her mother's favorite conversation topics ever since Charlotte's best friend, Caitlin, moved to Russia over the summer and left Charlotte and their friend Maddy behind. That's right, Russia. Caitlin's parents were English-as-a-second-language teachers, and they decided to take two-year jobs teaching English to Russian orphans, or some absurd thing like that. Who does that? And even if you do do that, can't you teach English to orphans in a place that has e-mail?

Well anyway, "meeting new people" was often a subset of "trying harder" and "getting involved" and "having a better attitude," and frankly Charlotte was tired of it all. She'd been hearing about this so much that she would do anything to stop it. Anything.

"Okay, Mom."

"What?" her mother started.

"Okay . . . I'll audition."

Mrs. Mielswetzski clasped her hands together. "Oh, Charlotte, that's wonderful! You'll have so much fun!"

She was actually beaming. Charlotte hadn't seen her look that happy in months. And something about the particular light emanating from her mother's face warmed Charlotte, and she felt suddenly different about the world. Yes, she would have fun! Yes, she could try! For the world was a place where you put yourself out there, where you tried things, and even if your best friend since you were four had just moved to the former Soviet Union, there were all kinds of people whose parents didn't want to teach orphans, and maybe they were worth meeting.

That mood lasted until Charlotte saw the cast list, on which her name was very distinctly absent and the names of some of her more banal classmates were very distinctly present, and Charlotte realized that she had been duped, and she was never ever going to put herself out there again, never going to "try harder," never going to "improve her attitude," and certainly never ever going to "meet new people." Why would she want to meet new people when the people she already knew were asking her to humiliate herself? So she had planned to tell her mother when she got home from school on this day—that, and that this was all her mother's fault and she was never listening to her ever, ever again.

But of course she forgot all of that as soon as she picked up the kitten, and when she saw her parents in the kitchen, instead of wanting to yell or flee, she was absolutely delighted—for she could tell them about the world and all its extraordinary kittenesque things. She did not know that they had been waiting for her for quite some time because they, too, had news—news that they promptly forgot when they saw the gray and white creature in their daughter's arms.

"Oh!" said her mother.

"Oh!" said her father.

"She followed me home," said Charlotte.

"Well, she probably belongs to someone," said her mother.

"Almost certainly," said her father.

"Look at her fur! It's all dirty," said Charlotte.

"We'll put up signs," said her mother.

"And put a classified in the paper," said her father.

"Look how skinny she is," said Charlotte.

"She might have worms," said her mother.

"She might have rabies," said her father.

"Well, we should take her to the vet," said Charlotte.

"Yes, we should!" said her mother.

"Right away," said her father.

While Mr. Mielswetzski called the vet and then checked the newspaper classifieds, and Mrs. Mielswetzski called the lost and found at the Humane Society— for these are steps everyone should take when finding a kitten, because someone may be missing it very much—Charlotte opened a can of tuna for her new friend.

"What's your name?" asked Charlotte.

"Meow," said the kitten.

"Are you a girl kitten or a boy kitten?" asked Charlotte.

"Meow," said the kitten.

"Do you want to go to the vet?"

"Meow," said the kitten.

The vet could see them right away, so the Mielswetzskis piled into the car. It was not an hour later that Charlotte found that her kitten was a girl (Charlotte had thought so), did not have rabies (good), did have worms (nothing some pills wouldn't take care of), was certainly underfed (poor kitty), and was likely a stray. They should put up signs and put an ad in the newspaper, but if no one claimed the kitten for one month, she would be an official member of the family.

Charlotte was not worried. They could put up all the signs and take out all the ads they wanted. The kitten had chosen her—it was fate, and Charlotte knew it. Charlotte might not be good for choirs or plays or school or sports or good attitudes or new people, but she knew that she was good for kittens. And kittens were most certainly good for Charlotte.

Mr. and Mrs. Mielswetzski were good parents and

good people, and while perhaps they would not have thought to go out and get themselves a cat—the time was never quite right, maybe next year, maybe for Christmas, it's important not to rush into anything—if one were to fall into their laps, they would certainly let it stay there.

"She *is* awfully cute," said Charlotte's father on the way home from the vet.

"We better not get too attached," said her mother.

"But it would sure be nice," said her father.

"Well, there's no doubt about that," said her mother.

"We should pick up some supplies," said her father.

"Oh, yes," said her mother. "The cat will need supplies."

And pretty soon the Mielswetzskis had not only a cat, but two ceramic cat dishes, a bag of premium kitten food, one scratching post, some clumping litter, a litter box with a hood, assorted balls and accoutrements, three toy mice, two boxes of catnip, and one sorely needed soft-bristled brush.

"What are you going to call her?" asked her father, putting the bags in the car.

"At least until she's claimed," said her mother, getting into the front seat.

"Bartholomew," said Charlotte.

It just came out of her mouth—"Bartholomew"—

but maybe that, too, was fate. Because Bartholomew is an excellent name for a cat, even if the cat is a girl cat and Bartholomew is a boy's name. Because cats need names, even if you are going to pretend the cat is temporary (when you know it is not). Because you can shorten it to Mew, which is really the most fabulous nickname for a cat ever. And because Bartholomew was currently curled up fast asleep on Charlotte's lap.

"Once upon a time there was a cat with no home," Charlotte whispered to Mew. "And there was a girl with a home but no cat. But then the cat found the girl, and the girl took the cat to her home, and then they moved to Prague together and opened a coffee shop and lived happily ever after."

But Bartholomew was not the only surprise in store for Charlotte that day. At dinner that night—take-out Chinese food from the restaurant next to the pet store—Mrs. Mielswetzski suddenly slapped her forehead.

"Oh!" she said, looking at her husband.

"Oh!" said Mr. Mielswetzski, looking at his wife.

"We completely forgot."

"In all the excitement!"

"We have news."

"Good news!"

"At least we hope you think it's good news," said Mrs. Mielswetzski.

"I'm sure she will," said Mr. Mielswetzski.

"Well, you never know."

"Oh, she'll be thrilled!"

Charlotte waited. It often took her parents some time to get to the point. Sometimes she thought that they were actually one person who had been divided into male and female parts by a mad scientist. Anyway, she was in no hurry; her parents' idea of good news did not quite match her own—it tended to involve an outing to History Days or a bout of family therapy. Besides, no news could possibly be better than the news currently curled up on the bench right next to her. Charlotte let her hand rest on Mew's softly breathing belly.

"Well," said Mrs. Mielswetzski, "I've been talking to Uncle John. . . ."

Charlotte perked up. Uncle John and Aunt Suzanne lived in London with their son, Zachary, who was Charlotte's age. The Millers had all come over one summer when Charlotte was six—Charlotte had vague memories of kicking around a soccer ball with her cousin, who kept insisting on calling it a football, and at the time she had thought he was very, very stupid. In the last couple of years Charlotte had repeatedly tried to convince her parents to go to London to visit them—not that she was desperate to visit family she barely remembered, but she was quite interested in going to England. The Mielswetzskis kept saying they might go sometime, when the time was right, maybe next year, maybe for Christmas. Charlotte almost had them convinced this summer, but then Aunt Suzanne's mother died, and Charlotte's mother and father said it wouldn't be right. Charlotte wanted to go to London so badly—life certainly couldn't be so banal in London. She had thought maybe she could even spend a year there sometime, and then she would "try harder" and "meet new people" and "have a better attitude." Someday she was going to live there and take photography lessons; her mother said she'd send her to photography lessons right where they were. That totally missed the point. London sounded like the coolest place in the world—though, let's face it, anything for Charlotte would have been better than where she was.

"Well," Charlotte's mother smiled, "Uncle John is going to be transferred back here in the winter! They're going to live right near us. The whole family."

Charlotte tried to mask her disappointment. So much for her glamorous new life abroad. She scratched Mew's ears comfortingly.

"But that's not all," her mother said. "Uncle John and Aunt Suzanne didn't want Zachary to have to start at a new school in the winter. So . . ." She held out her hands expansively. "Your cousin is going to come live with us. Isn't that great?"

Charlotte blinked. *Great* wasn't quite the word. *Bad* wasn't the word either, by any means. It was neither great nor bad, it was entirely without greatness or badness. It was neutral. It simply was. Like school lunch or piano lessons, her cousin's impending arrival seemed to be just a fact of life, one more ordinary thing in what had been—until just that afternoon—an exasperatingly ordinary life.

But Charlotte tried to be enthusiastic for the sake of her mother, and her father smiled at her and said, "See? I knew she'd be delighted." And her mother beamed and said, "Oh, honey. It will be like you have a brother!" And Charlotte smiled and did not say a word, not a word; everything she had to say was expressed by her hand on her kitten's gently humming back.

So all was well in the Mielswetzski house. Charlotte was happy, for the first time in months, and her parents were happy too. They believed everything that they had said to their daughter about Uncle John's transfer and about the reasons for Zachary's sudden move. They had no reason not to; the story certainly made sense. But the fact is, Uncle John had not quite been honest with his sister. He was going to be transferred in the winter, yes, and the whole family would be moving, yes. But he did not mention that he had actually requested the transfer and that winter was the soonest he could get it. He did not mention that the whole reason for the transfer was to move his son away, as soon as possible, and the fact that he was being abruptly taken out of his school and shipped off to America had nothing to do with his education. So Mr. and Mrs. Mielswetzski could not be blamed at all—the liar here was Uncle John. But you must not be too hard on him. He was desperate.

CHAPTER 2

Mr. Metos

CHARLOTTE WAS ONE MONTH INTO THE SCHOOL YEAR
at Hartnett Preparatory School, and thus far the year
had proved to be just like all the other years, except
more so. Eight of the girls in her class, whose names all
began with *A*, had left for the summer as brunettes and
had come back as blondes. They paraded through the
hallways like an eerie airhead cult, and just as their hair
had lightened, they seemed to have faded a little—they
had lost form, character, color, as if their very atoms had
spread out and could barely be distinguished from the
walls around them. Charlotte wondered if they had all

fallen victim to some elaborate brainwashing scheme. She didn't know whether to feel proud that she had escaped that fate or insulted that the brainwasher didn't want her.

But the girls' transformation was far overshadowed by that of identical twins Lewis and Larry Larson, who had gone to fat camp and come back shadows of their former selves. The change had thrown all of the rest of the boys into a strange predicament—since Lewis and Larry had once been tremendously fat, the other boys had, in their banal way, believed the twins should be teased, but since Lewis and Larry were no longer fat, the boys could find nothing to tease them about. This quandary had thrown the eighth-grade males into a state of dull disquiet as they pondered the nebulous nature of the universe.

So the girls had faded and the boys were in a state of constant melancholic unease, and thus there spread a pall over the entire eighth grade.

All the teachers noticed it. Nobody shouted out the answers in class anymore, nobody even raised his hand. Attempts at discussion resulted in vast silences; lectures were greeted with glassy-eyed stares. The most vibrant and popular students seemed to be living inside a gigantic ball of existential goo.

One by one the teachers changed their approach.

Even the most mild mannered of them became fierce and confrontational, sending an unrelenting barrage of questions into the classroom, picking out defenseless students and daring them not to answer.

Charlotte found it all extremely annoying. She had been able to get through her school years without attracting attention either way thus far. She, as a practice, raised her hand in class once a week—enough so the teachers didn't get suspicious that she wasn't doing the work, but not so much that they might actually expect anything of her. It was a delicate balance.

Charlotte did a good portion of her schoolwork usually, whatever was required to keep her out of trouble, which was all she really cared about. Last night, of course, Charlotte hadn't done a lick of work because of all the kitten-related excitement. There'd been so much to do! She'd had to call her friend Maddy and take pictures to send to Caitlin (which would probably arrive next summer), and then she'd had to watch the kitten as she played with some invisible something that went darting all around the living room, and then she'd had to provide a lap for Mew to snooze on once all that darting around was done. It was a lot of responsibility and did not leave time for doing algebra equations or reading about the causes of World War I. So Charlotte simply approached her teachers and told them the truth.

"Mr. Crapf," she told her math teacher, "I didn't do the homework last night. My mom sprained her ankle and we took her to the emergency room and it took forever, and by the time we got home, it was really late and I had to help Mom."

"Your poor mother!" said Mr. Crapf. "Is she all right?"

"Yeah. She's elevating it. It should be much better in a few days."

"Well, tell her to feel better. You can make up the assignment when you have time."

"Oh, of course! Thanks a lot!"

As for history, Ms. Bristol-Lee had taken to giving them pop quizzes, which seemed awfully un-American to Charlotte. So Charlotte turned the quiz over and wrote a long letter to Ms. Bristol-Lee about how her parents were fighting and it was a really hard time for her right now and she just wasn't able to focus on her reading, but she was trying, she was trying really hard, and she was seeing a counselor to help her through this difficult time, but reading about world war was more than she could take right now.

Okay, so not the truth, exactly. To Charlotte, truth was a flexible instrument, one that could readily be shaped to fit her needs. Charlotte may not have been, in her own estimation, good for much else, but she could talk her way out of any situation. It was a useful skill in a world that was constantly expecting more out of you than you wanted to give. And usually a good story was so much more interesting than the truth.

As for her classmates, Charlotte had been cutting an even wider swath around them than usual this year. Charlotte did not think much of existential angst or artificial hair color. She would certainly never alter her own hair; Charlotte was not one of those redheaded heroines who bemoaned her fiery locks. She had no desire to fake blond highlights or, as her mother's stylist had suggested, tone down her color with some nutmeg shades. If you were to ask Charlotte for one adjective with which to describe herself, she would say, "Redhead." And that was that.

She was a redhead, and she did not truck with teasing boys or tinting girls. She and her friends could not be bothered with social structure; they had their own pursuits—Caitlin (when she was still there) had her music, Maddy had her straight A's, and Charlotte had her hair.

In a week Charlotte would also have a cousin from England, which would be interesting. Zachary was black, too, and that would confuse everyone for a while, as Charlotte was not. ("Is he adopted?" people would always ask when they saw pictures. No, silly. Her uncle had married a black woman, see?) And perhaps a new arrival with a British accent would give the blond girls something to focus their attention on, and maybe then their molecules would inch back together and they might be slightly less boring.

Or so Charlotte was thinking while sitting through English class at the end of the school day. English had once been Charlotte's favorite subject (back when she had such a thing); she read quickly, actually liked learning vocabulary words, and had a peculiar fondness for rules of grammar and usage. It made a good defense against teasing—when Chris Shapiro would tell her that when you had red hair, it meant you were part mutant, she would simply tell him his modifier was dangling and would stalk away, leaving him looking quite bewildered. Plus she just loved stories. They were always full of strange and interesting worlds, so far away from the one she lived in. Charlotte could not help but feel that the great tragedy of her life was that it would make an absolutely terrible story. What, then, was the point? Once upon a time there was a girl named Charlotte. The end. She had to make the rest of the stuff up to make the story any good.

Anyway, her English teacher, Mrs. Dinglish, had retired. Charlotte had raised her hand many times a week for Mrs. Dinglish. Her replacement was Mr. Metos, and Charlotte couldn't help but think there was something funny about him. He was the tallest man she'd ever seen; she came up to about his belly button (not that that said much—Charlotte was still waiting for her growth spurt, and she was beginning to think it would never come). And he was really pale and thin, paler than Charlotte even, with hair so black it was blue. He always had the shades drawn in class, and she never saw him eat anything in the cafeteria. Charlotte thought he was probably a vampire—while she'd never actually seen anyone who drank blood, she was sure if she had, that person would certainly have looked like Mr. Metos. Charlotte took to covering her neck with her hands so he wouldn't get any ideas.

Mr. Metos certainly took to the new teaching style with the glee of an unabashed bloodsucker, and most of the students found that during his classes their general torpor was mixed with an overriding feeling of terror.

But, for the time being, Charlotte could relax a little bit; they were doing a unit on Greek myths, and Charlotte was rather knowledgeable about that subject. She hadn't had to do the readings all week. She loved Greek myths; they were all such good stories. When she was young, she had had a big atlas-size book of them that she read again and again. She would lay the book flat on the ground and trace over the illustrations with her fingers. She could still see the pictures when she closed her eyes—of poor vain Arachne, who was turned into a spider by Athena, crawling across the tapestry that had offended the goddess; of foolish Pandora, who opened the box that let all the world's evils out; of Perseus flying away triumphantly with the Gorgon's head. The only ones she hadn't liked were the pictures from the stories about the underworld—grim Hades opening up the earth and dragging beautiful Persephone down to the shadows; the endless, dark landscape of the underworld, dotted with drooping trees; the dour king and reluctant queen standing like grieving stone in the cold, colorless cave of a lair, with their three-headed dog, Cerberus, grimacing awfully (with one of his heads, anyway).

The underworld, appropriately enough, was the topic of the day's class. Charlotte thought Mr. Metos looked like he would know a lot about it. Too bad there were no vampires in Greek mythology, at least as far as she knew.

"The underworld," he said, "is ruled by Zeus's brother Hades. When the Olympians began to reign, Zeus, Hades, and Poseidon divided up the world. Zeus became the lord of the sky; Poseidon, the water; and Hades got the realm of the dead, which is sometimes called Hades as well. No one knows where the underworld is—some say it's over the edge of the world, others say it lies just beneath us and there are secret entrances everywhere.

Now, what do we know about the underworld?" Mr. Metos's eyes soared about the room for a moment, then quickly alighted on prey—in this case, the unfortunate Brad. Mr. Metos stared at him, waiting.

"Brad?" he prompted. "What do we know about Hades?"

"Um . . . it's hot," said Brad meekly.

Wrong, thought Charlotte.

"Wrong," said Mr. Metos. "Hades is nothing like the hell we know and love. So when someone says something is hotter than Hades, that's really not saying much. This gets to my next question. Who goes to Hades? . . . Elizabeth?"

Elizabeth—a *natural* blonde—was one of those students who had gotten by her entire school career without ever saying a word, so this year whenever she was called on, she turned a most curious shade of magenta. "Ummm," she whispered, "bad people?"

Wrong, thought Charlotte.

"Wrong," said Mr. Metos. "Everyone goes to the underworld after death. In Greek mythology there is no heaven or hell. Everyone goes to the same place. Once there, great heroes are led to the Elysian fields, great villains are doomed to various kinds of torment. But most of us just sort of hang out in the world of the shadows. What happens when you die, does anyone know? Enid?"

"You go to heaven!" squeaked Enid.

Charlotte rolled her eyes.

"I mean in Greek mythology, Enid," said Mr. Metos drily. "Do you know?"

Enid knit her eyebrows together uncomprehendingly and shook her head.

"When you die, the messenger god Hermes leads your spirit into the underworld. There the ferryman, Charon, takes you across into the world of the dead—if you can pay. The Greeks always buried their dead with a coin under their tongue. If you don't have a coin, you have to find the paupers' entrance into Hades. Once you're taken across, you're never to return."

And so he went on, talking of King Hades himself and of the underworld, while Charlotte's mind drifted a little, floating around in space until it ended up somewhere very near her kitten, where it stayed for some time.

"Charlotte?" Mr. Metos's voice cut through her reverie. Charlotte jumped.

"Huh?"

"Ms. Mielswetzski," he said languidly, "do you know how Queen Persephone came to live in the underworld?"

Charlotte closed her eyes and opened them again. She took a deep breath. She did know, and she would be able to tell the whole class if only Mr. Metos would stop looking at her. "Hades, um, kidnapped Persephone from Earth," she said quietly. "He opened up the ground and just took her."

Mr. Metos smiled. It was a strange sort of smile, one that only his mouth participated in. His eyes still looked stern. "And then what happened?"

"Well"—Charlotte gulped—"her mom was a goddess. The goddess of the harvest."

"Demeter. Yes. Keep going, Charlotte."

"And, um, she was so sad about her daughter that she wouldn't let any grain grow, so the people starved. And so Zeus told Hades he'd have to let Persephone go. But Hades tricked Persephone into eating some pomegranate seeds, so she had to stay."

"That's right. Once you've eaten the food of the dead, you are bound to the underworld. But Zeus didn't want the people to starve. So he worked out a compromise. For six months Persephone would stay on Earth with her mother, and since her mother was happy, the earth would bloom. And for six months Persephone has to live in the underworld, and during that time nothing grows on Earth. That is why we have seasons." He rubbed his hands together, then nodded toward Charlotte. "Very good," he said. Then he turned away. "Now, there are several stories of mortals going into the underworld and coming out again. It's a bit of a rite of passage in epic tales. Can anyone name one? Eric?"

Charlotte exhaled deeply. She hadn't spoken so much in this class all year, and she hoped she would not have to again. All of the kids were looking at her like she was some kind of redheaded supergeek. It wasn't like that at all; she was just a redhead who'd had a book when she was a kid. Jeez.

That night Charlotte had the strangest dream. She was running through a field by herself, on the most beautiful day the world had ever made. And then suddenly she heard a loud cracking sound. It went on and on. And then the earth began to open. A man appeared in front of Charlotte—or something very like a man—a very tall, thin man in a tuxedo, with yellow eyes and white skin. And he lunged toward Charlotte and she started to run, but everywhere she went, the earth opened up in front of her. And then there was nowhere left to run. The man-like man grabbed her and jumped into the great, dank chasm. And then she was falling, and she heard a rumbling, and the earth closed up, and all was dark.

When she woke up, she said, "That was the strangest dream."

"Meow," said the kitten.

For the next week the Mielswetzskis busied themselves with preparing for Zachary's arrival. Mrs. Mielswetzski spent several days degirling the guest room—taking down the fluffy curtains, stripping the bed of the flowered sheets and comforter, and replacing it all with a nice masculine taupe. "We want your cousin to feel at home," she said firmly. Charlotte thought that with the huge grown-up bed and the big private bathroom, Zachary would probably do just fine.

Charlotte's mother seemed to be getting more and more nervous as the day approached, and she spent her time constantly questioning Charlotte about her behavioral plans.

"You'll be nice to your cousin?" asked Mrs. Mielswetzski.

"Of course, Mom," said Charlotte.

"You'll show him around school?"

"Of course, Mom," said Charlotte.

"You'll introduce him to your friends?"

"Of course, Mom," said Charlotte.

"You'll help him catch up in his classes?"

"Of course, Mom," said Charlotte.

"I mean, you'll be really nice, Charlotte. You'll really try hard?"

"Mom!" said Charlotte.

"Because sometimes you can be a little, well, prickly."

"Mom!" said Charlotte.

"Well, honey . . ."

Despite the fact that her own mother thought she was prickly, Charlotte felt that life was distinctly looking up, and perhaps she would not run away and catch a boat to Paris quite yet. Bartholomew had taken to sleeping on her bed, and that's all she really needed out of life. The kitten had charmed her mother and father, too—she spent her evenings sleeping in the lap of one or the other, when she wasn't doing a mad dash around the perimeter of the house. She had the strangest habit of running to the dining room, leaping on the table, skidding all the way across on the slick surface, and flying off, front arms spread out like a kitten superhero. She walked over tables, dressers, credenzas, bookshelves, weaving in and out of Mielswetzski vases, photos, and other decorative accessories, sometimes avoiding them, sometimes leaving a trail of destruction in her wake. At about four in the morning she would start pouncing on Charlotte's feet, meowing loudly and gnawing on her toes. Charlotte would get out of bed, pick the kitten up, put her in the hallway, and regretfully shut the door behind her.

The Mielswetzskis were of a mind to think all this sleeplessness and destruction was cute, as is constitutionally required of a kitten owner, and every night when the family sat down to dinner, Charlotte's mother would say, "Well, no one called about Bartholomew today."

And her father would say, "I didn't hear anything either."

"But it's early yet," her mother would add quickly.

"That's true. We mustn't get too attached," her father would agree.

And Charlotte would smile, listening to the sound of Mew's feet prancing through the living room.

At night she would get in bed next to her kitten and whisper, "Now, Mew, are you going to be nice to my cousin?"

"Meow," said Mew.

"Are you going to introduce him to your kitten friends?"

"Meow," said Mew.

"You'll help him catch up in his kitten classes?"

"Meow," said Mew.

"Are you sure? You can be a bit fuzzy sometimes."

"Meow," said Mew.

"Well, okay then. Good kitty," said Charlotte. And she would fall asleep happily with Mew next to her, unaware that in a few minutes she would be dreaming of falling through the earth again.

CHAPTER 3

Zee

Zachary Miller arrived on Saturday night, along with Charlotte's uncle, who had flown all the way over from London to drop off his son. Charlotte told her mother that she thought this was a bit excessive and thirteen-year-olds were perfectly capable of making the journey by themselves, and international travel had gotten rather sophisticated since the invention of the airplane, and the language difference between England and America was not so great that Zachary wouldn't be able to cope in the airport, but Charlotte's mother told her that if she were sending her child to Europe to live, she'd want to come drop her off too, missy.

The Mielswetzski household was in a flutter all day. Bartholomew was running up and down various walls. Mrs. Mielswetzski changed the curtains in the guest room ("*Zachary's* room") again to a nice masculine gray flannel, for fear the boy would find all the taupe overwhelming. Mr. Mielswetzski spent the day making his special chicken cacciatore. Mrs. Mielswetzski bought a cake, and Mr. Mielswetzski decorated it with WELCOME HOME, ZACHARY, which, if you asked Charlotte, was overdoing it—but once again, nobody had asked her. They took great pains to decorate the dining room—Mrs. Mielswetzski put up balloons, and Mr. Mielswetzski put up streamers. Bartholomew began to do furious laps around the entire room, buzzing over the table and under the chairs, trailing streamers and balloons behind her until an hour before the Millers' plane was to arrive, when Charlotte found her passed out on the floor, wrapped in paper streamers and Scotch tape.

"Well, I guess she didn't like the decorations," said Mr. Mielswetzski.

"Or maybe she liked them too much," said Mrs. Mielswetzski.

So Charlotte and her father spent the next hour removing streamers, tape, and kitten from the dining room, while Mrs. Mielswetzski drove to the airport.

Two hours later the cake was decorated, the dining room cleaned, the tablecloth laid, the table set, the chicken cacciatored, and the Mielswetzski family car was pulling into the garage. Charlotte was in her room putting on her green sweater, which looked excellent with her hair. Charlotte had a strange urge to impress her unknown cousin from London, even if she didn't know what to think about his arrival; no matter what, it never hurt to look your best, and maybe if Zachary liked her, he would take her back with him to London. She heard the garage door open and pursed her lips, wondering how her life was about to change.

"They're HERE!" shouted Mr. Mielswetzski.

"I SEE," shouted Charlotte.

"Well, come on DOWN!" shouted Mr. Mielswetzski.

On her way down the stairs Charlotte stopped at the landing to see if she could catch a glimpse of her cousin, but it was too dark outside—all she could make out were dim forms. She took a deep breath and headed to the kitchen.

"Are you excited?" asked Mr. Mielswetzski.

She shrugged.

"That sweater looks beautiful on you. I'm sure your cousin will like it."

Gross, thought Charlotte, wishing she had worn something else.

But before she could protest, the door opened. "Here we are!" sang her mother.

There was a flurry of motion then—Charlotte was given a large hug by someone who was probably Uncle John, while her parents bobbed around beside them. Charlotte felt herself being steered in the direction of the living room, and before she knew what had hit her, she was standing in the living room alone with her cousin, who was holding a glass of soda (with ice and a lemon wedge), while the door closed gently behind them.

Charlotte stared at Zachary, who was looking blankly at the icy, lemony, soda-y glass in his hand. He was tall, a whole head above Charlotte, and very thin, like a boy who could run very fast when called on. But he didn't look like he had done much running lately; his brown skin seemed very sallow, his eyes were sunken in, and his face was gaunt. He looked tired—as anyone might after an all-day flight, Charlotte reminded herself.

"Was your flight okay?" she asked. It seemed like the thing people said.

"Um, yeah," he said. "Bit long."

"I bet," Charlotte said. "I've never been on a flight so long. How long?"

"Uh . . . seven hours," he said.

Words sounded so much cooler out of Zachary's mouth. Charlotte wished she talked like that. Maybe when she went to England someday, she would pick up a nice accent, then even when she said stupid things, no one would notice because her voice was so cool. It's one thing to get together with all your friends and dye your hair blond, it's another thing to have a British accent.

"So," Charlotte said, "do people call you Zach or, uh—"

"Zee," he said. "I like Zee."

"Cool," said Charlotte. Well, Zee was certainly much cooler than she was. He would be a good person to have on her side, assuming he didn't completely disown her for being a baboon, which he probably would.

"Yeah," he said.

"So, um . . ."

"So."

"Well." Charlotte took a deep breath. "You're going to start school on Monday?"

Zachary—Zee—yawned, a full-face yawn that seemed to stretch to his hairline. His brown eyes watered. "Sorry," he said formally, "I'm really knackered."

"What?"

"I'm *knackered*," he repeated loudly.

"Oh," said Charlotte.

"So, yes," he said, wiping his eyes. "I'm going to your school. We'll be in the same year?"

"Yeah, I guess."

"You can give me a tour," said Zee.

Charlotte relaxed a little. Maybe he didn't think she was a super-loser-freak—even if she had been acting like one, he was too tired to notice. "'Course I will," she said. "No problem."

"Brilliant," he said softly, which Charlotte thought was a bit of an overstatement. "So, um, how is it? School?"

"Okay," Charlotte shrugged. "It's school."

"And . . . your, uh, classmates . . . what, uh . . ." He shifted a little. "What are they like?" He was looking at her strangely.

"Oh, you know . . ." Charlotte shrugged.

"Anything . . . odd?" he asked.

"Odd?" Charlotte stared at him.

"Oh, you know. . . ." He bit his lip. "Is everyone . . . feeling . . . okay?"

"Feeling okay?" Charlotte blinked. "You mean . . . are the kids sick?"

"Yeah. You know"—he laughed a little—"does your school have a plague? Bubonic or, um . . ." He trailed off. He seemed to be trying to make a joke, but Charlotte could not for the life of her figure out what the joke was. It must be a British thing, she thought.

"Well, there's a plague of blondness," Charlotte said.

He blinked at her and opened his mouth, but just then a loud crash came from the dining room. Charlotte and Zee exchanged looks. Mr. and Mrs. Mielswetzski emerged from the kitchen. They all went into the dining room, to find the entire tablecloth scooted over to one side of the table, broken plates on the floor, and a very scared-looking Mew frozen under the table.

"Oh my goodness," said Mr. Mielswetzski.

"Oh my goodness," said Mrs. Mielswetzski and Uncle John.

"Poor kitty," said Charlotte.

The five of them stood staring at the mess for several moments. Mrs. Mielswetzski let out a heavy sigh, and Mr. Mielswetzski clapped his hands together.

"Well," he said. "Shall we eat in the kitchen, then?"

"May I help you, Uncle Mike?" said Zee with utmost politeness. Charlotte gaped at him. Oh, great. That's all she needed—a cousin with a *good* attitude. She could see he was going to make her look very, very bad.

At dinner the family made polite conversation across the small kitchen table, as polite as could be when you were constantly elbowing the person on your right. Charlotte was elbowing Uncle John and being elbowed by her mother. Charlotte excused herself the first couple of times, but soon she gave up. There were better ways for a growing girl to expend her energy.

Zee, though, issued a formal apology each time he elbowed Mr. Mielswetzski. The first few times Charlotte's father assured his nephew that it was no trouble, no trouble at all, it can hardly be helped, don't worry yourself over it, young man, I'm elbowing my wife right this minute. But as the elbowing and apologies accrued, and it became more and more apparent that all his jovial assurances were for naught, the vitality was slowly sapped from Mr. Mielswetzski, and by the end of dinner he was practically helpless.

It wasn't just the elbowing. Over the course of the dinner Charlotte watched, amazed, while her cousin comported himself as if he were eating with the Queen. Everything was "please" and "thank you" and "excuse me." His napkin rested cleanly in his lap, his posture was impeccable, and his knife stayed perched, blade in, on the rim of his plate. "My, so polite," her mother kept saying.

"Thank you, Aunt Tara," said Zee.

"Don't worry," whispered Uncle John to Charlotte. "Half the British kids act like this. It's in the water. Makes us all look like a bunch of drooling apes."

Charlotte glared at him. He didn't notice.

She studied her cousin through the dinner, through the chicken cacciatore and the cake and the clearing of the table (with which he insisted on helping). She studied him when the whole family adjourned to the dining room to clean up Mew's mess—despite Mrs. Mielswetzski's best efforts to send the weary travelers to bed. She kept replaying the conversation in the living room in her mind. *Maybe he's really paranoid about getting sick*, she thought. *Maybe he's an athlete, or he had a friend who died of the black plague and for the rest of his life he's been afraid he'll get it too. It's not a rational fear—but then, fear is not rational, is it? Or maybe he was just cra—mentally ill.* (Her mother did not like it when she referred to people as crazy.) *She'd read about people like that; they think germs are everywhere and are always washing their hands and stuff. Or maybe he thought that American schools were really, really dirty.* Charlotte wanted to ask him, but if he really was nuts, it probably wouldn't be polite to mention it. *Once upon a time there was a weird boy named Zee who suffered from a strange fear. . . .*

Or so Charlotte was thinking as they picked up the last shards of plate and pieces of silverware from the dining-room floor. Mr. Mielswetzski swept, Mrs. Mielswetzski went to shake out the tablecloth,

Charlotte put the silverware in the dishwasher, and Zee accidentally stepped on Mr. Mielswetzski's foot.

"Oh! Uncle Mike!" exclaimed Zee loudly. "Oh, I'm so sorry!"

"No," sighed Mr. Mielswetzski, "it's fine."

When Charlotte went to bed, Mew did not join her. Charlotte left her door open and waited. Mew did not come. Finally she got up and went to find her cat.

It did not take her long. When she passed by the guest room—no, *Zachary's* room—she saw a hint of fuzziness behind the half-open door. She stopped and peered in (which was almost certainly not polite) and there, snuggled up next to her cousin's head, was Bartholomew.

I didn't say be *that* nice to him, she thought.

Charlotte made her way down the stairs to the kitchen for a glass of water and perhaps—just perhaps— a kitty treat to be placed conveniently in the doorway to her room, but she stopped just outside the kitchen door. Uncle John and her mother were talking in voices that suggested they did not want to be disturbed.

So Charlotte crouched behind the doorway to listen.

"I really appreciate your taking him like this," said Uncle John.

"I keep telling you, it's our pleasure," said her mother. "I think it will be good for Charlotte, too."

Charlotte bristled. *And why, exactly, is that?* She would have liked to stomp in and ask, but that probably wouldn't have been a good idea, so instead she just waited.

Alas, Uncle John wasn't nearly as interested in Charlotte as Charlotte was. "Well, Suz and I are really grateful."

"Anyway, it's all for a good reason, right?" her mother said. "It's so exciting that you got transferred back here. You've been gone so long!"

"Right," said Uncle John quickly. "A stroke of luck."

Charlotte thought this was the most boring conversation she had ever eavesdropped on. *If adults are going to talk in quiet voices, they have a duty at least to say something interesting.*

But then Uncle John cleared his throat. "Listen, um, Tara . . . I . . ." Charlotte could not help but notice that he sounded extremely uncomfortable. She perked up.

"What?" Charlotte's mom asked.

His voice got very low then, and Charlotte had to keep her body very still to hear. "If Zee says or does anything . . . unusual . . ."

Unusual? thought Charlotte.

"Unusual?" said her mother.

"Just . . . anything."

"John . . . he's a teenage boy," Charlotte's mom said gently. "I think he may have a license to be unusual."

"Well . . ." Uncle John coughed a little. "True. But . . . anyway, if you notice anything . . . you'll let me know?"

Charlotte had already noticed several things, this conversation being high on her list. There was something weird about her cousin, that much was true. Uncle John knew it, but whatever it was, he certainly wasn't going to tell her mother. Charlotte waited for more explanation, but none came. Her mother and Uncle John soon started to be very boring again, and Charlotte, forgetting all about her kitten treat, went up to her room, where she could think in peace.

CHAPTER 4

Doors

In the immense sprawl of suburbs around Charlotte's hometown, conveniently located off one of the vast freeways that encircled the area, just minutes from the international airport and accessible from several major bus lines, there stood an enormous mall. This mall, better known as the Mall, was the biggest mall in the United States (though not in North America. That distinction belongs to the Mall in Vancouver, British Columbia. If you want to be picky). Each floor of this mall was more than half a mile around. The Mall had 520 stores and sprawled over 4.2

million square feet. It had the largest indoor amusement park in the nation, with thirty rides, including a roller coaster, a Ferris wheel, and a water ride thingy. It had a fourteen-screen movie theater and more than fifty restaurants—including several that billed themselves as dine-u-tainment. It had a bowling alley, an aquarium that housed 4,500 creatures (including sharks), a theme park entirely devoted to cereal, and a blimp made with almost 140,000 LEGOs.

The Mall was Big. It was Huge. It was Mega. But despite its size, the Mall was generally very well laid out. All of the stores sat on the central avenues, so none could be missed. Egresses were well marked and easy to find. There were plenty of restrooms, and large kiosks stood at convenient locations, displaying large, easy-to-read maps for the benefit of the bewildered Mallgoer.

There was, however, a small hallway that did not appear on any of the maps. Most people did not even know it was there. You could pass it right by, swinging your shopping bags and drinking your large soda or fruit smoothie, and not even notice the nondescript corridor that lurked somewhere between the store devoted to foot sculptures and the store that sold cheese.

If you did not notice the nondescript corridor, you certainly would not notice the nondescript door at the end of it, nor would you notice the nondescript sign with nondescript letters that read, nondescriptly, NO ADMITTANCE.

No one who worked at the Mall thought much about that door. Certainly no one used it. The security guards assumed it was for the maintenance people. The maintenance people assumed it was for the cleaning staff. The cleaning staff assumed it was for Mall officials, and Mall officials didn't really think about it at all.

If any of these guards, people, staff, or officials were to try to open that door, he or she would find it very much locked. But no one ever tried. Whenever anyone wandered down that corridor, he found himself possessed of a strange incuriousness and, for added measure, an overwhelming urge to go to the food court and buy a nice jumbo pretzel.

Now, let's leave the door for a moment. Let's leave the corridor and the jumbo pretzels, the cheese store and the dine-u-tainment. Let's leave the Mall altogether and travel about ten minutes away, over the interlocking freeways and the bright rows of suburban houses, to the home of a man we'll call Frank. This Frank was not a pleasant sort. He had a black heart, and black teeth to match. He scowled and grumbled at every man, woman, girl, boy, baby, dog, and kitten that he saw. All Frank loved on Earth were his tomato plants, to which he murmured and sang like he had just given birth to them.

Now, Frank had very nice tomato plants, and they made lovely tomatoes, juicy and plump, but really . . . isn't there more in life? Should one really devote every morsel of one's love, to the exclusion of the rest of the world, to something that can't even decide if it's a vegetable or a fruit?

No matter. Frank will not trouble us for long. One day—just two days after Zee arrived at the Mielswetzskis'—Frank went out in his yard as usual to sit among his babies and talk of their hopes and fears, only to find some bugs had eaten away at his plants overnight.

Frank let out a high-pitched shriek. Flocks of birds from several neighborhoods away flew from their perches. Shaking his hand at the sky, Frank swore vengeance then and there, not just against those bugs, but all bugs. He began to stomp wildly around the yard, looking for mosquitoes, flies, ants, and yes, even lady-bugs, and he slapped at (flying bugs) or stepped on (crawling bugs) every single one. Frank saw a particularly large grasshopper and lifted his foot high in the air, ready for a particularly crushing stomp, when he felt a strange pain in his chest.

Ouch.

The pain grew and soon became unbearable. To Frank, it felt like his heart was getting ready to explode, and he had a pretty good idea that it actually might.

Frank knew. He knew what was about to happen, and he still used all his might to stomp his foot down on the grasshopper with a great thwap. If he hadn't, perhaps he could have been saved—but he did. So, then and there Frank died, killing himself through his own meanness.

No one, not even the tomatoes, would mourn.

A few moments after Frank's death the door in the Mall opened. A form slipped through, a messenger of sorts, with winged sandals and a winged hat, and he moved so quickly through the air that no one saw him at all. People in the Mall saw a flash, maybe, felt a small breeze, a mere tickle of the air, but as soon as it was there, it was gone again and thus forgotten. Oh, nothing, they say. Let's go to the food court. Those jumbo pretzels are so good, aren't they?

The Messenger whizzed through the Mall, out the doors, and up to the sky. He arrived at Frank's house in moments, where he found the dead man sprawled in his garden.

Nice plants, thought the Messenger.

He opened Frank's mouth to check for a coin and shook his head. He didn't know what was wrong with people these days. He buzzed right through the walls of the house, circled around, found an old, stained sofa in the living room, checked between the cushions, and pulled out a quarter. Then he flew back to Frank, stuck the coin under his tongue, and knocked on his forehead three times.

A few minutes later Frank and the Messenger were zipping toward the sliding glass doors of the Mall. When Frank saw where they were headed, he muttered, "I should have known." Frank had never much liked the Mall.

And in the blink of an eye Frank and the Messenger were standing in front of the nondescript door.

There are doors like this door all over the world. Their locations change as civilizations change, old ones simply fade away and new ones pop up all the time. They tend to be hidden in plain sight, where vast crowds of people congregate, where the air fills with the cacophony of life. There are doors like this door all over the world, but this particular door at this particular time was unique because there was a man waiting on the other side of it. Or something very like a man.

This man-like man was quite tall, perhaps seven feet tall, and extremely thin, with hollow cheeks and deep-set eyes. His face was white—not Caucasian white, but white white—his lips were gray and cracked, and his eyes were a sickly shade of yellow. He stood stiffly in the shadows with a strange kind of grace, and he wore an old-fashioned tuxedo with tails and a white tie.

He had followed the Messenger up through the long,

winding caves when Frank's time had come; he had been too late to make it through then, so he waited in the shadows behind the door for it to open once more. He would not miss this chance—who knew when the call would come again?

And when the door did open, he pressed himself against the stone wall of the cave, as he did every time, while the Messenger and the dead man (that would be Frank) sped through. He waited while the large door slowly swung shut, then, at the last second, when the Messenger was well out of sight, the tuxedoed man caught the door and slipped through into the bright expanse of the day.

CHAPTER 5

Get Ready

CHARLOTTE AND ZEE ARRIVED AT SCHOOL A HALF HOUR early on Monday so she could give him the grand tour. It had already been determined that Zee would share Charlotte's classes for the year, since she could help him catch up. Which sounded like a great deal of extra work to Charlotte, but nobody had asked her.

As her mother kept reminding her, Charlotte was supposed to introduce Zee to her friends. This would not take long. With Caitlin gone, that only left Maddy. The threesome had become a duo. It was okay. Maddy was cool, when she wasn't worrying about school.

Charlotte always said that Maddy cared so much about school that Charlotte didn't have to; Maddy worried enough for two people. But Charlotte liked her because she had no patience for twits or jerks either—though for Maddy it was probably because they interfered with her studies.

There were girls Charlotte was friendly *with*—Elizabeth-who-never-talked, and Molly-the-ballerina, and Gretchen-the-goth-girl, who didn't like *anyone*. But as for tell-all-your-secrets-to, three-hour-long-phone-call, maid-of-honor-at-each-other's-wedding, best-friends-forever friends, Charlotte was distinctly lacking. Someday, when she hopped on a bus for Brazil, that might change.

She didn't really explain any of this to Zee. In some seismic departure from her norm she introduced him to absolutely everyone, even people she didn't like (she wouldn't have been able to tell you why)—and absolutely everyone seemed to size Zee up as someone they might like to have on their side. His accent, his clothes, his countenance, and some ineffable je ne sais quoi seemed to mark Zee as one of those cool but accessible kids that everyone likes. It was incredibly annoying; Zee was clearly drinking some sort of weird potion that made him perfect in every way. Even Gretchen-the-goth-girl seemed impressed with him and immediately started to ask Zee about bands Charlotte had never heard of. His Zee-like reticence was taken as an alluring mysteriousness, and he was immediately marked as a babe by Audrey, Angie, Andrea, and both Ashleys, who indeed had all gained more shape and definition at the sight of him. He ran circles around everyone during the soccer game in gym and was quickly deemed the man by Chris and Brad and their ilk. Even the teachers seemed charmed by his politeness and formality—qualities that, for any other new kid, would have earned him a serious wedgie, but not Zee. After an entire day of being asked which one of them was adopted, Charlotte began to wonder if the question had more to do with respective coolness than any confusion over ethnicity. It was all very typical of her life.

The last class of the day was English. Charlotte and Zee walked down the hallway together, and everyone had a smile for Zee. Charlotte was surprised he still bothered talking to her.

Zee leaned over to her and muttered, "People are very friendly in America."

Charlotte raised her eyebrows. "Sure," she said.

"It's nice. When you meet people here, they don't introduce themselves as, like, the eighth earl of Asherton."

"Sure," said Charlotte.

"And the teachers are so relaxed."

"Sure," said Charlotte.

"So . . . " Zee said, "next is literature, isn't it?"

"English. Yeah. At the end of the hall."

"Do you like it?"

Charlotte shrugged. "Well, we used to have a wonderful teacher, but Mr. Metos—"

Zee stopped suddenly. He stared at Charlotte. "Metos?"

"Yeah," said Charlotte, looking at him. "Why?"

Zee turned his head. "Oh, nothing," he said. "Unusual name, that's all."

But the way Zee said "Oh, nothing" was the way people talked when there was Definitely Something. Charlotte peered at her cousin and said slowly, "Well, he's an unusual guy."

Every time Charlotte walked into Mr. Metos's classroom, she felt as if she were walking into a crypt. The room had an air of dusty, dark things, things you would be advised not to touch. She kept one eye on Zee when they entered the room, but when he saw Mr. Metos, his face only looked puzzled.

Mr. Metos sat at his desk in the front of the room while the students filed in, writing in his attendance book. Probably deciding whose blood he wants to drink first, thought Charlotte. She took a deep breath.

"Mr. Metos?" she said quietly. "Um, this is my cousin Zee—Zachary Miller. He's new."

Slowly Mr. Metos lifted his head from his desk. His eyes went right to Zee's face. He looked at Zee for what seemed like ages, long enough to make Charlotte want to squirm. Bet Zee won't think everything's so relaxed here now, she thought. Indeed, he was eyeing Mr. Metos strangely, almost suspiciously.

"Well, Zachary," Mr. Metos said. "You're coming in at the end of our unit. How are you on your Greek mythology?"

"I have some schooling in that subject," Zee said.

"Good, good," said Mr. Metos, rubbing his hands together. "Why don't you see me after class and we can discuss how we can catch you up."

"Yes, sir," Zee said. Charlotte had not yet told him you weren't supposed to call teachers "sir." She would. Someday.

Today's class was on Prometheus. Again Charlotte knew the story well. Prometheus was a Titan who had fought for Zeus in his wars against Cronus. So Zeus gave him the task of repopulating Earth, and Prometheus made humans, molding them out of river clay in the shape of the gods. Prometheus loved his creations and wanted humans to be better than animals. But Zeus was content to let people stay primitive, another beast on the earth. And humans were not faring well in the world. So Prometheus stole fire from the gods and gave it to the humans so they could keep warm and cook food. The fire also taught them to look upward, to the heavens—to think and to dream.

Zeus was not happy. Gods never want people to have knowledge. So, as punishment for defying him, Zeus chained Prometheus to a mountain, and every day an eagle came to gnaw on his liver. Every night Prometheus's liver would regenerate so it could be gnawed on again the next day. This last part always seemed especially excessive to Charlotte.

Mr. Metos seemed to think it was excessive too. "Prometheus did not understand why Zeus would make man and then leave him in the dark. He wanted Zeus to bless man, and when he didn't, Prometheus took it upon himself to do so. Prometheus was known as the Friend of Man but was tormented for generations because of that friendship. But there was more to it than that. Prometheus was essentially telling Zeus that in his treatment of man Zeus was proving himself unworthy to be a god, and Prometheus decided he would have to nurture and protect man himself. So"—he turned to the class—"can anyone think of another situation where the gods abused mankind?"

Humankind, Charlotte thought, doodling. Charlotte

spent the class making a picture in her notebook of a man chained to a cliff with a big eagle heading right toward him. She was not a very good drawer, and her eagle looked more like a weird-looking giant bat. She wondered if Mr. Metos turned into a bat at night or if that was just a myth.

Next to her Zee was paying careful attention to Mr. Metos like a good boy. He had probably never doodled in class in his life. British boys probably didn't do that; they were too busy making friends and being polite and stealing people's kittens.

After class Charlotte put her books together slowly and stood in the doorway. She was torn between wanting to run out of the classroom and wanting to see what Mr. Metos would say to Zee. Anyway, she was supposed to watch over her cousin, and Uncle John might not want him to get his blood drained on his first day.

Zee looked at her. "Um, I'll catch up with you," he said. "I've got to talk to Mr. Metos for a minute."

"I know," said Charlotte. "I can wait."

"No, no," said Zee. "Don't trouble yourself. I'll meet you on the steps." And then he closed the door.

Charlotte sat on the front steps of the school, watching as all of the kids filed out around her. It was still oddly warm; no one was wearing a coat. By Halloween everything might be covered in snow, and Zee would have to hurry up any mysterious postclass meetings if he didn't want Charlotte to freeze to death. Of course, she thought, looking at her watch, she might still be here then. Once upon a time there was a girl named Charlotte who sat in the same place for six years, and no one noticed her.

"Charlotte?"

Charlotte looked up. Her history teacher was standing above her, shielding her eyes from the sun and smiling kindly.

"Hi, Ms. Bristol-Lee," Charlotte said.

"Charlotte . . ."—she crouched down and put her hand on Charlotte's shoulder—"I wanted to talk to you for a second."

Uh-oh, Charlotte thought. She braced herself to hear more about her potential.

"Listen," the teacher leaned in. "I just want to say, what you're going through, with your family . . . I understand."

Not potential? It took Charlotte a couple seconds. Oh, yeah. Pop quiz in history. Didn't do reading. Parents fighting. World War I. Right.

"Thanks, Ms. Bristol-Lee," she said, nodding slowly. "That really means a lot."

"My parents were divorced when I was your age. I

know it's hard. Now, I just want to let you know that I'm here for you." She patted Charlotte. "Sometimes parents forget that what they're doing affects their kids. If you want someone to talk to your family about what you're going through—"

"Oh!" Charlotte said. "Wow, that's really nice. But you know . . . it's gotten much better. They got a new counselor, and she's done wonders. I really think they're going to be able to work it out! Plus Mom's on a new medication and, uh . . . she's really much less moody." Charlotte grinned like the happy, well-adjusted thirteen-year-old she was, then added pointedly, "They're really trying to put all their troubles in the past."

Ms. Bristol-Lee broke out in a huge smile that almost made Charlotte feel guilty. Almost. "Oh, Charlotte, I'm so glad! Keep me posted, okay? And take care of yourself. . . ."

"I will," Charlotte nodded, eyes big. "Thanks."

Ms. Bristol-Lee squeezed Charlotte's shoulder, then went on her way. Charlotte exhaled heavily.

She sighed and put her chin in her hands. The stream of students coming out of the doors was wearing thin now, and still no Zee. She stretched her legs out and thought of all the things her weird cousin and her creepy English teacher might be saying to each other.

"Hey!" Another voice interrupted Charlotte's reverie. She looked up to see the cat-eyed glasses of Maddy staring down at her.

"Hey," Charlotte grinned.

"What are you doing?"

"Waiting for Zee. He's talking to Mr. Metos. Probably getting his blood sucked."

"Char!" Maddy looked behind her. "I like Mr. Metos. He's . . . interesting."

"*Interesting* is right," Charlotte said. "Vampires are extremely interesting."

"I doubt he's a vampire."

"Well, maybe he's a werewolf."

"For a werewolf he sure gives a lot of homework," she said, patting her big purple assignment book. "And if he is, Zee better get out of there. Full moon tonight."

Charlotte looked at her watch again. "I'm *really* hoping he comes out before dark. If he doesn't, getting eaten will serve him right. . . . Are you getting picked up today?"

"Nah. I'm gonna walk. Mom's got Pilates. . . . Anyway, Zee's awfully cute."

"I know," Charlotte sighed long-sufferingly. "There's something weird about him, though."

Maddy grinned. "Is he a werewolf too?"

"I'm serious!" Charlotte said. "Something's up with

him." She told Maddy about her first conversation with Zee and what she had overheard Uncle John say on Saturday night. "And, I don't know, I swear when I mentioned Mr. Metos, it was like he knew his name."

"Huh!" Maddy bit her lip and thought for a second. "That is weird."

"I know!" said Charlotte. "There's something going on with him, Maddy. Something strange. Zee has a secret, I know it."

Maddy nodded. "Look, I gotta get home, I've got piano. We'll talk more about it tomorrow, okay? Keep your eyes on him! We'll figure it out."

Charlotte smiled. They made their good-byes, and Charlotte watched as her friend headed off down the street.

Charlotte kept her ears open and her eyes peeled that night, but she didn't have any new information to give Maddy the next day. But Maddy wasn't in homeroom anyway. Charlotte thought she must have had an appointment or something, because Maddy had never missed a day of school before in her life. But she wasn't in science, either, and when Charlotte looked at the list of excused absences on the teachers' announcement board, she saw her friend's name: MADELINE RUBY— ILL.

Weird, Charlotte thought.

She didn't get a chance to call Maddy that night, though. Zee stayed after school to try out for the upper-school soccer team (every once in a while when a kid was super good at something, they let an eighth grader play on the upper-school teams), and she stayed with him on her mother's instructions. It was worth it to watch the coach's eyes bug out when Zee played. He might be weird and a cat thief, but Zee could sure play soccer. Charlotte didn't know whether to feel bad that she had no actual talents or to be proud that Zee was on her side, so she settled for both. Then they went out to dinner because Uncle John was going to leave the next morning. So by the time they got home, it was way too late to be calling sick friends, as much as you might want to. All you could do was start your math homework, know that your friend would probably be back in school the next day, and watch wistfully as your kitten snuggled up on your cousin's lap.

But Maddy wasn't in homeroom the next day either, and Charlotte could not help but feel uneasy. During her free period she found herself going from classroom to classroom, collecting homework assignments for her friend, even though she hadn't willingly spoken to so many teachers before in her life.

"That's good of you, Charlotte," each teacher said. "What's wrong with Madeline?"

"I don't know," Charlotte said quietly each time. And something in her voice seemed to make the teachers quiet too.

After school Zee went to soccer practice (for, naturally, he had made the team) and Charlotte walked the six blocks to Maddy's house, clutching a red folder of assignments that Charlotte had spent all of English decorating.

It had finally gotten cool enough to be October. Two days ago the trees lining the sidewalks had been green; now they were all bright red, and as Charlotte walked along, she felt a few brown leaves crunch against the sidewalk. The air smelled of burned things. The wind had a faint chill in it, and perhaps that, combined with her apprehension over Maddy's two-day absence, was why she felt that something was not quite right in the world around her, almost as if she were being watched.

Charlotte pressed the little round iron doorbell at Maddy's front door and heard the familiar, cheerful chirping echo through the inside of the house. She'd done this thousands of times since the girls became friends in first grade, after a discovery of a great mutual affection for Play-Doh.

But this time the bell faded out and she heard nothing. No sound coming through the hallway or rushing down the stairs to greet her. Just silence. And Charlotte's heart flipped a little. But then, there, firm adult foot-steps sounded in the house, and Charlotte exhaled.

Maddy's mom opened the door, looking weary. There was something different about her, and it took Charlotte a few moments to realize this was the first time she'd ever seen Mrs. Ruby without the light pink lipstick that Charlotte had come to think was her own natural (albeit waxy) coloring.

"Oh, Charlotte," said Mrs. Ruby. "Hi." She smiled faintly and leaned against the doorway. A moment passed.

"Um," Charlotte said. "I brought Maddy's home-work." She held out the folder weakly. She had a strange urge to drop it and run in the other direction.

"Oh!" Mrs. Ruby exclaimed. "Of course. I'm sorry, Charlotte, I'm just . . . that's very nice of you. Come on in."

She held the door, and Charlotte walked in, clutch-ing the folder tightly.

"Maddy will be glad to see you," Mrs. Ruby said quietly.

"Yeah, um . . . what's wrong?"

"I don't know. She's just—I don't know." She shook her head. "I came home on Monday to find her just col-lapsed on the couch. She could barely talk."

"On Monday? I saw her leaving school. She was fine."

"Well, she wasn't when I got home. And she got worse all evening. We went to the doctor yesterday, but . . ." She shook her head. "Well, let's go see her, huh?" Mrs. Ruby smiled tightly at Charlotte, and then held out her hand like she used to when Charlotte was six. Charlotte took it, and together they walked up the stairs.

The shades were drawn and the lights off in Maddy's room, and Charlotte could barely make out her friend in the mass of covers on the bed. Mrs. Ruby went over to her. "Honey? Are you awake? Charlotte's here to see you!" She sounded oddly cheerful, in that way grown-ups can. "Come on over, Charlotte."

Maddy was buried deep inside several layers of blankets. Her head was propped up on three large pillows, but under the covers the rest of her body seemed flat against the bed, useless, like an old rag doll. Her eyes looked shadowy, and when she smiled at Charlotte, the effort seemed to drain her more. Charlotte sat down on the edge of the bed and sucked on her lips.

"I'll leave you girls," said Mrs. Ruby. "But only a few minutes, okay, Charlotte?"

And then she was gone, and Charlotte sat on her friend's bed and thought about how she had absolutely nothing in the whole wide world to say.

CHAPTER 6

Get Set

CHARLOTTE DID NOT SLEEP WELL THAT NIGHT. FOR A few days she had fancied herself on the periphery of some great mystery, one that had begun with the sudden arrival of her British cousin and then seemed to encompass her English teacher as well. But suddenly Charlotte wasn't living in a mystery anymore, in a fantasy world made of dark secrets and hidden tunnels and vampiric teachers and foggy London nights. Now Charlotte lived in this horrible world where her best friend could get so sick she couldn't lift her head.

And Maddy had been just fine at school that day,

absolutely 100 percent fine. Better than that. She'd been *Maddy*, all cat-eyed glasses and mischievous smiles, with purple socks that matched her assignment book. The girl in the bed was just a shadow of her friend.

She hadn't told her family about Maddy, not yet. She didn't really know what to say, and somehow the words "Maddy's got something weird" or "Maddy's really sick" sounded useless to her, like a crumpled-up lunch bag. So at dinner, when her mother said, "You're awfully quiet, honey," and her father said, "Is there something bothering you, dear?" she just shrugged and said she was tired. The Mielswetzskis believed in giving children their own emotional space, so they did not prod, but merely turned back to Zee and listened to him talk about how much he was enjoying his new school.

Charlotte couldn't even toss and turn—she had taken Bartholomew to bed with her that night, for she had great need of Mew's kittenness, and the cat had dutifully passed out tucked right into Charlotte's stomach. This was a thing too wonderful to be disturbed, so Charlotte lay with her hand on Mew, staring at the wall and thinking of her shadow of a friend.

It was hard for Charlotte to get out of bed the next morning; all she wanted to do was stay in her bed with

the covers pulled over her head and never ever, ever
get out. Every piece of clothing Charlotte put on that
morning was gray, from her hair elastic to her socks. It
set the tenor for the day well. She'd never noticed before
how colorless the school was—the walls and floors were
all the same noncontroversial beige, and it fit
Charlotte's mood perfectly. Every splash of color that
she saw seemed to hurt her eyes.

Zee, on the other hand, was strangely exuberant—
more so than was natural for a thirteen-year-old boy, if
you asked Charlotte. Whatever trepidation he had had
when he first arrived seemed to be gone, and he bounded
through school like a prisoner on his first day out.

He went through the hallways saying hello to people
Charlotte didn't even know. Of course, since their
schedule was the same, Charlotte had to walk from class
to class with him and his red sweater and his bright chatter, while everyone in the school greeted him as if now
their lives were shiny and free too. Thanks to her cousin,
the great malaise had gone away, and Charlotte very
much missed it.

Nothing was right anymore. All the social structures
were being thrown off. Zee was friendly with the mean
boys, the smart boys, the cool boys, and the formerly fat
boys. And those boys, as a result, were being—if not
friendly—at least civil to one another. The girls, mean-

while, had all started to be nice to Charlotte, as if she could get to Zee for them. She'd liked it better when they were all angsty, she decided. At least then they'd stayed out of her way.

In the locker room after gym she was accosted by one of the Ashleys, who had never spoken to Charlotte before in her life.

"Char!" she said brightly. "How are you?"

"Fine," Charlotte said, letting her suspicion show.

Ashley smiled toothfully. "You know, that's a nice sweater. It really tones down your hair!"

Charlotte sighed. "Thanks."

"Not that your hair's not pretty."

"Yeah," Charlotte turned back to her locker.

"Hey, I was wondering . . . you know your cousin?"

"Yes," Charlotte said. "I do."

"Well, um . . . does he have a girlfriend? Like, back in England?"

"Yes," Charlotte turned to face the girl. "He has six girlfriends, and they all have their natural hair color."

Ashley reddened and bit her lip. Charlotte felt a momentary pang of regret, which she quickly stifled. What would happen—the girls would never speak to her again? They didn't now, and she didn't think they had anything interesting to say anyway. Whatever. The world was too gray and heavy for regret. None of it mattered.

The rest of the day girls with dark roots in their hair were whispering and pointing at her. Charlotte walked along staring at the ground, trying to will the flushed color out of her cheeks. Even Zee stopped trying to communicate with her, and Charlotte found herself trailing along well behind her cousin and whatever bright bunch was traveling with him.

By the end of the day the entire school was cutting a wide swath around Charlotte, as if they had all gotten the memo. In English, Gretchen-the-goth-girl nodded approvingly. Charlotte spent the class running her pen back and forth across her notebook just to see how black she could get the paper, and darn the consequences.

But after class, as she was stalking through the door, Mr. Metos stopped her.

"Ms. Mielswetzski?"

Charlotte's neck prickled. Perhaps consequences should not be taken so lightly after all.

She turned slowly. "Yes, Mr. Metos?"

He stared down at her, his dark eyes precise and unwavering. "Ms. Mielswetzski, I am told that you are collecting assignments for Ms. Ruby. Is that correct?"

"Oh!" Charlotte exhaled. "Yeah, I am." This morning one of the counselors, Mrs. Spackelor, had asked her to keep collecting the homework until Maddy was back at school. She had not gotten anything from Mr. Metos, since she was in his class too and could just tell Maddy the assignments. Anyway, she was too terrified to talk to him. Like, say, now. With any other teacher she could spin a golden tapestry of lies, but Mr. Metos scared all the artistry out of her and she became a bumbling idiot. Talking was her only skill, and he took it away from her. "I told her about the reading and the test and stuff," she sputtered. "I didn't think—"

"No, no, Ms. Mielswetzski. It's perfectly fine," he coughed. "Would you tell her not to concern herself with the rest of this unit? Madeline seems to have things well in hand."

"Oh!" Charlotte blinked. "I will!"

"Good, good." He leaned back on his desk. "Mrs. Spackelor said Madeline might be out for some time. Do you know . . . do they know what she has?"

"Um . . ." Charlotte bit her lip. "No. Not yet."

"I see." He nodded slowly, still looking at Charlotte. He opened his mouth but then shook his head slightly. "Well, you tell her to feel better," he said briskly.

Charlotte nodded, wide-eyed. Mr. Metos released her from his gaze, and she began to make for the door, when he added:

"Oh, and Ms. Mielswetzski? In the future, if you would like to practice your modern art, would you not do it during my class?"

"Yes, Mr. Metos," she squeaked, and scurried out the door.

Perhaps everything would have unfolded differently had Zee not gotten a concussion at a soccer game on Sunday morning. Perhaps the whole story would have come out earlier, and Charlotte could have taken precautions or warned everyone or something. . . . Perhaps then the Footmen would have moved on to some other plan at some other school, and this would have been some other girl's story, and Charlotte could have gone on with her ordinary life, which really wasn't so bad once you looked at the issue carefully.

But it didn't.

Because Zee got a concussion at a soccer game on Sunday morning. It was just one of those things that shouldn't have happened, except that it did happen. It was late in the game, and the score was tied 3-3; Zee had two of the team's three goals, and the Mielswetszkis couldn't have been prouder. Until . . .

The goalie for the other team was an All-Metro senior and had a particularly high drop kick, which he aimed at a very burly midfielder, and Zee ran in to make the steal. The two jumped for the ball at the same time, and the midfielder threw his elbows out to push off Zee, headed the ball, then headed Zee. The heads knocked with a sickly thud that seemed to reverberate through the field, and both players were on the ground. The midfielder got up. Zee did not.

The referees appeared around him, then the coach, then the team, then the other team, then the ambulance. The Mielswetzskis had gone to the game, of course, and Charlotte's mother rode in the ambulance with Zee, while Charlotte and her father drove to the hospital.

They were back at home three hours later. He would be fine, he had a concussion, he needed to lie down for a few days, they should watch him carefully, they should wake him during the night, and absolutely no soccer or any other physical activity for two weeks. Any strange signs, any vomiting, any difficulty in speech or movement, any personality change, and they should take him straight back to the ER.

At home they propped Zee up in the den with blankets, lots of root beer, and just about every new release the movie rental place had. Once he was set, Charlotte watched as her mother sat next to him, held his hand, and began to apologize.

"Oh, Zachary, your father's going to kill me."

"It's not your fault, Aunt Tara," Zee said sleepily.

"He's absolutely going to kill me. You're here barely a week—"

"It's all right, Aunt Tara."

"It's not all right! You got a CAT scan!"

"Which was normal. Aunt Tara, I promise he won't kill you. I won't let him. He really hasn't killed anyone in a long time." Charlotte watched, wide-eyed. The attempt at humor would not work, she knew; Charlotte had seen her mother like this before. Her imagination was more out of control than Charlotte's. It was best just to agree with her before things got out of hand.

"I should never have let you play soccer with the upper-school boys."

Like that.

"Aunt Tara!" Zee's eyes widened. "It has nothing to do with that, this happens all the time!"

Charlotte winced.

"Oh, it does?" Mrs. Mielswetzski exclaimed.

Charlotte tried to signal to Zee to cut his losses. This was not the time to reason with Tara Christine Miller Mielswetzski, and if Zee kept talking, she might never let him leave the house again. But he was opening his mouth, even though his face was pale and his eyes were shadowy and his head looked so heavy against the pillow.

Charlotte coughed. "Hey, Mom?" she said. Her mother's head whirled to her. "Um, weren't you supposed to call the nurse when we got home?"

"Oh my goodness!" said Mrs. Mielswetzski. "Oh my goodness!" She sprang up and out the door.

Neither Charlotte nor Zee moved for a moment. They listened to Mrs. Mielswetzski's footsteps as they went through the hallway, down the stairs, and into the kitchen. A door closed. They both exhaled. Zee's head tilted slightly, and he whispered, "Thanks!"

"Yeah," Charlotte shrugged. "Let's watch a movie."

Zee's days of bed rest meant he was not in school on Monday, Tuesday, or—just to be safe—Wednesday. As a result he was not there to notice that the school seemed to be slowly emptying out. On Monday, Ashley, Angie, Lewis, and Elizabeth were absent. On Tuesday, Chris, Brad, Gretchen, Audrey, and Larry were gone too, along with half of Charlotte's homeroom. By Wednesday nearly one third of the students in the school were out. Every class had empty seats, and the traffic in the hallways between classes was noticeably lighter. This happens in schools, of course. One day somebody sneezes, and the next day half the school is out sick. It happens every year, twice a year; nothing to worry about, really, though it is perhaps—this time—a little early? Still, it happens. The students will stay home, one by one, and then they will come back, one by one, and there will be all sorts of missed tests to proctor and late assignments to grade and make-up work to, well, make up—or so discussed the teachers in the faculty room, as they do every time.

"It's like a germ incubator in here," said Ms. Dreeper, a science teacher.

"The student body is a fraction of its former self," said Mr. Crapf, math.

"It's as if the black plague has swept through our school," said Ms. Bristol-Lee, history.

"It's the end of the world," said Mrs. Benihana, drama.

"I suppose we'll all get sick too," someone sighed.

"Yeah, I'm beginning to feel it already," another lied.

"You know how it is in schools. On Monday one student sneezes, and on Tuesday half the school is out."

"What is this? Cold? Sore throat? Stomach?"

"I don't know. . . ."

Everyone in the faculty room looked at one another. They shrugged. They shook their heads. No one spoke. Nobody knew. At least, no one who was saying. Physical examinations were normal, blood tests were normal, everything was normal. Nothing was wrong with the kids, except that they were clearly sick.

By Wednesday afternoon parents had called parents, doctors had called doctors, and all of them had called Mr. Principle, the principal. Whatever it was, it was becoming an epidemic, and parents of students who were not afflicted had no desire to send their children to ground zero. Twenty students gone on Monday became fifty on Tuesday became eighty-five on Wednesday, and that was just too many for Mr. Principle's own comfort. Stranger still, a few more phone calls showed whatever was afflicting the students seemed largely restricted to the middle school—and mostly *his* middle school. There were ten freshmen and five sophomores out in the upper school, and five fifth graders in the lower, but in the other grades attendance was completely normal.

With the help of the board and the headmaster and the lawyers, Mr. Principle came to the conclusion that there would be no school at Hartnett Prep Middle on Thursday or Friday. It was a long weekend anyway, and that would give everyone a chance to recover, he could get the building examined and cleaned just to make everyone happy, and really, no one needed to be calling in the Centers for Disease Control, that would be really extreme at this point. There was no need to panic. You know how it is at schools. On Monday one student sneezes, and on Tuesday half the students are out sick.

The principal called the parent council leader. The parent council leader called the homeroom parents.

The homeroom parents called all the families. And, from their perches in the sitting room, Mr. and Mrs. Mielswetzski called in Charlotte.

Charlotte found her parents poised in their usual chairs, with books in their laps that they were decidedly not reading. Both Mielswetzskis had a look of some combination of concern and suspicion that made Charlotte want to back away slowly.

"Um, you wanted me?" Charlotte asked, biting her lip. She didn't know what she had done wrong, but there was obviously something.

"Charlotte," Mrs. Mielswetzski said, "what's this about a flu?"

"Oh!" Charlotte relaxed a little. "Yeah. A lot of kids are sick."

"Quite a lot, I gather," Mr. Mielswetzski said.

"I guess," Charlotte shrugged.

"You didn't say anything!" said Mrs. Mielswetzski.

"I guess not," Charlotte said. She hadn't. She still hadn't mentioned Maddy to them. There was nothing to say.

"Are you feeling all right?" asked Mr. Mielswetzski.

"Totally," said Charlotte.

"Are you sure? We could call the doctor."

"Nah, I'm totally fine!" said Charlotte.

"Well . . . they've called school-wide sick days for

tomorrow and Friday. So many kids are sick they want to investigate," said Mrs. Mielswetzski.

"Or at least cover their butts," said Mr. Mielswetzski.

"Really, Michael," said Mrs. Mielswetzski.

"Well, it's true, dear," said Mr. Mielswetzski.

"Wait," said Charlotte. "What? A sick day?"

"Yes," her mom nodded. "There's no school Thursday or Friday."

"Really?" said Charlotte.

"Really," said her father.

"Sweet!"

And before her parents could say anything else, Charlotte ran up to the den to tell Zee. He was supposed to go back to school on Thursday—really he could have gone back on Wednesday, but Charlotte's mother liked to be extra careful, and so she had exaggerated the doctor's orders a wee bit.

"Hey, Zee! Guess what?" Charlotte burst in to find Zee sitting up, flipping through their history book with a dazed expression that she thought probably had nothing to do with the concussion. Bartholomew slept peacefully on his lap.

"What?"

"You don't have to go to school tomorrow," said Charlotte. "Not all week!"

Zee closed the book. "I'm much better, really. Please, tell your mum—"

"No, no," said Charlotte. "I mean there's no school the rest of the week."

Zee's eyebrows went up. "Why?"

"Oh, bunch of kids are sick. They want to cover their butts."

"Wha—?" Zee said.

"Lots of kids are sick. So I guess—"

"Wait," Zee leaned forward. "How many?"

"I dunno," Charlotte shrugged. "Maddy's got it. She's been gone for a week."

Zee leaned toward her and grabbed her arm. Bartholomew fell off his lap. "What is it? What does she have?"

Charlotte stared at him. "I don't know! Nobody knows. She can't get out of bed, it's really awful, she's just lying there—"

Zee fell back into the couch. "Oh no." His hands flew to his face. Charlotte and Bartholomew stared.

"What?"

"It's my fault," he said slowly. "It's all my fault."

Charlotte could not stand it anymore. "What's your fault? Zee, what's going on?"

Zee had lost all color in his face. He seemed to be shaking. "They *followed* me."

PART TWO

Now, the Beginning

CHAPTER 7

The Last Summer of Grandmother Winter

Six months ago Zachary Miller had been an ordinary boy living an ordinary life in an ordinary part of the ordinary city of London (for, despite Charlotte's feelings on the matter, London is very ordinary if you grew up there). Zee liked music, he liked football (that's British for soccer), and most of all he liked Samantha Golton, the dark-haired forward on the girls' school team. He had spent quite a long time trying to name the exact shade of brown of her hair—it was richer than "nut," yet not as red as "mahogany" or as black as "raven." He had finally settled on "chocolate," which had the added benefit of connoting something extremely delicious.

Samantha was the fastest girl in her year at Feldwop and Egfred's School for Girls, and Zee was the fastest boy in his at Feldwop and Egfred's School for Boys. Zee thought it was time for some coeducation.

At night he dreamed of a summer running back and forth across football pitches with Samantha, practicing his passes with her, but there were a couple of problems with this scenario.

Problem Number One: He was going to spend the summer in Exeter living with his grandmother and training with the summer club there. Zee was actually really looking forward to going; he always came back from his summer holidays fit, well fed, sun drenched, and happy. But he did not know how he could survive ten weeks without a glimpse of those dark tresses rippling behind her as she ran, like the waves of a cocoa-dark sea.

Problem Number Two: He had never actually spoken to Samantha.

Not that there hadn't been plenty of chances. F&E offered plenty of opportunities for (well-supervised) interaction between the girls' and boys' schools. In addition to various formal social functions there was the drama club, the yearly F&E Olympics, and the chess club—which, due to its coeducational nature, was far more popular than it reasonably ought to have been.

But Zee did not do drama, he was terrible at chess, and he was unwilling to fake it for the sake of either club. He grew so quickly that tuxedos never seemed to fit him right, and anyway, most of the social events seemed designed for people with Roman numerals after their name. He had watched the girls' team play a few times, and he'd become friendly with some of the members of the team. He even went running occasionally with their captain, Nicki, who lived down the street from him.

But he had never been able to talk to chocolate-haired, almond-eyed Samantha; in fact, he had never been able to talk *near* or *around* chocolate-haired, almond-eyed Samantha. In fact, if you took any preposition and put chocolate-haired, almond-eyed Samantha as its object, what you'd get was one mute Zee. He thought it would be better at least to babble incoherently, the way Chad Blightmere did *near* or *around* Nina Desai—at least then Samantha would know he was there. But alas. Her very presence in a room turned him perfectly still and mute, a lovesick banister.

So even if he were going to stay in London, he could not frolic, because a banister does not frolic. In Exeter he could frolic all he wanted, but that frolicking would be entirely Samantha-free.

Or so he thought.

One day, just as spring was easing into summer and he had already mentally begun to pack for his trip, Zee went to see a senior girls' match with Nicki. On their way home they talked buoyantly of the match, of their teams, of school, and of nothing in particular.

"You going to play this summer?" Nicki asked.

"I'm going to Exeter," Zee said. "I'll play with the club there."

"Pity," Nicki said.

"Nah. I like it. My gran's there, and I stay with her."

"Every summer?"

"Yeah. My dad travels for work in summer. Mum's a teacher, so she goes with him. Gran's fun."

"Is the club any good?"

"Ah, they've got some brilliant players. The club attracts people from all over, and we always win the district."

"Oh," Nicki gave a shrug, as if to say that winning a district isn't a big deal when that district isn't London. "No girls' team, I suppose."

Zee blushed. "No."

She nodded. "Well, there's some sort of camp at the university there this year, and they actually let girls play. One of ours is going to be there in July."

Zachary stopped. "One of yours? Who?"

"Samantha Golton. The forward. Know her? She's almost as fast as you."

Zee's eyes popped open. "Samantha?"

"I see you do know her," Nicki grinned. "Shall I put in a good word for you?"

"Yes. No . . . I don't know!" Zee grabbed her shoulder. "What should I do?"

"Sam's cool. Why don't I, you know, lay the groundwork?"

"No! No! Don't!"

"Okay, okay. Why not?"

"Because . . . because . . ." Zee stopped. Why not, indeed? Because either Samantha wouldn't be interested and then he'd have to curl up in a corner and die, or else she might be interested and then she'd try to talk to him and he might not be ready and then he'd embarrass himself and would have to curl up in a corner and die. Either way the consequences would be dire. Dire!

For the last three years, ever since his parents had enrolled him in Feldwop and Egfred, Zachary Miller had worked on his football game. His parents had insisted on sending him to a school that still wanted to train lords and ladies, whereas Zee wanted to go to a school where all the real people were, the ones who lived in *this* century. But F&E was known as one of the "best" day schools in the country, and he suspected that neither of his parents realized that in some ways that just meant that F&E attracted the "best" people.

All of the students at F&E were *something*. Most of those things involved having the most land or the longest name or the highest aristocratic rank or the most drops of blue blood or, at the very least, the most money. Zee didn't belong to that world. His dad was an American businessman, his mother was a school-teacher and the daughter of immigrants. Most of the boys there belonged to something very old, very insular, and very, very, very white—something that people with grandmothers from Malawi and grandfathers from South Africa were not a part of. There were not a lot of biracial earls of Northumberland, nor were there many brown faces at F&E, no matter how many times the administrators took pictures of Zachary, Matthew Hollywell, and/or Phil Higsby for their promotional brochures.

But the opposite of *something* is *nothing*, and Zee had no interest in being nothing. He was determined to find his place at F&E. And since he could never be *something* based on bloodline, he would have to settle for merit. But he could not be the smartest. Zee was smart, cer-tainly—consistently around tenth in his year. But F&E attracted its share of young geniuses, the kind of boys who were in the chess club for the actual chess—like, for instance, Phil Higsby, who was nationally ranked. Zee could not be the best singer because, while he had a nice voice, he was no match for the still-soaring soprano of wee little Boyd Brentwaithe. He could not be the best at cricket because he thought cricket was dull, or at polo because he wasn't a total twit, or at debate because he preferred it when everyone just got along. But if he worked, if he practiced and trained, he could be the very best football player, and that—at F&E, like at any other British school—was truly *something*. There he had the lineage; his parents may not have been peers of the realm, but his mother was the University of Exeter cross-country champion, and his dad had played basketball and baseball at the University of Minnesota. Zee had speed, he had talent, he had mental and physical agility, and he had drive—plus he'd been kicking around a football ever since Grandmother Winter gave him his first one when he was three.

And Zee was the best. There was no denying it. There were rumors they were going to let him play for the senior team next year, a year early. He was the best, his teammates revered him, and he was *something*.

But no matter what, he was never as happy as when he was in Exeter, playing football all day and spending his evenings with Grandmother Winter. The boys there came from all over the West Country, and they were just *people*; they went bowling and wore T-shirts and didn't care about which fork to use, and they were Irish and Asian and African and sometimes all three.

And they were good. Much better than the F&E team, even the much-lauded senior team. Zee was just average on the club team, and in Exeter being average was just fine with him.

All of that was perhaps why Zee was even more nervous to hear that Samantha Golton would be in Exeter for July. Samantha was a part of the world of F&E, where all the boys carried their somethings around with them like medals of honor. Exeter had cows, and he had to carry nothing with him at all. He could just wear blue jeans and play football and be with Grandmother Winter, who made excellent lemonade and lots of cake, who took him to museums and bought him ice cream and laughed at his jokes, and who seemed to think he was really something.

But nothing that summer was to be as expected.

One night, a week before he was to leave, his mother sat him down with a sort of ominous-sounding "I want to talk to you about this summer." Zee's first thought was that she had found out about Samantha and wanted to give him love advice.

"Um, okay."

"Your father's travel schedule is light this year," she continued, "and he's got some holiday. I thought we might come out to Exeter in July and visit with you and Gran, if you don't mind."

"Really?" Zee said.

"Yes. It's been a while since I've visited my mother. We'll just come for two weeks or so."

"Okay," Zee said. That was fine, especially if it would be just for a couple weeks. And it was much better than love advice.

"And your dad thought we might invite Aunt Tara and Uncle Mike and Charlotte up for August, too. They've been talking about coming over."

"To Exeter?"

"No. London. We'd come back."

"But . . ."

"Wouldn't you like to see your cousin Charlotte?"

Zee bit his lip. He barely knew his cousin Charlotte. They had gone to visit when he was six; he had dim memories of kicking around a football with her at a time when he'd never heard the word *soccer*, and he had thought she was playing a weird joke on him. It's not that he actively didn't want to see his cousin Charlotte; his feelings on the matter were entirely neutral. But August was not for London, no matter about Samantha Golton. August was for Exeter and lemonade and freshly baked cake and the sort of floury, sort of talcum powdery, sort of lotiony smell of Grandmother Winter's home.

Grandmother Winter almost did not invite her grandson to stay with her that summer, for she knew that during the summer she would die.

Once in a while Grandmother Winter knew things. Some of those things were small things. She always knew where Lolita Thornbridge had left her keys. She always knew the specials at the Flying Horse and when they were out of pies. And she always knew, every year, what her daughter was getting her for Christmas. (Though every year she pretended to be surprised. Because it's not nice to take the fun out of life for people.)

And some of the things were big. She knew when she left home when she was twenty that she would never go back. She knew when she met Zachariah Winter in Liverpool one rainy day that she would marry him. She knew when she was pregnant that she would have a girl and then no other children. She knew when her daughter was pregnant that she would have a boy, that that boy would be named Zachary, and that he would be the most precious thing on Earth to his grandmother.

And one day in April, while she was watering her rose bushes, she was struck with the knowledge that she was going to die that summer. Her death would be quiet and painless, a good death as far as deaths go. But it would most certainly be a death.

Well.

Once the initial shock had worn off, Grandmother Winter found that she was not upset about dying—she had lived quite a good number of years, thank you. In fact, she had been alive all of her life, but she had never been dead, and it seemed an interesting thing to be. And her husband had been dead for ten years. It would be nice to be in the same realm of existence as him again.

Of course, she regretted having to leave her daughter. She regretted the sorrow she would cause. And she regretted that she would not be with her grandson as he grew older—yet she also knew that somehow she would never really go away from him. Whatever death held, she would find a way to watch over him. Grandmother Winter had a way of getting what she wanted when she set her mind to something.

The one problem with the whole scenario was that she did not want her grandson to have to see her die. But every time she tried to come up with an excuse for why she would not be able to host him this summer, her brain came up empty. And every time she was ready to reach for the phone to call the Millers, something distracted her. Somehow she knew that no matter what she did, her grandson would be there with her when she died—that this, like her death itself, was unavoidable.

So he would come. They would have one last summer together. She would not tell him how it would end, because there was no point in his being sad for one more second than he had to be. He would come, and she would give him the best summer she could, she would give him a lifetime of grandmotherness, and when the end did come, she would make sure he knew that she would always be there.

For Grandmother Winter sensed something inside Zee. Something that was all closed up, hard and tight, when she saw him in London, something that unfurled when he was there in Exeter over the summer. She had tried to talk to his mother about it, but Suzy did not see it, in the way that sometimes parents cannot see what is in front of them. "Of course he's more relaxed over the summer," she had said. "It's summer!"

So now Zee would not have his summers anymore, and whatever it was that made him expand, she would simply have to help him find it on his own.

CHAPTER 8

Grandmother Winter's
Last Words

When Zee arrived in Exeter on June 8, he found that his grandmother had gone mad.

Not clinically mad. Not mad like talking-to-people-who-aren't-there mad or forgetting-to-wear-trousers mad or hello-I'm-the-Queen-how-do-you-do mad; but rather, mad in the way that a person can be completely normal all of your life, and then one day you discover she's completely gone off her rocker.

For when Zee arrived at Grandmother Winter's house—he had taken an early train to surprise her— he found her baking. This was not unusual in itself;

grandmothers bake, and Grandmother Winter was no exception. But usually she baked a cake a week, on Sundays, and Zee would have a slice a night and count the progression of the week by the diminishing eighths of the cake round. Zee never let her throw the cakes away when they were stale—Friday's wedge might be dry and old, but it was still Friday's wedge, the crumbly vestiges of the week, and it contained an implicit promise that on Sunday there would be fresh, whole cake again.

But on this day when Zee walked in the door of his grandmother's house, the whole place smelled as if it, too, had been baked, from the overstuffed furniture to the flowery wallpaper to the bright, thick carpet. His nose led him to the kitchen, where he found Grandmother Winter and not *a* cake, but *cakes.* Many, many cakes. He saw ten cooling cake rounds of various shapes, sizes, and colors waiting to be assembled into something extremely delicious, and judging from the heat in the kitchen, he knew there were more baking in the oven. He saw bowls everywhere, dripping with batter, and open canisters of flour and various and sundry sugars, empty boxes of cream, and several chickens' worth of eggshells in the sink. As for Gran, she stood at the stove working at a saucepan filled with a creamy substance that Zee knew was a few squares of chocolate, some egg whites, and a splash of rum away from becoming Grandmother Winter's inimitable chocolate icing.

When Gran looked up and saw him, a magnificent smile broke out on her face, the kind of smile that reminds you what a wonderful thing it is that there are grandmothers in the world, and she put down her saucepan and hurried to him.

"Zachary! You're early!" she said, giving him a flour-covered hug. "Everything's such a mess. You weren't supposed to see this!"

Zee hugged her back, then gestured toward the mess in the kitchen. "Gran! You've gone mad!"

She laughed, "Perhaps."

"Are you having the whole town over?"

She winked. "I couldn't help it. I was just so excited to see you. I couldn't decide which kind to make, so I made them all."

"I can see that!"

"Come help me with the icing. Make yourself useful."

And so within moments Zee found himself wearing one of Gran Winter's most grandmotherly aprons, whipping sugar and cracking eggs into the gooey mess while his grandmother looked on approvingly, for she had personally taught him to crack and divide an egg properly, and there were not many thirteen-year-old boys in all of England who could do so with such skill and grace.

In fact, Grandmother Winter had not gone out of her baking mind; the cakes were not all for Zachary alone. Somewhere around dusk the doorbell began to ring, and one by one his friends from the summer team appeared on her doorstep. Every one gave Zee an enthusiastic handshake or a man hug or a slap on the back, and every one was given a large piece of cake, and as they all talked and laughed through the evening into the night, Grandmother Winter never mentioned that her grandson had made the raspberry icing himself.

The first weeks of summer passed quickly for Zee. He woke up early in the mornings to find his grandmother making sausages or omelets, or sometimes working in her garden, or sometimes curled up on her big green easy chair with the paper or a mystery. She saw him off to training during the days and welcomed him home at night. Some nights he went out with the team, but mostly he came home to be with his gran. Some nights they cooked together. Zee learned to make Bolognese sauce, which made the whole neighborhood smell of spices; poached fish with the texture of cream; curry thick with potatoes. Some nights they sat down together to watch the sort of television shows eighty-two-year-old grandmothers were supposed to love and thirteen-year-old boys were never ever, ever supposed to admit to watching, much less enjoying, and certainly not gossiping with their grans about afterward.

Then, on the weekends, Grandmother Winter took him to some absurd tourist destination, the type of thing they had done together when he was six and hadn't done since. The first week, when she suggested they go to the cathedral and take the tour, he thought she was kidding. But they did it; they even had tea in Tinley Tearoom. Zee ate his fill of scones with Devonshire clotted cream, and they pretended to be Americans. They went to Rougemont Gardens, they went to the House That Moved, they went to the moors and to the quayside. They watched the swans, they ate ice cream, and they rented a pedal boat and went out on the river. Zee told his grandmother that they had tourist things in London as well, and she told him firmly to keep pedaling, smarty-pants.

Zee felt relaxed, happy, and for a few weeks he was able to keep his mind off Samantha. He could put her away, like the rest of London. He would know when she arrived, and he could deal with it then. For the twenty-minute walk from Gran Winter's house to training took him right past the university fields. Really, it was the most direct route.

The summer camps were well on their way by the time Zee arrived in Exeter. His first week of training, the university fields were filled with young kids—ten-and-unders scrimmaging on makeshift half-size pitches. The third week the kids got a little bigger, the eleven-and twelve-year-olds practicing headers or passing the ball back and forth endlessly up and down the pitch.

And then one day in early July, on his daily trek home, Zee found that the children had been replaced by girls. Beautiful, wonderful girls, with muddy cleats, fierce footwork, and indomitable insteps. And in the middle of them all, executing a dribbling drill with deli-cious precision, was Samantha Golton, the muddiest, fiercest, most indomitable of them all.

Zee froze at the sight of her. He had known all along that one day he would see her there, but knowing Samantha Golton is going to be in a place and actually seeing Samantha Golton in that place are entirely dif-ferent phenomena. He wanted desperately to flee, but since he was frozen, there would be no fleeing. There would be no moving at all. Ever. He was going to stay planted next to the bleachers on the lower football pitch of the University of Exeter athletic fields while the sun slowly set in the hills. The girls would end training, they would head to the locker room, then home for the night, and Zee would be there, still and watchful, and by the next morning, when the sun came up again, he would be covered in fresh dew.

Or he would have been, had someone sitting in the bleachers not suddenly blown a whistle, and had every single one of the beautiful, wonderful, fierce girls not turned her head in his direction, and had Samantha's gaze not fallen directly on him.

Zee unfroze. His feet popped awake and carried him swiftly behind the bleachers, where he caught his breath, began to blush furiously, then proceeded to head home, shaking his head and muttering to himself the entire way.

After that Zee considered changing his route. This one was obviously fraught with peril.

But it was the most direct way home. Zee decided simply to keep his eyes straight ahead when he walked by the lower pitch. If he didn't see Samantha, he would be much less inclined to humiliate himself in some way or another. He could ignore her all summer and wait to humiliate himself in London. Zee stuck to his plan—he never let his eyes waver, and he was proud of his determination and focus. These were qualities a good football player should cultivate.

On the last Saturday before his parents were to come join them in Exeter, Zee and Gran Winter spent their day walking around High Street. Grandmother

Winter kept trying to buy Zee things—new cleats, a new coat, even some CDs with decidedly ungrandmotherly content.

Zee was busily trying to explain to his grandmother why he didn't need anything and why she shouldn't be spending money on him and just what exactly that one album title meant, when Zee heard it.

Her voice.

Directed at him?

He looked around wildly. There, walking right past him, so close he could—oh, better not to think about it—there she was, arm in arm with two girls. She was smiling at him. His jaw dropped. And then she said the most beautiful word he'd ever heard:

"Hi."

Hi!

The other girls nodded at him in greeting, and the trio walked on, whispering to one another. Zee stood in the middle of High Street with his mouth open.

She said, "Hi!" He couldn't believe it. Hi means Hello, and Hello means, well, Hello! It means . . . Greetings! . . . Salutations! It means, I know who you are and I wish to acknowledge your presence. In fact, I salute you!

Zee watched the girls disappear into the crowd, contemplating *hi* and all its myriad wonders. Grandmother

Winter watched him watching them and smiled softly.

"Who's that?" she asked casually.

"Girl from Feldwop," Zee said.

"Very lovely," she said.

"Yeah," Zee shrugged, then added with a strange laugh, "You know, half the Feldwop girls are hoping to marry one of the princes."

Grandmother Winter tilted her head. "I don't know," she said thoughtfully. "She doesn't look as horribly dull as all *that*."

She grinned at Zee, who grinned right back. His body unfroze, and he laughed. "Let's hope not."

"Come on," said Grandmother Winter. "Let's go look at shirts."

That night Zee sat awake in bed and thought about the entire *hi* incident. She knew him. That amazed Zee. Of course, she'd seen him play before and they'd been at events together, but that was no reason for her actually to know him. To have noticed him.

He maybe could have said something back. Something like "Hi." Or "Hi, Samantha." But that might have been too much. And who knew what she would have thought then.

Zee didn't know what to do. Clearly he couldn't keep walking by the fields pretending not to notice her. He would have to find another route.

So he didn't see Samantha for another week, and he began to relax a little. The week was busy anyway—his parents had arrived, and his father had a strange love for tourist sites. So they visited all the standards again, this time without the irony, and they didn't pretend to be Americans because his father actually was one.

On the next Saturday, Zee had a match. His parents came to the game to cheer him on, but Grandmother Winter stayed home. She'd been feeling a little off for the last few days, and Zee told her it would be all right if she missed *one* game.

So his parents sat in the bleachers and watched, and right in front of them sat three girls, one of them with chocolate-colored hair.

Zee didn't even notice her until late in the second half, which was good because otherwise he might have fallen on his face. As it was, he was having a good match—he'd scored a pretty nice goal to tie it up in the first half. By the time he saw the chocolate hair, he was too exhausted to freak out in any way, shape, or form. And when the three girls approached him when the match was done, he didn't even run in the other direction.

Samantha smiled at him. "Hi."

"Hi!" Zee said. That went very well, he thought.

"Um . . . I'm Sam Golton. I'm at Feldwop too."

Zee coughed. "I'm Zachary Miller," he said.

"I know!" She laughed. "Hey, we're going to the Grecians match next Saturday. Do you want to come?"

"Um . . . yeah," Zee said.

"Brilliant. We'll meet you at the gate."

Zee nodded. He no longer trusted himself to speak. He might start babbling, or he might refuse out of fear, or he might introduce Samantha to his parents, who were standing off to one side pretending not to be watching the entire thing.

When he got home, Zee ran up to Grandmother Winter's room and told her what had happened. Grandmother Winter, who had arranged herself so she looked awake and well when she heard the family come in, winked at him. "See? I told you she wasn't dull."

And then everything changed, and Samantha Golton did not matter anymore.

The next day when Zee got up, his grandmother was not in the kitchen making sausages or pancakes or omelets. She was not outside gardening, and she was not in her big green easy chair reading the paper or a book. And Zee knew. He did not know how he knew, but he knew.

"Where's Gran?" Zee demanded of his mother, who

was sitting at the kitchen table drinking tea and staring blankly at nothing.

"She's having a lie in," she said quietly.

"She is?"

"I went in twenty minutes ago. She's still not well." A flicker of something passed over his mother's face. "I'm going to check on her again in a few minutes . . . to see if she needs anything."

Zee bit his lip. "Do you think we should . . . call the doctor?"

"She said not to."

He gulped. "Do you think we should anyway?"

His mother put down her tea and sighed heavily. She closed her eyes for a moment and then looked at him and said, "Maybe you can talk to her?"

"I'll go," he said. "I'll go."

But twenty minutes later there was no doctor on the way and no ambulance, either. There was just Grandmother Winter in her bed, resolute and strong in her dying. *It's time,* she said. *They cannot help me,* she said. *It is my last wish to be here, like this, with my family,* she said. *Are you going to deny an old woman her last wish?* she said.

Grandmother Winter had a way of getting what she wanted. So the Millers sat in her bedroom, not calling the doctor, not calling an ambulance, not able to do a

single thing to stop what they had known would someday have to happen, that they had hoped so fiercely
would never happen. Zee's mother sat by the bed and
held her hand, while Zee sat next to her with his hand
on his grandmother's shoulder, and Zee's father stood
behind them, touching his wife's back.

She spoke with them all, quietly, lovingly, caresses of
breath against the dark. And Zee waited his turn and
tried with all his might not to run from the room, from
this moment, from the utter certainty of what was
about to happen. He tried so hard to keep his hand on
her shoulder, firm and true. He tried so hard to keep
from dissolving completely, so his grandmother would
see him solid and present and strong.

And then she beckoned him closer, and he leaned
toward her, and she smiled a little and told him, firmly
and truly, "I will always watch over you. Never doubt
that."

He did not doubt her, not one bit. You never doubt
Grandmother Winter. In that moment Zee—who had
never considered an afterlife, and even if he had, certainly would not have believed in it—felt with his entire
body, from his toes to his tear-filled eyes, that she was
telling the truth.

Grandmother Winter took a big breath in, a loud,
urgent breath—and then Zee saw something flash in her

eyes, and what he did not know was that his grandmother was having her last premonition. Her face darkened, then she turned to her boy, her beloved Zachary, and pulled his ear right to her mouth.

It would be her last breath, and with it she said two distinct syllables to Zee. But he did not understand them and would not for several more months. How could he? For when he leaned in close to her, close enough to smell the floury, powdery, lotiony smell of her, Grandmother Winter had whispered:

Me-tos.

CHAPTER 9

A Brief History of the Underworld as It Pertains to Charlotte Mielswetzski

For a very, very long time King Hades—King of the Dead, The Unseen One, The Illustrious, The All-Knowing, The Receiver of Many—ruled the Underworld in peace. In the beginning there were some mishaps—the Persephone business and the whole Heracles to-do—each and every one caused by some rupture of the world of the Living and that of the Dead. No more, though. Hades learned his lesson quickly enough. There would be no more journeys into *his* Underworld for disoriented vagabonds with pretensions to myth or muscle-bound, snake-wrestling goons with delusions of grandeur. There would be no more sorrowful supplications from pretty-boy amateur musicians, no more frat-boy bride-stealing pranks, and (yes, he took responsibility too) no more bursting the earth open to kidnap pretty, young maidens. "Let them have their world and let us have ours," he would say to the Queen. "Never the twain shall meet!"

So a millennia or three ago Hades locked the doors and threw away the key, metaphorically speaking. No Admittance. No Exit. There would be only one way for mortals to get in, and once that happened, there would be no getting out.

After all, he would say to the Queen, Death is not a place from which to come and go, to stop by for a holiday, for a quick jaunt— Oh, I know, let's stop by Death for a quick bite to eat and maybe some gelato. That'd be splendid.

Through his minions he let word slip about some of the more extreme fates one could meet in his backyard. That, combined with an unforeseen sociopolitical shift in the Upperworld, gave his domain a reputation as a wholly undesirable place to visit. No one willingly goes to a nine-level torture chamber; when your welcome mat says ALL HOPE ABANDON, YE WHO ENTER HERE, it tends to keep out the riffraff.

The Underworld was no hell, of course; at least

Hades didn't think so. Sure, if you had been really, really bad (like, in the upper one half of one percent of all time bad), his Department of Eternal Rewards would send you to Tartarus and devise something suitably punitive—monkeys swinging by your entrails for eternity, say—but your average Joe would be just fine.

Really, Hades tried to be a good king. As he said to himself, if his lot in life was to rule the Domain of Death, darn it, he would be the best Domain of Death ruler the world had ever seen. He tried to keep his subjects reasonably comfortable—or at least make sure they were not *un*comfortable. After all, they would all be together for a very long time. A very, very long time.

And once Hades passed his Decree for Underworld Preservation and Sanctity, the realm ran very smoothly for a good number of years. The King himself was so much happier without having to deal with mortals, and Immortals (people with god or demon blood) were governed by a strict invitation-only policy that kept out anyone who might mean him ill.

But nothing (other than Death) lasts forever, and as the centuries passed by, the Underworld became a more and more difficult place to manage. The problem was simply the lack of turnover in the population; people kept moving in, but no one ever moved out.

"Times change, and the Underworld must change with them," he would say to the Queen. "We must adapt!"

Hades may have been a Greek god, but that didn't mean his leadership practices had to be ancient. There were any number of great business minds in the Underworld, and Hades could spend as much time as he wanted picking their brains, sometimes literally. You can't manage a burgeoning nether realm on your own, he learned. Not if you want to survive in today's competitive atmosphere. Organize. Delegate. You're only as good as your weakest link.

He began to appoint various Regents and Vice-Regents, Directors and Chairs, luring Administrators from the Universe's ever-growing pool of Immortals with the promise of flexible hours and a good pension plan.

By the turn of the twenty-first century the Underworld had become a vast network of Divisions and Departments and Directories, with plenty of Subdivisions thrown in for good measure. Hades himself could barely keep track of them all, but it did not matter. Every Division and Department had a firm organizational structure, a careful and clear hierarchy that was quite literally etched in stone. The Assistant Managers reported to the Managers, the Managers to the Heads, the Heads to the Directors, the Directors to the Ministers, the Ministers to the Regents, the Regents to the Chancellors, the Chancellors to the Demigods, and the Demigods to the Lord of the Underworld himself. Any Assistant, Manager, Head, Director, Minister, Regent, or Chancellor who violated the carefully conceived management structure or (Zeus forbid) bothered Hades with the petty problems of his Division, would find himself living among the whip-happy Erinyes in Tartarus, where he could spend some time contemplating the benefits of adhering to management protocols.

As a result ruling the Underworld had become a much less hands-on process than it used to be, and Hades, who once tried to visit every corner of his realm, now barely left the Palace. He got daily briefings from Thanatos, his Chief of Staff, and Hypnos, his Domestic Affairs Adviser. The twin brothers really ran the place, and they did such a good job, such a very nice job. So as the Underworld expanded, Hades's duties contracted, and as a result he was able to enjoy the finer things of life. Or rather, death. It's only right. He's a god, after all.

What with everything left to his advisers, and his advisers' advisers, and so on, if there had been any trouble, Hades would really have been the last to hear about it. (The last except perhaps for his lovely bride,

Queen Persephone, who did not venture out into the Kingdom at all, nor did she have anything resembling a daily briefing.) But really, how much trouble could there be? The Dead are a listless sort, not prone to revolt—they're Dead, after all. And his management staff had all been carefully screened—though no longer by Hades himself, but surely they had been, hadn't they?

Hadn't they?

There was that one incident. But Hades was sure he had handled it effectively.

Really.

One night not so long ago, on the date of their anniversary, Hades was eating dinner with his wife. This was rare indeed; there were so many social duties involved with being King of the Underworld. Hades always seemed to find himself hosting dinner parties for various visiting Immortal dignitaries, luminaries, and/or personages, but on this particular night Hades wanted to spend some quality time with his wife, his queen, his bride, the love of his life, the answer to all his prayers, in the hopes that she might one day actually speak to him.

Usually on their anniversary or on Persephone's birthday or on Valentine's Day or sometimes Just Because, Hades would throw a large party in honor of the Queen. Unfortunately, the Queen didn't always bother to attend these functions, perhaps thinking that with so many guests he would not notice her absence. But he did. He always noticed. So this year he pronounced it would be just the two of them. Alone. Together. She'd have to come then.

He had their personal chef prepare all her favorites—beginning with a light pomegranate soup because Persephone could not resist pomegranate. He had the table set as if for their finest dinner party. He informed all of his household staff that he was Absolutely Not to Be Disturbed.

Together, the husband and wife sat in their places at either end of the long dining-room table, silver spoons clinking against china bowls, crystal goblets filled with the finest of wines, the flames of tall candles twinkling above silver candleholders, silk napkins folded like swans, shadowy servants bringing out large, steaming, silver tureens. The table could seat sixty-six, but on this night it was just the two of them—he in his white tie and tails, and she in a diamond tiara and one of the gowns she'd had imported from Paris (the city, not the man).

"Such a beautiful night, my love," he said.

Persephone sipped her soup.

"You look ravishing this evening."

Persephone took a bite of bread.

"The green makes your eyes look like emeralds."

Persephone coughed and turned to one of the butlers. "Would you ask the King to pass me the salt?"

The butler bowed. "Certainly, madam." He turned to King Hades. "My Lord, would you pass Queen Persephone the salt?"

"Certainly, my dear," said Hades, smiling at Persephone. He reached for the salt shaker, and that's when the heavy dining-room door burst open.

At the sound of the interruption Hades stood up, knocking his tall ebony chair over. The chair hit the ground with a deadened thump, and all the servants in the room jumped. Persephone took a long, languid sip of wine and sat back in her chair. In front of the door had appeared a tall, dark, angular shape clutching a bowler hat.

It was Thanatos—Hades's Chief of Staff, the demonic personification of Death, dark twin brother of Sleep, wretched son of Darkness and Night, with a heart made of iron and a soul that knew no pity, on whom the Sun never dared cast its blessed beams. And he was in a twit.

"My Lord," he said, breathing heavily, "there's a problem."

"Excuse me?" Hades said as if he really did not want to be excused at all.

"I-I-I'm sorry, Sir. But . . . there's a . . . problem."

"Well, fix it!" Hades roared. "Can't you see it's my

wedding anniversary?" Across the long table Persephone rolled her eyes.

Thanatos cleared his throat. "I know, Sir . . . I thought you'd want to be aware, Sir!"

"What is it?" Hades sighed.

"It's Philonecron, he . . . he—"

"Who's Philonecron?" snapped Hades.

"Assistant Manager of the Department of Sanitation, Sir. A grandson of Poseidon. He . . . he—"

"He what? Get out with it!"

Thanatos exhaled. "He has blood."

Perhaps we should pause here and explain a few things. You are, no doubt, not very familiar with life in the Underworld, nor with what it is to be one of the Shades who live there, unless you are already Dead. In which case you may skip this part.

A Shade is, simply, a dead person. Well, not a person, exactly. A Shade is the essence of a person, what the body leaves behind after Death. History has portrayed the Shades as dull remnants of Life, aimless and joyless shadows lacking in thought or will. This isn't entirely true—or at least they don't begin that way. The problem is, life for a Shade in Hades's Underworld is not exactly a red-hot, thrill-a-minute, madcap adventure sort of thing. One could call it rather dull, which one, if one is a

Shade, often does. As much as Hades may say he likes to make his subjects comfortable, he really doesn't care a whit for them, and all of the Dead know it. As a result, over time, the Shades tend to lose their will, their emotions, their personality, everything that connects them with Life.

But there is one thing that can change all that:

Blood.

Yes, this sounds completely disgusting. Any warmblooded human being finds the idea of drinking blood completely icky, oogy, squitchy, and well, just plain gross. But the Dead are not warm-blooded human beings. They are, well, Dead. And the only thing that can make them feel Alive again, if only for a brief time, is blood.

Blood is Life, and to the Shades in the Underworld the taste of blood, the feel of blood, gives them the thrill of Life again. As the blood courses through their bodies, the Shades thicken, gain substance, form, emotion.

There was a time, back before the Decree for Underworld Preservation and Sanctity was passed, when people would waltz through the Underworld all the time, carrying fresh blood with them. The smell would lure the Shades, who would crowd, clamor, and claw as if they had already drunk the stuff, as if merely the promise of blood gave them enough Life to fight for a taste.

But if you were the ruler of subjects who were half comatose by nature, any substance that transforms them into crowders, clamorers, and clawers would make you distinctly nervous. And the prospect of any old Tom, Dick, or Herodotus waltzing through your realm and being able to lure and excite your people would not be an attractive one.

Blood did not belong in the Underworld. It changed the Shades. Made them unruly. They couldn't control their actions. They began to have delusions of Life—and nothing is more disruptive to a realm of the Dead than delusions of Life. In his Decree for the Promotion of Underworld Hygiene, Hades proclaimed that blood would be strictly forbidden in the Underworld (excepting, of course, inside the Palace. Hades liked his boar extremely rare).

What Hades did not know was that not all of his employees obeyed his decrees scrupulously. And the most unscrupulous disobeyer of all was an Immortal named Philonecron.

Philonecron was actually born in the Underworld, the son of a daughter of Poseidon and one of the demons who staffed the employee mud spa. He grew up playing along the banks of the Styx, skipping through the Vale of Mourning, frolicking in the Plain of Judgment.

It wasn't bad, growing up in the Underworld. There were quite a lot of Immortal kids, actually; what with such a large number of Immortals working there, most of them only *tangentially* related to one another, romances sprung up right and left, and sometimes those romances resulted in families. Or at least children. Whether birthed, hatched, or regurgitated, new babies were a common occurrence in the Underworld.

And of course with children came institutional needs. And the Underworld adapted. Day care. A good school system. Interspecies medicine. Children are a nether realm's most valuable resource, and Hades made sure they were treated accordingly. And he was rewarded; most of the kids grew up to work in the Administration, serving Hades loyally (and eternally).

As a student, Philonecron took a long time to pick a career path. His teachers pronounced him highly intelligent but lacking discipline, the sort that would rather spend his time writing sonnets about gastronomical distress than doing his geometry homework. His first internship in high school was with the Erinyes in Tartarus, but his guidance counselors thought he seemed to enjoy the job a bit too much. After graduation from high school he worked in a few low-level agencies before settling in at the Department of Sanitation.

But Philonecron had other goals. He wasn't going to be a garbage man forever. He had a plan.

For, despite what his teachers thought, he had been paying attention at school. He'd learned all of his history well. And he knew that there was only one thing that mattered in the world, and that was power.

Philonecron wanted power. Not pretend power, like the bloated Managers, lording over Recreation or Meal Services as if they were kingdoms unto themselves. He wanted real power. He wanted everything. He wanted to rule.

Oh, not the Universe. He had no desire for the earth, for the stars and the heavens, for Mount Olympus and all it surveyed. That was too much. All he wanted was his own world, his home, the Underworld. Anyway, he'd learned well that people who tried to overthrow Zeus did not come to good ends. But as far as he could see, no one had ever tried to overthrow Hades. And Hades was ripe to be overthrown.

Over the millennia King Hades had become complacent, lazy. Everyone knew it; they were just too scared to say anything. He sat in the Palace counting his gold, mooning over the Ice Queen, and letting the Administrators make up work for themselves.

The Underworld wasn't supposed to be like this. It's the Underworld, for the love of Zeus—the Dark

Domain, the Realm of the Dead—it shouldn't be run like some two-bit provincial government. *Bureaucracy* isn't even a Greek word. The Underworld needed a strong ruler, a man with a vision, a man handy with a whip, a man who could live up to the promise of the domain, bring back the days when it meant something to be a Greek god. The Underworld needed Philonecron.

But getting the Underworld to realize this was another matter. Taking control would not be easy. Hades was firmly entrenched. And all his Administrators enjoyed their petty positions of power. Hades had them all in his shadowy hands. Philonecron knew the whole Administration was designed only to perpetuate itself— all the Departments and Sections and Agencies only assured the complacency of the people who worked there, and kept Hades wedged in his throne.

The Underworld was now designed to serve the Administrators—the Immortals who served in the burgeoning bureaucracy. None of it was for the Shades. The Shades were the true subjects of the Kingdom of the Dead, and yet no one paid them any attention at all. No one cared about the Shades.

Really, Philonecron did not care about the Shades either, but he wasn't about to tell them that. Because the Shades outnumbered the Administrators at least five thousand to one. If someone could only incite them . . .

It took him quite a while to get past all the Underworld Preservation protections and start collecting the blood. You couldn't just go waltzing through the doors to the Upperworld anymore; the only Immortal who could go through without a pass—besides Hades himself, and he never went anywhere—was Hermes, the Messenger. And there was just no bribing that guy. Philonecron had tried.

But he was not to be thwarted, and soon he figured out that since the Messenger was the only one who could get through the doors, all he would need to do was follow him out. The wing-footed fruitcake would be too busy showing off his speed to notice.

And he was. In and out of the doors of Death Philonecron went, lurking in the shadow of the Messenger. Even more so than he had expected—he had thought that once he was in the Upperworld, he would wander freely, yet once there, he found himself strangely drawn to Death, in fact, to the site of the same Death that had called the Messenger through the doors in the first place. He found, too, he could travel only so far from the Death before he was drawn back to it.

No matter. With Death, so often, came blood, lots of it, especially in this day and age. War and murder were everywhere, and firearms produced so much blood;

Philonecron wished he had invented them. Disease ate away at life bloodlessly, but in the vast, sterile buildings that housed the sick and dying there were great storage facilities of blood, almost as if someone there, too, had been trying to stage a coup in the Underworld. In a quieter Death scene, a heart attack by a lone man, there were always neighbors somewhere, sleeping too soundly to notice a quick exsanguination spell. Nothing too harsh. Just a couple of pints. You'll be a little dizzy in the morning. Rest up, drink some apple juice, you'll be fine.

Philonecron was patient. He spent years building up his supply, storing bottles in thick containers under piles in the refuse dumps. He knew they would keep; the Underworld was a natural refrigerator. The only problem would be keeping the Shades from sensing the blood too early—hence the use of the rubbish yard filled with the fetid flotsam of Administration life.

He lured customers gradually, peddling his product on his garbage rounds. "They'll be more where this came from," he would say. "Just you wait."

The Shades began to follow him on his rounds, lurking in the shadows to see if he might have something for them. He always did. More came, and still more.

"Come to the Vale of Mourning on the King's Anniversary," he would whisper. "I'll have something for you. Tell everyone."

The King and Queen's wedding anniversary was a Kingdom-wide holiday in Death. All Administration offices were closed. So you would think someone would have found it odd to see an extra-large garbage wagon making its way from the central refuse dump to the Vale of Mourning, but no one did. Nor did any of the Administrators think anything of the swarms of Shades that seemed to be following it. The Dead were an odd sort, prone to strange gatherings, and the Administrators didn't think much of it. Really, they didn't think about the Dead at all.

Even the Underworld Security Agency would be closed. The ten-foot-tall Sons of Argus, with their burly bodies and giant clubs, would be so full of wine and roasted Calydonian boar they wouldn't be able to see out of any of their one hundred eyes.

It was evening and a holiday. Time for fun. Time to frequent the ambrosia clubs and Anniversary galas. Time to drop by Tartarus (for Tartarus was always open for business) and watch the action, maybe buy a few souvenirs. Time to bathe in barrels of wine and darn the consequences. It's a holiday!

So there were thousands of Shades on the Vale that night, like a giant spectral army, all buzzing in expectation. And there, on top of his great wagon, was Philonecron, eight feet tall, swathed in a giant black robe, with a magnanimous smile stretched oddly across his pale, shadowy face.

"Drink up!" he shouted. "There's plenty for everyone!" He threw small jars one by one into the masses, and ghostly arms reached up and plucked them from the sky. "Don't be shy!"

More Shades came and still more; in front of Philonecron legions of Dead clamored and thronged. "I am Philonecron!" he shouted, hurling bottles everywhere. "Friend of the Dead!"

"Philonecron!" a few voices shouted, and then more. In front of his eyes the Shades were thickening, gaining definition, character, even speech. One by one the Dead had life again—they were laughing, hollering, shouting his name. And with definition, character, laughter, came something else. He saw it in their eyes. They had will. He had them.

"Would you like some more?"

"Yes!" they screamed, and he picked up the tremendous hose he had made from Minotaur intestine and began to drench the crowd.

And then he waited. He waited until every last Shade he could see had been touched by the blood. Hundreds, thousands of useless shadows becoming whole before his very eyes. And they had him to thank for it.

"Does King Hades give you blood?" he shouted.

"No!" they cried.

"No! He denies you the one thing you want most. Is that fair?"

"No!"

"Ladies! Gentlemen! What kind of a king denies his subjects what they most desire? What kind of a king deliberately keeps his people in shadow? Death need not be a phantom existence. With me, you could Live again!" He had been practicing this speech for decades. He had it all thought through. "The Underworld is not for the gods, but for the Dead! For you! It's time to take it back!" He raised his arms up in the air, so excited by the speech that he did not notice the cheers of the audience were slowly weakening.

"Rise up!" he shouted. "Rise up against tyranny! Rise up! Follow me! We will have a new rule in the Underworld!"

That's when he noticed the immense shapes approaching him. He turned to look. Six Underworld Security Agents were lumbering toward him, clubs poised, apparently not glutted on Calydonian boar. Six hundred eyes blinked menacingly at him. Ten Griffins swooped down from the sky, howling and cackling, their enormous claws poised to rip into his skin. Three Erinyes appeared behind him, the snakes in their hair hissing wildly. And with them was the black, willowy form of Thanatos, riding in on a black winged horse, staring at him with an eerie composure that was marred only by a slight twitch in his left eyebrow.

The Erinyes grabbed him, pulled snakes from their hair, and tied his hands with them. Before they could gag him, he shouted to the throng in front of him, "See what they do? See? Knock down the Palace! Free yourselves!"

But it was too late. The effects of the blood were wearing off. They were becoming Dead again, Shades, phantoms, useless. They milled around aimlessly. Their will was gone.

Philonecron was pulled away. Thanatos appeared and raised his hands to the crowd. The Vale was silent.

"Go your ways, everyone," Thanatos said, his voice carrying as if through eternity. "There is nothing for you here."

Philonecron had expected to be sent to Tartarus—where there was a special chamber for disloyal Immortals. He wasn't afraid. Pain only made him stronger. He would come out eventually, he would begin his collection again, he would have enough blood to sustain the Shades through revolution, and then he could sit on Hades's ebony throne and lock all the Shades up in Tartarus for good. It would take time, but he would begin again. He would collect blood for years, decades, centuries if he had to. He would not fail next time.

But he was not sent to Tartarus. The Erinyes dragged him into Hades's Palace. Hades stood before him, a mountain of cold rage.

"Philonecron," he said, his black eyes burning. "You are banished. You have betrayed me, and my world is forbidden to you now. You may never set foot in the Kingdom of the Dead again. You will spend all of eternity wandering through the empty plains of Exile." He turned to go. Philonecron squirmed. Hades stopped, turned, and added, "Oh, and have a nice life."

For one year Philonecron wandered around the outskirts of Death, forbidden by Hades's very words to cross the threshold into the Kingdom. He slept in a cave and spent his days wandering the outer banks of the Styx with the Unburied—the lost souls who, for one reason or another, Charon would not ferry into Death.

He practiced his spell casting (there was a great advantage to having a demon father) and performed experiments on the Unburied. He followed the Messenger into the Upperworld nearly every day to collect blood, but as the days went by, he could not help but despair. He would never have enough, he could never keep the Shades alive long enough to overthrow Hades. He was a general with no army.

Then one day something happened. He was out on a blood-gathering round; the scent of Death had taken him to the body of an old woman somewhere in England. She had died peacefully, bloodlessly, and Philonecron would have to look elsewhere. But something struck him about the tableau in front of him. It was a typical deathbed scene: a family—a man, a woman, and a boy—tears rolling down their cheeks, heads bowed, whispers hanging in the still air. But there was something unusual about it. Something off. Something that caught his eye. The light in the room—no, no; the position of the body—no, no. It was the boy. There was something strange about the boy.

Philonecron could not believe what he was seeing. But it was true. There was no denying it.

The boy's shadow was loose.

CHAPTER 10

Creative Problem Solving

GATHER SOME CLAY FROM THE BANKS OF THE STYX. You may have to bribe Charon to look the other way, but that's easily done. It would be better to use clay from the other bank, the one in the Underworld, but you cannot go there. So you make do.

Take the clay. Soften it well with Stygian water.

Form it into the shape of a man.

Pause for a moment and think about your place in history, think about how the Titan Prometheus did just this, so long ago, to make the race of Man.

Well, not quite *this*.

Take one Unburied. Don't use force. Be gentle. You need his loyalty. Tell him you will make it worth his while. Tell him you are going to change things.

Show him the corpse of clay.

Tell the Unburied to lie down. Right inside it. It won't hurt a bit.

Watch as the clay embraces his shadowy form.

Now take an urn of ram's blood. Pour it over the body. Don't be shy. Drench the clay.

Say the magic words.

Wait.

Wait . . .

Purse your lips.

Think.

Take an urn of human blood. Pour it over the body. Drench the clay. Don't be shy.

Say the magic words.

Wait.

Wait . . .

Purse your lips.

Think.

Raise up your arm.

Mutter a few words.

Let the skin on your arm open, then the vein, and let your own blood, your half-demon-half-god blood, drip over the clay form.

Say the magic words.

Wait . . .

There!

Behold.

A limb twitches. And again. Clay skin adheres to clay bone. Unburied spirit relaxes into molded form. Fingers wriggle. Eyes open. Mouth. He blinks up at you, you nod, and he slowly lifts his body out from the ground that birthed him. Clay falls from him. He stands, he looks his body up and down. Feet. Shins. Knees. Thighs. Hips. Stomach, chest, shoulders, arms . . . it's all there. He is a man, or something very like a man. His body seems to stretch before your eyes, the stocky frame becomes too tall now, too thin, soon he stands as tall as you do, you, his master, but he looks as though you could break him with a glance. His death-white skin stretches tautly over his frame. His face is like a white clay skull. His eyes are yellowed, like memory. His lips are gray and scaly.

Well, you say, looking him up and down.

And then you make more.

Soon you have twelve—a good number, an Olympian number—and you line them up, one by one, murmuring to them, murmuring to yourself. You have twelve, all identical, except for the letter of the alphabet you carve into each of their foreheads to signify the order they were made. You have twelve of them in front of you, their clay skin crackling, their every bone painted in shadow, and you hold your arms out magnanimously and say:

My children. My people. How beautiful you are.

We are one, you and I. We are the same.

We are citizens of Exile, and I am your leader.

Together we will make a Kingdom.

But we will not be content to stay here, for we must take back what has been denied to us.

Soon we will rule the Underworld.

But we need an army. And you are going to help me get it.

Their eyes drink in your meaning. You survey them up and down. Your eyebrow arches. You clear your throat. You clap your hands together and say:

Right . . . let's get you some clothes, shall we?

CHAPTER II

———◆·◆·◆———

Zee and His Shadows

THE MORNING AFTER HIS GRANDMOTHER'S DEATH ZEE woke up feeling odd. This was to be expected—his grandmother had just died, and her death had been an unwelcome intruder in dream after restless dream the night before. So when he awoke, he found himself feeling achy and exhausted. He was torn between letting sleep carry him off again and trying to shake it off and face the day. But if he fell asleep, he'd eventually have to wake up and remember all over again that Grandmother Winter was dead.

Zee decided that once was enough. He rubbed his

eyes and stretched in the bed. He sat up. As soon as he was upright, a wave of dizziness flooded over him. His eyes filled with black, then the whole world seemed to go black, and he lay back down again. He exhaled, squeezed his eyes closed, and slowly sat up.

Much better.

He yawned, stretched, and stood. . . .

And had to sit down again.

After a few minutes of steady breathing Zee managed to get up without any more problems, though his muscles still felt like dried-out clay. And his chest was filled with a burning, hollow feeling that was not remotely physical.

Eventually Zee made it to breakfast, where, once again, his grandmother was not. His mother was there, sitting in the big green easy chair in the living room, wrapped in an afghan and staring off at nothing. She gave Zee a long hug and touched his cheek. Zee made his way into the kitchen, feeling his muscles protest a little. His father was scrubbing some pots in the kitchen sink.

"Hey," he said gently. "Can I make you something?"

"Sure," Zee said.

Mr. Miller opened the fridge and took out a big pack of sausages and some eggs. He poured a tall glass of orange juice and brought it over to Zee, squeezing his shoulder softly. Zee drank the juice down.

"How're you holding up?" his dad asked quietly.

Zee shrugged. His dad sat down at the table and put his arm around him. They sat for a moment, and his father seemed about to say something but then stopped when he noticed Zee's face. "You know," he said, "you look awfully pale . . . are you feeling all right? I mean physically. . . ."

"Yeah, um . . . I feel a little off today."

"Well," Mr. Miller said, standing up, "let's get you a nice big breakfast, shall we?"

After breakfast (eggs and many, many sausages, which did help Zee feel better) his father sat down and talked to him gently about what would happen next. There would be a small funeral on Friday in Exeter. Afterward Mr. and Mrs. Miller would stay for a week or two to tie everything up. It would be a lot of work, and Zee could go back to London after the funeral if he wanted.

Zee did not want. He wanted to stay.

Summer was over for Zee in July, replaced by the strange season of mourning. Zee quit the football club—he walked to training on Monday to tell them, cutting through the university fields by unconscious habit and not even noticing that he was looking away—and spent his days helping his parents pack up

Grandmother Winter's house. There was no way he could play anymore, and he'd be leaving in a couple weeks anyway. But a few of his friends from the club came to the funeral, dressed in suits that had been hastily shipped from their homes all over the West Country. Zee thought that it was pretty great of them to come. More would have been there, his friend Ben told him, but some of the guys on the team were sick.

"I've been feeling weird myself," said Zee. "Dizzy."

"Naw," said Ben, "this is something more. They've got it bad. Flat on their backs. Totally useless to the club now. Gits. Plus we've lost our best forward!" Ben nudged Zee.

"The best if you don't count the other four," Zee said.

"Well, yeah," grinned Ben. "That's what I meant."

Zee thanked them all profusely for coming and promised to come by training before he left. He got invitations from three boys to stay with them next summer so he could play with the club again. He told them he'd think about it, but he didn't mean it. As much as he liked the club, summer in Exeter would not be summer in Exeter without Grandmother Winter.

"Hey," Ben said, "some of us are going to the Grecians game tomorrow. I don't know if you can, but . . ."

Zee inhaled sharply. He had entirely forgotten about

Samantha Golton. He couldn't watch the match, not now. But he had no way of contacting Samantha to let her know; he had no idea where she was staying.

"Can't," he said. "But listen, will you . . ." He trailed off. He couldn't just send Ben to give her a message. That would be . . . ill mannered. His gran had taught him better than that. He would have to meet Sam himself, tell her himself. He'd meet her, send her off to watch the match, then go straight home. "You say hi to everyone for me."

"Sure, mate. Come by next week, or we'll come get you."

The next day Zee took a bus to St. James Park an hour before match time and stood right in front of the gate. And waited.

And waited.

People flooded in around him, but none of those people was Samantha Golton. Or Ben, for that matter, or anyone else he knew.

Then, fifteen minutes before match time, he saw one of Samantha's friends a few yards away. He waved and she came toward him.

"Zachary! Hi, I'm Sarah. Sarah Rocklin."

"Pleased to meet you." Zee shook her hand formally, like a well-bred grandson would.

"Sam's not here yet?"

Zee shook his head.

"Have you heard anything from her?"

Zee blinked. "Uh, no?"

"Hmmm. She wasn't at practice yesterday, and neither was Padma. Sick, I guess."

"Oh!"

"There's something going around the dorms. I live in Exeter, so I'm not staying there, but training was pretty thin yesterday."

"Yeah, I guess ours was too."

"You guess?"

So Zee told Samantha's friend about his grandmother and the end of his summer and how he really was just there to tell them he couldn't come to the game—he was there because he couldn't be there, if that made any sense—and he had to be home to help his parents, and he was so sorry. He gave Sarah the speech he was going to give Samantha, which of course meant he would have nothing to say to Samantha at all, despite all his careful, considered preparation. Which meant that when Samantha did arrive, he would be left either repeating himself precisely and looking like a nitwit, or just stuttering aimlessly and looking like a nitwit.

But Samantha did not arrive, and neither did Padma. Zee and Sarah waited, and waited, talking of nothing until there was nothing left to talk about. They both began to shift and look at their watches and look off into the distance and shift some more. A half an hour after game time Sarah and Zee looked at each other and shrugged.

"I guess they're not coming," Sarah said uncertainly.

"They couldn't be inside?" Zee asked.

Sarah shook her head. "I've got the tickets."

"Should we call?"

"Sam doesn't have a mobile, and the dorm phone's useless."

"I hope everything's all right," Zee said.

But Zee could not help but feel that things were distinctly *not* all right. There was something sitting in his stomach, something apart from the hollowness left by his grandmother's death.

Zee couldn't have explained it to you. It didn't make any sense—there was nothing unusual about people getting sick, after all. But suddenly Zee was overcome with a sense of unease—somewhere, somehow, he sensed that something was very, very wrong.

"Um . . ." Sarah bit her lip. "I think I'll just go over to the dorms and check on them? Maybe they just forgot."

Zee looked at his watch. He was supposed to be back by now, but he knew he couldn't just leave Sarah to go off by herself. And whatever was wrong, he simply had to know.

"I'll come with you," he said.

When Zee and Sarah went to the dorms, they found Samantha, Padma, and most of the other girls in their beds, looking as if some specter had visited them and taken their souls. Sarah immediately called her mother, and soon the girls had been taken off to the hospital. Zee spent the next week calling Sarah for updates, but she never called him back, and soon he learned she had gotten sick too.

The mysterious illness swept through the young people of Exeter. One by one they took to their beds and simply could not get out again. The whole town began to panic. People could talk about nothing else. What on Earth was taking their children?

For it was only the children who were sick; as of yet there wasn't a single case of an adult with the symptoms. Some doctor on the local news one night called it the Pied Piper flu as a result, and the name stuck.

Zee watched as everyone he knew fell ill. He talked to their parents and read the newspaper and listened to various proclamations from doctors, and nothing would quell his unease. His parents weren't helping—they kept threatening to send Zee home on a train, and he had to fight to stay. It wasn't the Piper flu. Whatever needed to be done for Grandmother Winter, he would do it. Then he could leave.

So his parents quizzed him every day on his health. But Zee was fine. Whatever had ailed him was passing— day by day he felt less dizzy, less tired. Perhaps he had gotten the thing and it had affected him differently. Perhaps his immune system had fought it off. Perhaps he had never had it at all.

It seemed he was the only one.

His club called off the rest of their season for lack of a team, and the football camps were shut down. By the end of that week everyone Zee knew in Exeter, including Samantha, had been fetched by worried parents and taken home.

The only good news was that none of the kids seemed to be getting any worse—everyone stayed exactly the same. From the little Zee could gather, no one could find anything physically wrong with any of them. No one could explain their complete collapse. And no one could make them better. All anyone knew was that the Piper flu was entirely confined to Exeter, and it didn't seem to be contagious—there weren't any new cases developing around the afflicted kids who had been taken elsewhere.

The Millers themselves left Exeter two weeks after

Grandmother Winter died. They had sold her house and closed her accounts and sold off her furniture—except for the big green easy chair, which Mrs. Miller was having shipped home. The Millers may have hurried things a little at the end, but they didn't tell Zee that. They needed to get out of there. Whatever plague or poison or fungus or flu had felled Exeter's children would not get their boy.

It was with a tremendous sense of relief that the family found London was as hale and hearty as it had been when they left. Zee called all his friends and found them quite well, thank you. He met with his best friends, Phillip and Garth, for dinner the day after he got back, and they were quite well too, and all their friends were quite well, and for one night Zee put away the Piper flu and that big ol' uneasy lump. Football practice would start in two weeks and school in four, so the boys resolved to spend the rest of their summer enjoying themselves as much as they possibly could before the exigencies of school put fun to a tragic end.

As for Samantha Golton, Zee stopped off at Nicki's house on the day he got back to find that Samantha had been taken to the south of France with her family. Nicki didn't know much more—she was no better, but no worse. And yes, Nicki was feeling quite well, thank you. And so were the rest of the girls. Everyone was just great. Absolutely everyone.

Well, everyone didn't stay great for long. Two days later Garth was sick. Then Nicki. Then Phillip. It went on through his neighborhood, and through their friends, and through friends of their friends. One by one the Piper flu picked off Zee's friends, his casual acquaintances, even people he didn't like.

When Zee heard about Garth's illness—then Nicki's, then Phillip's—he wasn't even surprised. He was horrified, yes, panicked, yes, but not surprised. He had known it would come.

He wasn't uneasy anymore. The creature in his stomach had transformed itself into something much more powerful than unease. Now he was filled with fear and dread, and some kind of strange apprehension. There was something wrong, something really wrong, and it was something strange, something unnatural—and it was something to do with him.

But what?

There was no answer, just dread. He could barely eat or sleep. Every time the phone rang, he jumped out of his skin, sure that on the other end would be news of someone else who had fallen ill. His parents, who had at the first appearance of the Piper flu in London begun to talk of sending Zee to America, spent their time whispering and watching.

One night Zee decided he could not stand it anymore. He could not bear this alone. He was doing nothing, accomplishing nothing, and people were suffering.

He sat his parents down at the kitchen table, leaned in, and whispered, "I have to talk to you."

The Millers exchanged glances. "What is it?"

"It's the Piper flu."

Mrs. Miller sat straight up. "Are you feeling sick?"

"No, no, I feel fine. But . . . but . . ." Zee trailed off. He didn't know how to say it. He knew his parents sensed something was wrong. Even he could see how pale and tired he looked, and Zee was not prone to notice his own appearance.

"What? Zachary, what's going on?"

He coughed. "I think, um, I think it's something to do with me."

His parents both looked perplexed. They exchanged another glance, then his father asked gently, "What do you mean?"

"The flu. I think it's something about me. I mean, look, everyone got sick in Exeter. And now we come back here, and suddenly everyone's sick here. And it's all my friends. It's right here. It's not all of London, or we'd be hearing about it in the paper or on the news or something. It's just us. It's just . . . around me. . . ." Zee's face flushed. He could hear how he sounded.

"Sweetheart," Mrs. Miller asked, "are you saying you think you're carrying something? That you're infecting people?"

"No, not really . . . well, maybe . . ."

"Well," Mr. Miller said slowly, "you know, they've decided it's not contagious."

"I know. But I mean, think about it."

"Zach," his father continued, "just because these are the cases we know about doesn't mean these are the only ones. I mean, of course it seems like it's only all around us. But it's probably not. There could be some poor family in Birmingham who thinks they're carrying the plague too." He laughed slightly. Zee did not.

"Honey," his mother said, "if you're feeling ill, we'll take you to the doctor. I mean, you certainly were a little off for a while. We can find out for sure. That will set your mind at ease."

"And Zach," his father added, "I know you must be scared and upset. But it's not your fault. Believe me."

Zee thought if his parents exchanged any more meaningful glances, their faces would freeze that way. He couldn't make them understand. They wouldn't understand. There was only one person who would understand, and she had just died. Grandmother Winter would have believed him. She would have been able to help him. They would have figured this out together. But Grandmother Winter was gone, and he was all alone.

Preterm sports started two weeks before school for Feldwop students. On the first day just over half the team showed up for Feldwop's football practice, and as the days went on, fewer and fewer students came. Then the tennis team was hit, then rowing, then rugby. Even the chess club suffered. Finally the preterm training sessions were called off completely, for utter lack of participants.

Without training, Zee had plenty of time to see the doctor and do whatever else his parents wanted him to do, though he did not think it would help any. He had made a mistake by telling his parents what he thought— now they were just more worried, they suspected he had gone quite mad, and he was only more alone.

Mrs. Miller took him in to the doctor at the first available cancellation. She kept saying that they would get to the bottom of this, that they would help him feel better, but Zee could not help but feel that it was *her* fears she wanted to alleviate. His parents were acting suspiciously gentle with him, as if he were going to pop at any moment.

Zee didn't know what his mother had said to the doctor—perhaps something along the lines of "My son's gone barmy." But Dr. Widmapool was kind and thorough. Zee did not mention the Piper flu; indeed, they did not discuss it at all. Zee could not help but wonder if the good doctor wasn't relieved to see a patient who could sit upright.

Dr. Widmapool poked and prodded, both literally and metaphorically, and then sat Zee and his mother down.

"Well, Zachary looks just fine. I don't see any sign of this . . . this syndrome."

"Good," said Mrs. Miller.

"There is one thing in his blood work: He's a little anemic. That means your iron count is a little lower than it should be, Zachary. That may be why you were feeling dizzy and fatigued. Anemia happens, and it's not dangerous. But it's not something you normally see in healthy young boys. It means either you're not getting enough iron in your diet or else you've had some kind of blood loss. Are you a vegetarian?"

"No," Zee said.

"Have you lost any blood for any reason? An injury?"

"No," Zee said.

"Well . . . as I say, sometimes this happens. I don't see signs of anything serious. I'll want to monitor those levels. But I think a good vitamin regimen should cure you right up, and you won't feel so worn out."

"There's nothing else?" Mrs. Miller asked.

"No. No signs of infection. Other than the anemia, Zachary is a healthy young man. Though he does seem to be exhibiting some of the symptoms of stress . . . I believe that may be causing his sleeplessness and appetite trouble. I think this is perfectly understandable, given the, um, situation. Zachary, I'd like you to talk to someone. I have a name."

So Zee found himself in a psychiatrist's office. He was fairly sure this was also to make his mother feel better. With a few nice pink pills maybe whatever delusions he was having would go away, and they could all stop whispering and worrying and go back to being a normal family.

"I'm not a nutter, Mum," he told her.

"Oh, honey, I know. But you have been under a great deal of stress, and he can help you with that. Dr. Widmapool thinks it will help you sleep."

"Whatever, Mum," he said. It wasn't like he had anything else to do. It wasn't as if he could do anything to help all his sick friends. He might as well chatter away with a shrink while the Piper flu took all of England.

So he humored his parents. He sat in Dr. Vandimere's office for an hour. They talked of life in general—the upcoming school year, his activities, his plans for the future, even football, though Zee got the distinct impression Dr. Vandimere didn't know his flick header from his foot trap. Every once in a while the doctor would try to work in a more direct question, and Zee would parry as politely as he could.

"You haven't been sleeping well?"

"Bit rough."

"Tell me about your dreams."

"My dreams?"

"Yes. Is there anything you dream about that you remember in particular?"

"Doors." The word just popped out of Zee's mouth. He'd had no idea it was in there. But once it was out, he realized it was true. He dreamed of doors. At night his brain filled with them. Long, narrow corridors; hidden hallways; small, dark staircases—and at the end of them, doors. Simple, nondescript doors, the kind you could pass by a thousand times and never notice. But in Zee's dreams he wanted desperately to open them, to see what was on the other side. He could feel it, there in the psychiatrist's office, the urge to reach his hand out, wrap it around the knob, and turn. . . .

"Doors?" Dr. Vandimere repeated eagerly. He leaned in.

"Moors," Zee said. "I'm frightened of the moors. Hound of the Baskervilles and all that." He widened his eyes. "I have nightmares!"

"Ah," said Dr. Vandimere. He made a note.

"I was sorry to hear about your grandmother," the doctor said.

"Yeah," Zee said.

"You were very close."

"Yeah."

"And then the Piper flu hit."

"Yeah."

"A lot of your friends got it."

"Yeah."

"How did that make you feel?"

Zee blinked. "Uh . . . well . . ." He cut off. He was trying to be polite, but the doctor was getting awfully personal. Really, he was a perfect stranger.

The doctor shifted in his seat. "There've been a lot of cases of this flu."

"Yeah."

"And a lot of your friends are sick."

"Yeah."

"Both in Exeter and here."

"Yeah."

"The flu might even seem to be . . . following you."

Zee raised his eyebrows.

"You know, Zachary"—the doctor smiled gently—"sometimes things happen we can't understand. Sometimes bad things happen to people we care about. And when something bad happens to our friends or family, but not to us, we feel guilty. We don't know why we should be exempt, and sometimes we even begin to feel that what's happening is our fault. But it's not our fault. . . ."

Dr. Vandimere went on while Zee's ears burned. He was never ever, ever going to speak to either of his parents again. He had enough to deal with without being patronized. There was something going on, something strange and terrible, and the whole world thought he was crazy. He was just going to have to figure this out on his own.

It did not take long.

The day after his appointment with Dr. Vandimere, Zee walked to the tuck shop to get a sandwich and drink; he was on his own for dinner, as his parents were going to a meeting at Feldwop about the Piper flu that evening. Zee had wanted none of that. But he did want a sandwich, preferably a turkey one, and perhaps some crisps. All his brooding had finally caused him to work up an appetite.

So he walked the few blocks to the shop, and as he walked, he found himself extremely aware of each door he passed. There were so many of them; there were doors everywhere, countless, and they all seemed to be beckoning to him.

It was a little strange.

And there was something else, something even stranger. Zee suddenly found himself very aware of the back of his neck, like the skin itself had sentience. The feeling traveled down his spine, electrifying his back. His head tingled. His legs seemed aware and alive. And then suddenly he knew with absolute certainty what he was feeling:

Zee was being followed.

In the movies whenever people realize they are being followed, they act extremely cool. They continue walking calmly, confidently, while carefully planning their next move.

Zee did not act cool. Zee stopped right where he was and looked around wildly.

There was no one there, no one at all, just Zee alone on this sunny, door-lined street. Zee turned around and around and tried to find someone, anyone, but there was nothing.

He got his sandwich. He got his crisps. He even got a pickle. He walked back home slowly, still paranoid and prickly, swiveling his head this way and that.

He turned the corner and saw a young man on the other side of the street. It made Zee feel strangely good—he hadn't seen another young person in days, and Zee had to fight off the urge to run and talk to him. But the boy seemed preoccupied with something. He was stopped in the middle of the sidewalk, looking around curiously. Zee half nodded at him as he passed, then turned the next corner.

That's when he heard the scream.

Zee whirled around and ran back around the corner. And then he froze.

The boy was no longer alone. Two men, or something very like men, were with him. The man-like men were extremely tall, extremely thin, and extremely pale. They were wearing old-fashioned tuxedos, and their skin looked like dirty plaster. One of the man-like men was holding the boy, the other was reaching into the boy's chest, which was giving way like jelly. The boy was screaming. Zee stood, absolutely unable to move, while the second man-like man started pulling out something long and black and flimsy from the boy's chest. And then the boy stopped screaming and seemed to collapse on the spot. The second man-like man took the black thing and folded it up like fabric, while the first picked up a shiny black physician's bag and held it open with an accommodating nod. The second smiled graciously and carefully tucked the black thing away, while the first tapped the boy on the forehead three times. The second took the bag, latched it, and gave his partner a satisfied nod, and they both brushed off their hands. Then the first one noticed Zee. He nudged his friend and pointed, and the two ran off.

Zee still stood in his spot, staring at the crumpled heap of boy. The boy weakly lifted his head, stood up, and stumbled around, and still Zee stared. The sun seemed to illuminate the boy, and that's when Zee noticed.

The boy had no shadow.

Zee exploded into a run. He ran and ran, he ran all the way home, and then he did not leave his house until his parents put him on a plane headed out of England.

CHAPTER 12

The Footmen

PHILONECRON HAD PLACED A DISCREET ORDER WITH the Underworld's best tailor. It cost him an arm and a leg (though not his), and Charon required his usual "service fee" for smuggling messages and goods back and forth from Exile. But Philonecron was not afraid to pay for quality, and he would have only the best for his Footmen—for that's what he had decided to call his new servants. He believed excellence inspired further excellence, and his would not be some hastily stitched, poly-blend, puckery-seamed, one-size-fits-all coup; no, no—Philonecron's revolution would be pearl buttoned, satin trimmed, and completely pucker-free.

This particular tailor had a reputation for working quite swiftly, as you might if you had two dozen arms (and were ambidextrous to boot), and in just two days Philonecron found on his doorstep (or what would have been his doorstep if he hadn't been exiled and weren't living in a godsforsaken cave—but, you know, stiff upper lip and all that) twelve promising-looking packages wrapped up in the tailor's own freshly shedded skin.

At the sight of the packages Philonecron let out what can only be called a squeal—as if he were a young girl on Christmas morning rushing to the tree to find a golden-haired puppy while a hush of snow fell over the world. A squeal is not a sound one might associate with an evil genius, but evil geniuses are people too (or in this case, not really), and they experience involuntary vocalizations just like you or I.

Philonecron squealed, and his squeal reverberated through Exile. The ground shivered, the stalagmites rattled, the stalactites trembled, the Unburied quavered, and the twelve buck-naked Footmen stood up as one and moved to attend to their master—who was more than a little moved by the gesture. He watched, marveling, as they lined up in a careful arc in front of him, precise and proud.

Philonecron sighed with pleasure. The men regarded him blankly, faces etched out of shadow and clay. He smiled munificently back at them and gestured to the packages. "Hold out your arms!" he sang, and, like that, twelve long, spindly pairs of arms dutifully shot out, ready to receive whatever burden he might bestow on them.

"Close your eyes!" he trilled, and twelve pairs of yellow eyes disappeared behind twelve pairs of heavy gray-white lids.

"Are they closed? . . . Good! Don't open them until I tell you to!" With great ceremony Philonecron walked down the line, one by one putting a package in a pair of arms. The Footmen did not move. When he was done, he took his place in front of them. "Right, now open your eyes!"

The Footmen were not very experienced at this sort of thing, and anyway, they tended to take their orders quite literally. So it took some coaching for Philonecron to get them to look down at the bundles their gray-white arms were embracing.

"Yes! Yes!" He held his arms out magnanimously. "They're for you, my children! Go on! Go on! Put them on!"

It wasn't for several more minutes that Philonecron was able to get the Footmen to unwrap their packages, examine the garments, and then put them on. He never would have believed it before, but inbred, mindless loyalty does have its drawbacks.

But Philonecron's spirits were not to be dampened, and he in turn closed his eyes while his men dressed, and did not open them again until they were all lined up in their new finery.

And what he beheld made it all worthwhile. When his eyes opened, he let out a gasp. He shook his head. He clasped his hands together. His eyes moistened.

"Why," he exclaimed, "you're all just so . . . *beautiful!*"

The Footmen were wearing exquisitely crafted tuxedos with jet-black jackets trimmed with silk, impeccably tailored to the angular contours of their wearers. They wore white ties, white gloves, with crisply starched snow-white shirts, white silk waistcoats, and impeccably folded white silk handkerchiefs poking out of the breast pockets. Philonecron could practically see his reflection in their shoes.

Something happened to the Footmen when they put on their finery. They altered, grew into their sartorial molds—almost as if they were made out of clay. Which, in fact, they were. The transformation was not physical, exactly; they had been blank, mindless automatons, and they had become, well, still mindless, but possessed of dignity, elegance, and grace.

"Exquisite," he breathed. "Just exquisite!"

The Footmen all smiled their very first smiles and bowed their heads graciously one by one.

"My goodness," Philonecron enthused. "You're all so . . . well bred!"

Well, really, it was only natural. They were made with his blood, after all.

"Now," he said. "Come close, my beautiful darlings, and I will tell you what we are going to do."

It had all begun with the boy. You know. The Death. The old English woman. The family tableau. The man, the woman, and the boy. Something about the boy. His shadow. His shadow was loose!

Right then Philonecron knew that all of his problems had been solved. But he did not know quite how yet.

He stared at the boy and he thought. He thought hard.

And then he came up with a plan.

A delicious, delightful, delovely plan.

A lesser evil genius would have taken the boy's shadow right away. But not Philonecron. One shadow does not an army make. He would leave the boy's shadow, but he would take his blood.

Just a little. Not enough to kill him or anything;

Philonecron had a feeling he would need the boy later on, and anyway, he seemed like such a nice boy. The boy would be fine—woozy for a while, but fine. Children are awfully resilient.

He couldn't take the blood right then, of course, with the boy conscious and his parents right there. Yes, denizens from the Underworld can walk around the Upperworld unseen, but it's fairly hard to take blood from someone without his noticing. Philonecron didn't want anyone to start getting suspicious and behaving rashly. He would have to wait until the boy was sleeping.

It was all right. He had plenty to do before then.

Philonecron spent four hours wandering the city, studying people and their shadows and the connections thereof. In the past he had regarded trips to the Upperworld as a necessary evil (that's *evil* in a bad way, nothing at all like *evil genius*, which is a wonderful thing)—you couldn't be a blood smuggler without visiting the realm of the Living. But he had always found these sojourns unpleasant—and it had little to do with all one had to endure just to come and go thanks to Hades's precious Security Decree. The Upperworld had become so *uncivilized*. The way people *dress* . . .

But on this day Philonecron felt nothing but joy as he orbited as far from the scene of the Death as he could. He loved the people, with their exposed legs and artificial fibers and white socks and vulgar shoes, for they were going to save him.

Since his first trip to the Upperworld Philonecron had always been fascinated by shadows. There was no such thing in the Underworld; shadows were a peculiar product of Life—something about the reaction between light and the Life Essence that allowed people and animals and things to exist in the Upperworld. (One of these days Philonecron would figure out what that Essence was so he could wander around the Upperworld unchecked, but that would be another evil plan for another day.)

But for some reason he'd never paid any attention to children before. Perhaps it was because they were loud and too full of Life, or perhaps it was simply because one did not tend to find children around scenes of Death. Or perhaps he simply had never before been looking for an army.

On this day, though, Philonecron sought out as many children as he could find, Life Essence and all. Much to his delight, he learned that the boy, whom he had begun to think of affectionately as Patient Zero, was no aberration. If shadows were caused by the interplay between light and Life, a child's was still forming. An adult's was inextricably bound to his body, but a child had a tenuous relationship to his own permanence, and thus, his own shadow.

And so the shadow could be taken.

It would take a little work, a good spell or two, and he might have to materialize to carry it off. He might need to do a quick time spell or freezing spell, since children tended to congregate in groups and there was no sense in scaring the little dears off before they did their service to his cause, was there? But none of that would be difficult. In fact, right over there, look! Two children of just the right age. Let's give it the old college try. Be careful now. Approach them softly. Mutter a few words. They're frozen now, they won't notice a thing. Reach into their bodies. . . . And there you go. Handle the shadows carefully, you don't want them to rip. That's right. Now, fold them up and put them safely in your breast pocket. Tonight you will experiment.

Philonecron patted the samples in his pocket with glee. It was a good start. There would be much left for him to do, of course. He would have to figure out how to enchant the shadows, how to turn them into soldiers. He would probably need to find a way to replicate them, for shadow collecting would be time consuming. And being around children tired him easily—now he was already beginning to feel the familiar stretching of his skin that meant he had stayed in the Upperworld too long, that this world of light and breath and time was beginning to wear on him. He would need some help.

Some servants to help him gather the shadows. He would so like to have servants.

His skin was beginning to look rashy, his inner organs felt like someone was tugging on them, and his mind was filling with clouds. But he had one more errand to run.

He went back to the scene of the Death—already that made him feel a little better—and found the boy's room. There was a nice chair in the corner, so he sat and waited. Darkness spread over the room, and soon the door opened and Zero came in and got into the bed. Philonecron wanted to hug him, to cradle him, to sing him to sleep—you wonderful boy, you have changed the world. But instead he just sat and watched as the boy's breathing became long and steady. His chest heaved up and down so peacefully, and Philonecron took a moment to think of the great beauty of childhood and of the fragility of Life. Really, he thought, nothing is more precious than watching a child sleep. Then he got up, picked up the boy's arm, and drained some blood.

Mission accomplished, he headed to the nearest door to wait for the Messenger.

Philonecron had given the Footmen careful instructions on how to navigate the Upperworld. In a way, he hated to send them up there; they were such precious, pure creatures, and he was loath to corrupt them with the world of Life. But that's what they were for, there was no getting around it. And they proved quick and willing studies, eager to sip from his font of knowledge, to strive to improve themselves, to work to be the best they could be. They reminded Philonecron so much of himself.

He taught them a few spells, enough for shadow stealing, stealth, protection, and minor time manipulation. But he had no idea what it would be like for them up there. Would they be seen? How long could they stay? Would they be frightened? All he could do was give them as many tools as he could and then send them out into the world, heart in his throat.

His last gift to them, before their first journey, was a small vial of Zero's blood.

"Keep this close to you at all times," he said. "When you go into the Upperworld, you will find yourself drawn toward the site of a Death. Resist. Take out this vial of blood. Smell it. Then pick out the scent in the air and follow it. It will lead you to a boy. His name is Zero. When you find Zero, follow him. He will lead you to your shadows."

Sometimes Philonecron was stunned by his own genius. He could have sent his men out willy-nilly, but that would just waste time. Death so often led to blood, but rarely to children. *Children*, on the other hand, inevitably led to more of the little rascals. Of this he was certain.

He sent out two of the Footmen on the first day with an impassioned "Go out, my darlings, go out and conquer." He spent the next several hours pacing back and forth in his cave, unable to do anything either evil or genius.

But then there they were, at the mouth of the cave, with their cracking, flaky mouths set in satisfied grins. Philonecron stopped his pacing and stared at them. One by one they unfolded shadows—one, two, three, four, five, six, seven! Seven shadows for a few hours' work. The shadows were in perfect condition, not a tear in the bunch. And the two Footmen, the two glorious Footmen, bowed from the waist and left Philonecron to his shadows.

The game was on.

Philonecron set up a little evil laboratory in a spacious cave nearby where he could experiment on the shadows. He found he could replicate them, but only about a hundred per shadow before the original became worn.

It took some doing to enchant the shadows, and even when he did, they tended to float around like specters, not behave like good little soldiers. That would take some doing. Zero's blood proved essential for everything. He should have known—well, he did know. That's the sort of evil genius he was. Every single shadow got a drop of the boy's blood. Certainly any human blood would have sufficed to give them Life, but by giving them the blood from the same person—well, did he mention he was a genius? You'll see why later.

The Footmen all had their different methods of shadow stealing. Beta, Zeta, Lambda, and Mu liked to stop time before the children saw them, freezing the creatures in the most delightful positions, reaching in and grabbing the shadows, then leaving the children frozen until the spell wore off. Kappa, Alpha, and Theta chose to let themselves be seen, then freeze the children in their postures of horror, whereas Delta, Epsilon, Iota, Gamma, and Eta preferred not to stop time at all, letting the children scream through the whole process until they passed out. Variety being the spice of life.

During the day the Footmen went out, and Philonecron experimented on the shadows. At night they gathered in Philonecron's cave and he read to them, or played music, or lectured on philosophy or history or fine wine. Then the Footmen slept—they slept standing up, like little wax statues. They were so adorable.

And every day the pile of shadows grew.

Zero was proving extremely cooperative, too. Just when the Footmen had collected almost all the shadows from the town that they possibly could, the boy left. It didn't take long to find him, and when they did—oh, what a day! He had gone to London. London! They would never have to worry about running out of shadows now, as long as the boy wasn't some sort of housebound misfit. Which he wasn't. He was intelligent, social, athletic, involved, handsome! He was wonderful, he was perfect, he was *something*, he was Philonecron's little Zero. Philonecron had chosen perfectly, perfectly—how his shadows would be inspired by the boy's commands!

(Oops. Well, he let that slip, didn't he? Philonecron never could keep a secret. But he had learned from his weeks of shadow work that the final step in bringing the shadows to Life would be the commands of the human whose blood they had been enchanted with. That being Zero. He'd have to find a way to convince the boy to speak the words, but that shouldn't be a problem. He'd spent enough time with the boy's blood that he wouldn't have too much trouble with the mind control, and he'd already begun working on luring Zero down to the Underworld.)

Philonecron didn't even notice when things went

terribly wrong; he was too busy working in his laboratory training the shadows to become ethereal when
attacked. But for four days the Footmen came back
empty-handed. At night on the fifth day the captain of
the Footmen appeared in the doorway of Philonecron's
cave. Philonecron could tell just by looking at him that
something was amiss—not that the Footman betrayed
any emotion, but a good father always knows.

"My Lord. I am sorry to disturb you. But . . ."

Alpha was the only one of the Footmen who had
speech. Philonecron did not think it necessary for them
all to talk. He did so detest noise, and after all, what
would they say? One would be just fine; Alpha could
speak for all of them. Alpha's voice was barely even a
voice; it was as if he moved air around to form syllables,
as if the wind itself whispered in Philonecron's ear.
Really, it was quite pleasant.

"My dear. Come in. What's bothering you?"

Alpha bowed in response. "My Lord. There is a
problem."

Philonecron put his arm around his servant. "Well
then, we'll fix it. Tell me everything."

Alpha's face grew long, even longer than usual. "It's
Zero. He's stopped leaving the house."

"What do you mean?"

"He has not left his house in days. I believe"—he

cleared his throat—"I believe he encountered some of us in medias res, and he has not left the house since. I do not think he is coming out. I am so sorry, my Lord, I do not know how it happened. We were careless, and . . ."

The Footman cringed a little, as if Philonecron were going to beat him. Beat him! His little darling! No, no. Accidents happen.

And it didn't matter. If Philonecron were some kind of evil simpleton, they would have had to start over, find a new Zero, steal shadows all over again. But he was a genius—a *genius*—and geniuses always have a Plan B. The day after Alpha and Delta came back with the first shadows, he had taken a vial of Zero's blood, gone out into the Upperworld, and done an errand of his own. It had proved quite satisfactory.

"Fret not, my sweet," he said, squeezing Alpha's shoulders. "I have a backup plan."

PART THREE

The End of the Beginning

CHAPTER 13

Go

BACK IN THE MIELSWETZSKI DEN, CHARLOTTE STARED at her cousin while he haltingly told his story. Grandmothers, plagues, strange man-like men, and shadowless boys—she had no idea what to think. The way she saw it, there were three options:

    1. Zee was pulling her leg.
    2. Zee was certifiably loony.
    3. Zee was telling the truth.

Charlotte meditated on these options, conscious of her cousin's eyes on her. Even Bartholomew, who had listened attentively to the entire story, was watching her.

He didn't seem like he was pulling her leg, unless he was the best actor ever. It would be a strange joke—one that, frankly, required more imagination than her cousin had shown so far. And if Charlotte was to be fair, it required a lot more meanness, too. Zee might be a little strange, but he was not mean. She glanced at her cousin and blushed.

"You think I'm having you on?" said Zee quietly. His eyes dropped.

Charlotte squinted at him. She was becoming very good at translating British to English. "No," she said. "I don't think you're pulling my leg."

It was entirely possible that Zee was crazy. He certainly had been acting like it this entire time. There was some great mystery surrounding her cousin, and Uncle John had said something about him acting "unusual." This was unusual, all right. If she had a kid who told stories like this, she'd ship him out of the country too.

Plus, he had recently had a head injury. That could explain a lot.

But when Charlotte had first thought Zee was bonkers, on the very first night, it was because he'd kept asking if anyone was sick. And then everyone got sick. If he *was* crazy, he was awfully prescient, too.

And there was something else. The men. The tall, thin, man-like men in the tuxedos. When Zee was talking about the creepy men on the street, something in her brain had stood at attention, and her stomach rose in her belly.

She could close her eyes and picture those men, just as he had described—the strange, old tuxedos; the grayish-white skin; the freakishly chapped lips. She had seen those men before.

But where?

An involuntary shiver ran through Charlotte. That thing in her brain started to dance around urgently. She regarded her cousin carefully.

"You think I'm barmy?" muttered Zee.

Slowly Charlotte shook her head. "No," she mumbled. "I don't think you're nuts."

And that left only one option. . . .

Could he really be telling the truth?

Charlotte chewed on her lips. Her stomach was still floating around in her belly, and her skin felt prickly. She couldn't get the afterimage of those man-like men out of her mind. She looked up at her cousin, who was regarding her closely. His eyes were big, and for a moment he seemed very small. They looked at each other for a while, saying nothing. Zee gulped.

"So," he said in a whisper, "do you believe me?"

The words hung in the air. Charlotte couldn't help but notice how desperate he sounded. "I don't know," she answered truthfully. She closed her eyes. She shuddered. "Maybe?"

Zee exhaled loudly. "Okay. Okay," he said. "If you want, well, I know a way . . . I could prove it to you."

Charlotte ducked into her room to pick up what they would need, and then she and Zee walked down the stairs together as quietly as they could. Charlotte knew a confrontation with her mother was inevitable, but she still held out hope that the world was a magical, wonderful place where she could sneak in and out of the house without her mother even noticing.

"Charlotte?"

Alas, the world was not such a place.

"Mom?" Charlotte called innocently. She and Zee froze by the coat closet. Bartholomew, who had followed them downstairs, started running back and forth along the front hallway.

"What are you doing?" Mrs. Mielswetzski's voice carried in from the living room. Charlotte glanced at Zee.

"We're going out!" she said brightly.

"Oh, are we?"

Charlotte sighed as she heard footsteps approach. Her mother stood in front of them, hands on hips. "And just where do you think you're going?" she said in her very motherly way. Bartholomew started batting at her ankles.

Charlotte's eyes grew wide. "We have to give Maddy her homework. Zee wanted to come with." This is what made Charlotte a good liar; she was quick thinking, earnest, and remorseless. In fact, she was at her most sincere when she was lying. Her parents still hadn't caught on.

"Oh, did he?" Mrs. Mielswetzski gazed at Zee, and then back at Charlotte, in her *I know this is all your fault* kind of way.

"Mom, he's fine. He said he was feeling much better." Charlotte elbowed Zee in the kidneys.

"Um, yes, Aunt Tara," he added quickly. "I could really do with some exercise. I feel much better, but I really need some fresh air."

Charlotte exhaled. He had said just the right thing. Her mother was a great believer in fresh air.

Indeed, Mrs. Mielswetzski visibly relaxed. "All right," she said. "Just . . . be careful. Bundle up."

"Mom! It's really warm."

"Charlotte, there's something going around. You're lucky I'm letting you out of the house."

"Bundling up's not going to help," Charlotte muttered, glancing at Zee. She grabbed her coat.

Mrs. Mielswetzski had not heard. "I'm sure I'm going to regret this. I've never heard of them canceling school," she sighed. "You be careful out there. And your father says dinner's in an hour. Don't be late. And Charlotte?"

"Yes?"

Her mother's expression softened. "You're nice to help your friend. Tell Maddy I hope she feels better soon."

"Thanks, Mom." Charlotte smiled a little.

But her mom wasn't looking at her anymore. "What is that cat doing?"

Charlotte and Zee turned to look. Bartholomew was standing directly in front of the front door, staring at Charlotte and Zee. Her tail had puffed out to twice its size, and a low growling sound was emanating from somewhere deep within her. Charlotte and Zee took a step toward her and the growling grew louder. She backed up against the door and starting hissing.

"See?" Mrs. Mielswetzski said, laughing a little. "Even the kitten doesn't want you to go out."

Eyes wide, Charlotte approached Bartholomew, picked up the hissing, growling, scratching, puffy hell beast, and gingerly set her aside.

Charlotte had not been completely lying to her mother; they *were* going to Maddy's house. She had been truthful about the destination of their visit, if not the reason, the best lies having some truth to them, and all.

The cousins walked along in silence in the cooling evening air, while Charlotte mused further on Zee's story. It did sound crazy, but who was to say there weren't weird, creepy, tuxedo-wearing shadow thieves wandering around? It was possible. Anything's *possible*.

And, of course, Uncle John and Aunt Suzanne's reaction was so classic. Her parents would have sent her into therapy too. It would just never occur to them that he might actually be telling the truth.

And if it was true, none of them, neither the Millers nor the Mielswetzskis, were going to be any help at all. Which was so typical.

"Now," Charlotte said when they got to the Rubys' door, "let me do the talking."

Zee coughed a little. Charlotte rang the doorbell.

Mrs. Ruby answered the door, looking even more tired than before. "Charlotte? Hello. Come on in."

"Hi, Mrs. Ruby," Charlotte said. "I wanted to give Maddy today's homework. Oh, this is my cousin Zee."

Zee stiffened and stuck out his arm. "It's a pleasure to meet you."

Mrs. Ruby blinked and shook his hand formally. "And you, Zee."

"He's from England," Charlotte explained. "How's Maddy?"

"Oh, well . . . I'm sure she'll be better soon." Mrs. Ruby smiled thinly. Mrs. Ruby was not a very good liar. Charlotte's stomach turned.

Maddy's room was the same dark, cold place it had been when Charlotte last saw it, and Maddy looked just as lifeless as she had before. She smiled at Charlotte, but she didn't even lift her head, and for a moment Charlotte forgot why they had come.

"Hi, Maddy," Charlotte said softly, sitting down next to her friend. "Are you okay?" It was so dark in the room she could barely see her face.

Maddy shrugged.

Charlotte leaned in. "What's *wrong?*"

Maddy's eyes grew into small, round moons. "I'm just so *tired*," she said weakly.

"It's okay, Maddy," she said softly, grabbing her friend's hand. "You'll get better."

"I don't know." Her eyes traveled to Zee, who was standing in the back of the room. "Oh! . . . Hi . . ."

In the sickbed moment Charlotte had almost forgotten the reason for their trip, but at the reminder of Zee's presence in the room everything came flooding back to her. She stiffened, then said, too brightly, "Zee's here . . . he wanted to say hi."

"Oh!" Maddy said, casting a *You should have warned me* look at Charlotte. She moved, as if to sit up.

"No, it's all right." Zee stepped forward anxiously. "Don't . . . don't. I just wanted to say . . . I hope you feel better."

"So," Charlotte interjected breezily, "I've got your homework. Mr. Metos said you don't have to worry about the rest of the unit, isn't that nice? And do you know there's no school all week? So you won't be missing anything. Cool, huh? With the long weekend, that makes a whole week off. You'll be back in school with the rest of us on Wednesday. Then you can get back to helping me with my math." Charlotte smiled limply, while Zee stepped back into the shadows. Meanwhile, Maddy had faded into her pillows.

"Hey, um, Maddy?" Charlotte said tentatively. "Can we ask you something?"

"Yeah?"

"When you were walking home on Monday, you know, when you got sick? Did anything, um, happen?"

"Huh?"

"Oh, you know . . . did you see anything . . . weird? Or . . . anyone?" Charlotte eyed her friend carefully.

Maddy shook her head. "No. No," she whispered. "I

was just walking, and I don't know. I must have fainted or something. I was fine, and then I woke up on the ground. I could barely get home."

"And that's all?"

"Well . . . just about . . ."

"What else?" Charlotte leaned in. Zee, too, stepped forward.

"Oh, it's nothing. It's crazy. I just had this weird feeling. Like . . ." She didn't have to continue. Charlotte knew exactly what she was going to say, and her brain formed the words just as Maddy said them—*Like I was being watched.*

There was a knock on the door, and then Mrs. Ruby opened it slightly. A beam of light invaded the room, and Maddy visibly winced. "Charlotte? Honey, I think we should let Maddy rest now."

"Okay, Mrs. Ruby," Charlotte said. "I just need to show her something in the math homework."

"Well . . ." She entered the room, and Zee stepped back farther. "Charlotte, maybe now isn't the best time."

"It's really important," Charlotte said. "We'll just be another minute."

"It's okay, Mom," said Maddy quietly.

Mrs. Ruby sighed. "Okay, Charlotte. I'll be back up in one minute." She shook her head and then left.

Charlotte and Zee exchanged a look. Charlotte was

beginning to feel very sweaty. Maddy murmured, "Anyway, Char, we can wait on the math. . . ."

"No, no," Charlotte said, reaching into her pocket. "It's not math. I just wanted to give you some pictures of Bartholomew . . . I thought they might make you feel better."

"Oh!" Maddy said. "Yeah! Let me see. . . ." Charlotte held the pictures up to her friend, heart in her throat. "Zee, would you mind bringing over that lamp?" She motioned to the bedside table. "It should reach."

Zee moved quickly over to the table. Charlotte squeezed her eyes shut. She heard the sound of her cousin clicking on the lamp and then moving it toward them. She felt the beam of the light on her. Maddy started cooing over the pictures, and Charlotte slowly opened her eyes. She knew exactly what she would see; she had known all along. There were shadows from the photos, from Zee, and from Charlotte, but Maddy cast no shadow at all.

On the way home Charlotte and Zee walked close together through the dusk, talking in whispers. Zee seemed strangely relaxed; Charlotte supposed it helped that someone believed him finally. Charlotte was not relaxed at all, not one bit. Her mouth tasted sour, her stomach was burning, and her heart had expanded to six times its normal size. She shook her head.

"I don't understand," Charlotte said.

"Neither do I, really," said Zee.

"Why would someone take kids' shadows?"

"I don't know," said Zee.

"And why would it make everyone so sick? I mean, it's just . . . a shadow. It's not *real*. Is it?"

"I don't know," said Zee.

"Maybe they are real. I mean, how can you take them if they're not real?"

"I don't know," said Zee.

"But that's really weird," said Charlotte. "I mean, even if they are real, why would you want them?"

"I don't know," said Zee.

"I mean, it's obviously something evil. It has to be."

"I don't know," said Zee.

"And why are they following you? I mean, they clearly are."

"I don't know," said Zee.

"And what would they want with shadows, anyway?"

Zee stopped. He turned and looked at Charlotte. "Look," he said. "I've been thinking about this for a long time. A long time. *Constantly*. And I just don't know. It doesn't make any sense. I can't figure it out, and I don't see any way to figure it out. But"—he stepped closer and looked her in the eyes—"that doesn't matter. There's only one thing that matters."

"What's that?" Charlotte asked.

"How are we going to save everyone?"

Charlotte blinked. She had nothing to say to that.

"We're the only ones who know what's going on," Zee continued. "And no one will believe us. Something really bad is happening, and we need to stop it and we need to save everyone. Or"—he shrugged—"at least I do." He appraised her.

Charlotte still didn't speak. She felt distinctly like vomiting.

"Anyway." Zee started walking again. "This has got something to do with me. It's my responsibility. And I might be immune. For some reason they're not attacking me. I don't know why. I was the only one who didn't get sick in Exeter and in London, wasn't I? Of course, that doesn't mean . . ."

"What?" Charlotte said.

"Well . . ." He looked at her frankly. "I don't know whether or not they would attack *you*."

"Oh." Charlotte contemplated this for a moment. It sounded quite unpleasant. She bit her lip.

"Hey," Zee said suddenly. "Did you hear something?"

She hadn't. Something else had occurred to her. "You

know," she said slowly, "those guys. The men. I think I've dreamed about them."

"What?" Zee exclaimed. He stopped and stared at her.

"I swear. When you mentioned them before. It sounded so familiar. And I've just figured it out. I've dreamed about them."

"Like, how?"

"I think . . . they were sucking me into the earth." She shuddered. "Like Persephone."

"Sorry?"

"Oh. English. Greek myths. We were doing the underworld before you got here. We were talking about how Hades kidnaps Persephone and makes her his queen, and I guess I dreamed about that."

"Weird!" He thought for a minute. "So you were having a dream about something you were talking about in English, and those men were in it."

"Yeah."

"Maybe they have the power to work their way into normal dreams?"

"Maybe," said Charlotte.

"I dream about doors," Zee added offhandedly.

"Doors?"

"All the time. I'm always opening doors. It could be—" Zee stopped and looked around again. "There. You didn't hear anything?"

"No," said Charlotte.

Zee leaned in. "Come on," he whispered. "Let's go home."

And then Charlotte did hear something. Something sibilant and sneaky, something creepy and close. Her stomach dropped into her intestines. And she felt something too, something shadowy and sinister. Her skin began to prickle. . . .

"Zee!" she exclaimed.

"Run!"

But it was too late. There, right in front of them, were two man-like men, with gray-white skin and dead-looking yellow eyes set in a face like a skeleton's. Charlotte screamed, and the men smiled and bowed— and if you asked Charlotte, that was the creepiest part of all.

The cousins turned as one and began to run in the opposite direction. Charlotte was struck with the feeling that she was about to be sucked into the earth. Or worse.

She thought she was still screaming, but the world seemed absolutely silent all of a sudden. She could feel her feet running, but she wasn't sure she was moving. All seemed strange and still. She knew, somehow, that if she looked behind her, the man-like men would still be standing, still smiling, just as close as they were before.

The world was a lonely, terrible, cold place—and utterly silent.

Then, suddenly, a sound burst into the night—a loud motor, a squeal of tires, then a bright light. A car turned the corner and barreled down the street toward them. Charlotte and Zee ran toward it; Charlotte wanted to jump in front of it because getting hit by a car was surely better than what was about to happen to her.

She could hear her voice again and could feel her feet pounding against the pavement. She ran toward the car and heard her cousin doing the same. She didn't know where the men were, and she didn't want to look back to find out.

The car squealed to a stop right in front of them, the passenger door flew open, and a voice yelled, "Get in!"

Charlotte gasped. It was Mr. Metos.

CHAPTER 14

Mr. Metos Explains
it All

Charlotte and Zee sat side by side in the passenger seat of Mr. Metos's battered old sedan. Charlotte felt like her organs had been ripped from her body. Zee didn't look much better.

"What were you kids doing outside?" Mr. Metos muttered. He didn't sound like he wanted an answer.

It took Charlotte some time to regain power of thought. She sat huddled next to her cousin, who had his eyes closed and was slowly breathing in and out, as if to reassure himself that he still could.

They drove on in silence, block after block.

Charlotte put her brain back in place, then her throat, then her heart and lungs, then her stomach. It took some time to untangle her intestines, which seemed to be intertwined with her kneecaps.

That done, Charlotte could focus on her immediate situation. She had a thousand questions. As in, what on Earth was Mr. Metos doing there, what were they doing in Mr. Metos's car, and what in the world was going to happen to them now? Charlotte had a strange urge to open the door and run all the way home, grab Bartholomew, hide under the bed, and never ever, ever come out.

But then she would never find out the answers to these thousands of questions, and frankly, she really wanted to know, and besides, she didn't have any breath left to run.

Mr. Metos did not seem in a particularly chatty mood. He was a lot less frightening than the man-like men, but that really wasn't saying much.

Charlotte gulped. "Um, where are we going?" she asked quietly.

"To my apartment," Mr. Metos said brusquely. "We have much to discuss."

Charlotte's heart flipped. "I'm supposed to be home for dinner," she whispered.

Mr. Metos raised his eyebrows and just kept driving.

Charlotte huddled closer in to her cousin, who looked nearly catatonic. Eventually they pulled up behind a small white brick apartment building in a neighborhood full of such buildings. The only thing that distinguished this one from the others was a big sign that read, IF YOU LIVED HERE, YOU WOULD BE HOME BY NOW.

Charlotte could not argue with that logic.

Mr. Metos parked right next to the building. Zee awoke from his coma and dutifully began to open the passenger door, but Mr. Metos whispered harshly, "Don't." Zee quickly shrank back in his seat, and Charlotte didn't know whether to be comforted or even more frightened that Zee seemed scared of Mr. Metos too.

Charlotte and Zee watched while Mr. Metos got out of the car, closed the door softly, and began to walk slowly around the parking lot. He stopped a few times, looking around carefully. Finally he walked up to the passenger door, opened it, and hurried them out.

"Quickly, now," he said, ushering them to the building door. Up a flight of stairs they went, then another, then another, feet echoing noisily in the concrete stairwells. The lights buzzed and flickered overhead. Charlotte was conscious of Mr. Metos behind them, moving them with his gaze.

When they got to Mr. Metos's apartment, Charlotte

immediately thought it looked a great deal like his class-room—small, dark, and bare. There was a little, brownish kitchen to the right, in the sitting room was a tan couch on which rested a bed pillow and a folded-up blanket, and to the left Charlotte could see a room that seemed to be filled entirely with books. And right in front of her, on the counter, sat a small phone. And that reminded her:

"I have to call my mom. She'll think . . ." Charlotte gulped a little. "She'll think something happened to us."

It wasn't until she had finished dialing that Charlotte realized she had no idea what to say to her mother, who of course picked up on the first ring. Charlotte was a good liar, but really, how on earth was she supposed to come up with a plausible narrative if her mother picked up on the first ring? "Mom, hi!" she gasped. "Um, we ran into our English teacher walking home from Maddy's, and he invited us over to dinner. . . ."

There was a pause. "Your father made turkey burgers," said Mrs. Mielswetzski flatly.

"Um, it's extra credit," said Charlotte. As soon as the words came out of her mouth, she winced. It was her worst lie ever.

Mrs. Mielswetzski just sighed heavily. "Oh, well . . . they'll keep. Mr. Metos will be driving you home, I hope?"

"I'm sure," Charlotte grimaced.

"You better let me talk to him."

Charlotte panicked. "He's in the bathroom!" she said. "He's been there awhile! Um, I have to go. We'll be home in a couple hours." And she threw the phone back on its hook as if it were burning.

She looked up, blushing. That had not been her best performance. Mr. Metos was looking at her oddly. Zee was still standing in the entrance, staring at the door (which was also odd) and hugging his coat around him. It *was* awfully cold in there. Charlotte was suddenly conscious again of being a human, one who felt cold, hunger, exhaustion, and tremendous thirst. She stood by the kitchen and bit her lip. Mr. Metos was standing a little awkwardly, looking at both of them as if he'd never seen human children before.

"Um," Mr. Metos said, "you can sit down over there." He motioned to the furniture brusquely. Charlotte guessed he didn't entertain a lot. She nudged Zee, and together they plopped down on the sofa, which was awfully squishy. Charlotte wanted to wrap the folded-up blanket around herself, but she had a feeling that it was what Mr. Metos slept with, and that was just . . . icky.

Mr. Metos went over to the small kitchen and poured himself a glass of water. Then he moved into the living room and proceeded to drink it. Charlotte gulped.

"Uh, Mr. Metos?" she said in a very, very high voice. "Could I . . . could I have something to drink?"

Mr. Metos blinked rapidly. "Oh. Yes. Of course." He stood up and went to the kitchen. "Um. I have vegetable juice or, well . . ."

"Water would be fine," said Charlotte.

When Mr. Metos handed her a glass—which she had to share with Zee, who was looking at it longingly—Charlotte noticed that he couldn't seem to meet her eyes, and he might even have stammered a little. He was nothing like the teacher who stared down kids in class and made Charlotte fear for her neck. He was acting like one of the weird kids in gym class who always got picked last for the team. In this small, dark, underfurnished apartment he didn't seem like a monster anymore, but like a man. A kind of weird, very pale, socially retarded, vegetable-juice-drinking man.

Or perhaps once you've been chased by freakish, eight-foot-tall, skeleton-like goons in tuxedos, your creepy English teacher just isn't as scary anymore.

But just as Charlotte was finishing these thoughts, Mr. Metos seemed to regain himself. He leaned against the half wall in front of them and looked them over. "All right," he said. "Let's just get to the point. I'm going to tell you something, and this is going to sound very strange, but I must assure you that it is the absolute truth." He seemed to be regaining his teacherly composure, Charlotte noticed, now that he was instructing again. "Those men who were chasing you, well . . . they were trying to steal Charlotte's shadow."

A moment of silence. Mr. Metos looked probingly at both of them. Charlotte glanced at Zee, who glanced back at Charlotte. "We know," Charlotte said.

Mr. Metos blinked. "You *know*?"

They both nodded.

"I see." Mr. Metos raised his eyebrows. "What else do you know?"

"Well . . ." Charlotte bit her lip. "That's about it."

Then—slowly, carefully—Mr. Metos told them many things that they did not know. Like that the whole Greek mythology thing was actually true; they weren't myths at all. The Underworld was real too, all of it. And now there was a guy, a Phil something, and he was trying to stage a coup in the Underworld—with the help of twelve creepy man-like Footmen formed of clay and an entire army of shadows.

Well.

Upon reflection Charlotte decided that she was taking it all rather well. Which shouldn't have been too much of a surprise; after all, the day had been full of bends to the mind, and other parts of the body too, and Charlotte had really already been as surprised as she possibly could be. There was no more surprise left. Okay, Greek myths real. Underworld real. Coups with shadow army, creepy men made of clay, and Mr. Metos drinks vegetable juice.

Fine.

Charlotte pondered it all for a while, and Zee appeared to be pondering too in an equally unsurprised kind of way, and Mr. Metos watched them both ponder, perhaps surprised at their unsurprisedness—until Charlotte thought of something that did, indeed, surprise her.

"Hey," she said. "How do you know all this?"

Mr. Metos cleared his throat. "Well . . . there are those in the Underworld whose only loyalty is to money."

"Oh." Charlotte was wise in the ways of the world, and she got his meaning, though she couldn't help thinking that maybe Mr. Metos should spend a little less of his money bribing people and a little more on furniture. Still, it wasn't what she meant. "No, I mean . . . why do *you* know all this?"

"Ah. Well . . . I suppose you have a right to know. But this must be kept between us. Do you swear to me that you will keep this information to yourselves?"

They both nodded.

Mr. Metos stood up pedagogically straight and took

a deep, loud breath through his nasal passages. "I am a descendant of Prometheus," he proclaimed. He eyed Charlotte and Zee. "We are sworn to protect humans against the whims of their creators. It is quite a task."

Now Charlotte was surprised. "You're a god?"

Mr. Metos cringed. "A *Titan*, Charlotte. Not a god. I have Titan blood, yes. A little, though I am mortal. More important, I have the charge of Prometheus. The gods created man but do not help him. They're like parents who abandon their children. Humanity is nothing but a plaything to them, and now, Philonecron is treating people like lab rats. The whole history of man is just like this, the gods . . ."

But Charlotte had stopped paying attention. She'd been watching Zee, who had been quite quiet during this whole affair—even more so than usual. He didn't seem to be listening either—he was deep in thought and, once again, happy to let Charlotte do all the talking. Really, he was always deep in thought. He had been since she had met him. There were moments of irrational exuberance at school, but the rest of the time Zee was completely absent from the world around him. He stood in corners of rooms and hid in the shadows as if he weren't there at all. But where was he?

"Zee," she hissed. "Did you know this?"

He looked blank. "Sorry?"

"About Mr. Metos?"

Zee shook his head.

"But"—Charlotte scooted closer to him on the couch—"you knew his name. When I first mentioned him. And you were talking to him for so long after class that first day."

"Just about school things," Zee said, eyes wide.

Mr. Metos cleared his throat loudly. "If I might interrupt." He looked pointedly at Charlotte. "I took the opportunity on Zachary's first day to ask him some questions. It helped me unravel a few mysteries. I knew the Footmen had gone from England to here, but I did not know why. Zachary, I believe your grandmother's death was the moment when this all started. I believe they were present at her death and took notice of you. Then they began to follow you . . . tell me, after your grandmother's death did you ever feel strange? Weak?"

"Yes . . ." Zee was looking slightly dazed.

"They took your blood," said Mr. Metos. "They were using it to locate you and follow you."

"Oh . . ."

"But," Charlotte said, "why are you *here*? How did you know?"

"I just followed the Footmen," Mr. Metos answered. "I came when they did."

"That doesn't make any sense," protested Charlotte. "The men didn't come until Zee was here. You've been here all year."

"They were here long before that, Ms. Mielswetzski."

"But how? You just said they used Zee's blood."

"Charlotte, you must understand that in death, as well as life, blood is everything. The Footmen entered the Upperworld and used the scent of Zachary's blood to find Zachary and follow him in order to find children. Then, for some reason, the Footmen chose not to follow Zachary anymore. Perhaps they thought they had found all the shadows they were going to find in London, though that seems odd. I do not know. But suddenly they moved here, where the smell of Zachary's blood would lead them to another child that they could follow. You, Charlotte. Zachary's blood relative."

"Oh," Charlotte said.

"The Footmen have been following you, Charlotte, and taking shadows from the children you lead them to. Though I still don't know why they moved on from London."

"It was because of me," Zee said quietly. "I saw them. And then I was hiding. I didn't leave the house."

Mr. Metos nodded slowly. "Well, yes, that would do it. They didn't have you to lead them to the shadows anymore. So they found Charlotte. But now with you here they don't need Charlotte anymore. . . ."

He trailed off ominously, and nobody spoke for a few moments, thinking of all the places Mr. Metos might have gone from there.

"Mr. Metos?" Zee broke into the silence, his voice high and hesitant. "Did you, um, know my grandmother? Dalitso Winter?"

"Your grandmother? No. Why?"

"Oh." He shook his head slightly. "Never mind." Charlotte raised an eyebrow and looked at him, but Zee had retreated back into his pondering and clearly had no intention of elaborating. Well, whatever it was, she would get it out of him later.

"Well," Mr. Metos said, "the Footmen are here. They have collected a great number of shadows, and they will keep collecting them until Philonecron is satisfied. Perhaps they already have enough. I do not know. What I do know is that it's extremely important that you, Zachary, and you, Charlotte, stay safe. I believe they were trying to take Charlotte's shadow— or Charlotte herself—in order to lure you into the Underworld, Zachary. I believe they need you, Zachary, because of your blood. I believe they need you to utter the spell that will bring the shadows to life. Blood is everything, and they are using your blood to enchant the shadows. They need you for the final step."

Zee looked up. "I won't do it."

Mr. Metos said gently, "Unfortunately, Zachary, Philonecron has your blood, and he knows how to use it. Philonecron has been working with your blood, and I believe he can manipulate your will."

"What?" Zee asked.

"I believe he can control you. I believe once you get down into the Underworld, Philonecron can make you do exactly what he wants you to do. He knows how to talk to your blood, as it were."

Zee stared at Mr. Metos, horrified. Charlotte shuddered. "Mine, too?" she whispered.

"I don't know. You and Zachary don't have the same blood, but it is similar. I think he would have some power over you, but it wouldn't be as overwhelming as it would be for Zachary."

Zee was shaking his head slowly. Charlotte had a sudden urge to reach out to him, but she didn't dare.

"Listen to me very carefully," Mr. Metos continued. "He can make you do what he wants, Zachary. If he can lead you down to the Underworld, he will have all he needs to make his shadow army. And then, for the first time in history, there will be war in the Underworld.

And that is a war I do not want to see, because I am not sure Hades can win."

"Well, why does it matter?" Charlotte piped up suddenly. "So what if he overthrows Hades? It doesn't sound like he's so great."

Mr. Metos's gaze turned to her. "Well, Charlotte, if the shadows are sent into battle and destroyed, their owners will die. If Philonecron overthrows Hades, he will send your newly dead friends and all the rest of the Dead into a part of the Underworld that really is hell. Hades has no interest in the Dead, but at least he doesn't want to punish them. Philonecron wants all the Dead to spend eternity in torment. And since we will all one day die . . ."

Zee sat up. "He can't. He can't!"

It was the loudest he'd ever been, and Charlotte stared openly at him. And then she remembered his grandmother, and she gulped and looked at the floor, while Mr. Metos said softly, "I will not let him, Zachary.

"Now," he continued, "I want you two to stay inside the house. Do whatever you have to do, but they will have a harder time taking you from there. They need one of you, and I'm sure they wouldn't mind having both of you."

"But—" Zee exclaimed.

Mr. Metos held up his hand. "I am going to go down to the Underworld and stop Philonecron. I believe I can free the shadows, and then they will naturally go back to their owners. With no shadows, he has no army."

"How?" Charlotte asked. "How do you get down there? How are you going to free the shadows? How—"

"That is not your concern," he said sternly. "Ms. Mielswetzski, your concern is staying safe and keeping Zachary safe. I am counting on you."

Charlotte nodded. On any normal occasion she would have resented being condescended to—she was perfectly capable of doing things on her own—but in the case of going into the Underworld and taking on some evil Greek god named Phil, she'd let the adults take care of that one.

Mr. Metos drove them home, and they rode in the car in utter silence. Zee was off in his own Zee world again, and Charlotte was lost in images of the Underworld, drawn in gray and shadow.

When they arrived in front of the Mielswetzskis', Charlotte asked quietly, "How . . . how do we know when it's safe?"

"I'll come by," Mr. Metos said. "It won't be long. A day or two. I will be back."

Charlotte closed her eyes for a moment and an image of the Footmen appeared in her mind—they were there, behind her, reaching for her, ready to suck her into Death.

Her eyes popped open. "And . . ."—she didn't know she was going to say the words until they were out of her mouth—"will you be okay?"

Mr. Metos almost smiled. But not quite. "I will," he said firmly. "I will."

As they hurried up the path to her house, Mr. Metos watching carefully from the street, Charlotte found herself unconsciously wanting to take Zee's hand, but she didn't. Instead she clutched her arms around her chest and made her way quickly to the door.

CHAPTER 15

Good Kitty

Bartholomew, for one, was glad to see them home. When Charlotte opened the door, the kitten came bounding down the stairs and leaped toward Charlotte and Zee, landing just at their feet. She proceeded to rub herself against their legs, purring madly.

"She, for one, is glad to see us," Charlotte remarked under her breath, reaching down to pet her kitten.

Her mother, on the other hand, was not as glad. Or rather, she was *delighted* to see them safe and sound, but she had been *worried* because they were *late* and Charlotte had sounded so *strange* on the phone, and who was this Mr. Metos *anyway*, and what did Charlotte *think* keeping her cousin out with his *massive head injury*, and did anyone think of the *turkey burgers*?

Lecture received and apologies given, Charlotte led Zee into the kitchen, where Mr. Mielswetzski was cleaning up from dinner. He was not *delighted*, per se, to see them, but he was much less emphatic, and that was all right with Charlotte.

"What's with Mom?" she whispered. Zee hung back, looking uncomfortable.

"Oh, Char, she's worried," Mr. Mielswetzski said. "This flu thing has got her shaken, and she wants to keep an eye on you. She can't help it. *We* can't help it. You'll understand when you have kids."

Charlotte raised her eyebrows.

"Be patient with your old parents, my girl. We worry about you. That's all. If we act a little hysterical at times, it's just because we love you so much."

Charlotte's eyebrows sank. She looked at the ground. "Okay, Dad," she said quietly. Once upon a time there was a girl named Charlotte who suddenly felt a great attachment to her home.

"Now, can I get you anything?"

She and Zee exchanged a look. They had so much to discuss, but it suddenly occurred to Charlotte that there was a great beast gnawing its way through her stomach, and it would eat her and then Zee and then the whole house if she didn't get it some other sustenance quickly. From the way Zee looked at her—a sort of pleading wooziness—she guessed he felt the same way and simply didn't have it in him to say so.

"How about some of those great turkey burgers, Dad?" Charlotte asked.

"Coming right up," he said, flipping his spatula.

They ate quickly and quietly, the only sound the flatulent squeaking of the ketchup bottle. Charlotte tried to keep her mind off everything that had happened that day, otherwise she might vomit up the very delicious burger, and then she would be scared *and* hungry *and* vomity. Better just to try to focus on the dinner at hand.

But the quiet ended when the kitchen door opened and Mrs. Mielswetzski came through. She took one look at Charlotte and Zee and their ketchup-dripping turkey burgers. "What are you doing?" she exclaimed. "I thought your English teacher made you dinner? For"—and here she began to articulate very carefully—"*extra credit?*"

Charlotte's eyes popped. "He did!" she said quickly. "But . . . we're still hungry. There wasn't a lot of food. He's a vegan."

"Oh, is he, now?" Mrs. Mielswetzski squinted at

Charlotte. Was she finally, after all these years, beginning to catch on?

It was time to change the subject. Charlotte put down her burger and gazed at both of her parents earnestly. "Listen, Mom? Dad? I'm really sorry for worrying you. And I know things are scary right now. And Zee and I have talked about it"—she glanced at her cousin, who was staring at her with apprehension—"and we've decided we'll stay close to home the next few days. Until they figure out this flu. Okay?"

The faces of both senior Mielswetzskis softened at Charlotte's words, enough so she felt a little guilty for not being entirely truthful. But what was she supposed to say to them? There's a guy named Phil, and he wants Zee to enchant a shadow army to overthrow Hades, who really is King of the Dead, it's not just made up, and he's got some evil Footmen who are going to steal my shadow or kidnap me to get Zee down there, or something, we're not quite sure, but we know it's bad, so we're just going to stick around the house, okay? Home is, after all, where the heart is. And it's where the scary men aren't.

Meanwhile, Zee had that look on his face, the one that read, *I really want to protest but I can't because I'm British,* but she would have expected that. Zee wasn't a stay-put kind of guy. He was a talk softly (or not at all), run-out-and-solve-everything-himself-because-it-was-all-his-fault kind of guy. Well, not anymore, if Charlotte had anything to say about it. It was her job to watch him; Mr. Metos had said so. There was trouble, serious, apocalyptic trouble, and she was going to stay as far away as possible. Once upon a time there was a girl named Charlotte and she couldn't do anything right and she was a coward, and she was perfectly fine with that, frankly, because sometimes things are bigger than you. Going to France and living on her own and taking photography classes was one thing; going to the Underworld was something entirely different.

After dinner Charlotte and Zee sneaked upstairs, with Bartholomew sneaking right behind them. Charlotte led Zee (and the kitten) into her room and shut the door behind them—this was one conversation she did not want overheard; she couldn't very well look after her cousin if she was in a loony bin, could she?

Before sitting down, Charlotte turned on all the lights in her room, including the lamps, then she perched on her bed, picking up a bright pink, furry pillow and wrapping her arms around it. Zee sat on the foot of the bed, and Charlotte tossed him a pillow too, just in case. Bartholomew hopped up between them. The cat sat up, looking attentively at Charlotte.

The room felt so heavy, and Charlotte's lungs did

not seem quite up to the task of taking in the air. Zee looked to be having trouble too; he kept inhaling loudly and forcefully, almost as if to demonstrate that he still could. They sat for a time, trying to relearn the art of breathing.

After a while Zee picked up the purple pillow and began to play with the fur. He sighed heavily. "All I do is hide in the house," he said quietly.

Charlotte looked up. "Well . . . it's important!"

Zee shook his head. "There are men attacking my friends, and I hide in the house." He hit his hand against the pillow. Bartholomew started and turned her blue eyes on him watchfully.

"Well, look!" Charlotte exclaimed. "By hiding, you actually helped everyone. The Footmen left London because you weren't going anywhere, you weren't leading them to anyone."

Zee shrugged. "And they came right over here and began to attack everyone." Charlotte looked at the bed. "It's ironic, isn't it? They found me because Gran died. And she's the only one who'd know what to do."

"She knew about Greek stuff?"

"No, no . . . she just . . . I don't know. She knew things. She'd know what to do."

"Oh," Charlotte said, as if she understood, which she didn't. She casually reached over and began to scratch

Bartholomew on the head. "So . . . what was that about
your grandmother and Mr. Metos?"

"What? Oh!" Zee shook his head and looked away.
"Nothing. It wasn't anything . . . just a guess. . . ."

Charlotte eyed him. He started twisting the
strands on the pillow. He really didn't seem to
Charlotte to be the type to have a lot of hunches, but
she didn't think she could get anything else out of him
now. "Anyway," she said brightly, "we have someone
who knows what to do. We have Mr. Metos. He knows
all about this. He's going to take care of it. There's
nothing for us to do."

Zee raised his eyebrows. "How do we know?"

"Huh?"

"How do we know he's going to take care of it? How
do we know we can trust Mr. Metos? How do we know
what he says is true?"

Charlotte blinked rapidly. That hadn't occurred to her
and never would have occurred to her. Of course Mr.
Metos was telling the truth. Who on Earth would make
that up? She realized, too, that it had never occurred to
her before that a teacher might lie, and then she felt a bit
like a dork. "Why wouldn't we think so?" she asked.
"Everything he said made perfect sense. He knew about
the shadows, he knew about the men. . . ."

"Yes, but"—Zee leaned in and whispered—"doesn't

it seem awfully *convenient* that he was right there? I mean, he saved us *just in time*. How is that possible?"

"Well . . ." Charlotte paused. "I think he was following us. Watching us. Protecting us."

"Do we know that? How do we know if he's supposed to protect us or hurt us? Gran didn't . . ." He stopped and shook his head. "We don't know."

Charlotte squinted. "So . . . you want to just go out there? And do . . . what?"

"I don't know," Zee said. "But even if Mr. Metos is right, how do we know we're safe inside? I mean, why couldn't they just come in here and . . ." He trailed off.

"What?"

"And, you know, take *you*. Or your shadow. Or whatever."

Charlotte bit her lip. She hugged her pillow a little tighter. "I just think we should listen to Mr. Metos. . . ." She could hear how she sounded. All her life she'd been casting herself as some kind of heroine who would comport herself well in a story, if only there were one to be had—but now that there was danger and excitement and adventure, she was staying home.

"They took my *blood*, Charlotte!" Zee thumped his fist again. "They nicked my blood while I was sleeping, and they're using it to enchant an army made of the stolen shadows of people that I led them to . . . my *friends* . . . making them all incredibly sick. I have to do something!" He shook his head and quieted a bit. "Can't you see that?" he added, staring at her imploringly.

Charlotte's mouth hung open. It was the first time she had ever seen Zee talk like that. She didn't even know he had it in him. Any other time she'd compliment him or make fun of him or something, but on this particular occasion all she wanted to do was curl up on her bed with Bartholomew and cry. She swallowed. The air seemed only to be getting heavier. She didn't have a thing to say to Zee, nothing he would listen to, anyway, and she supposed, if she really thought about it, she could, yes, she could see what he was saying. And if she were in his position, she might feel the same way. Except she wouldn't be brave enough to say it.

"So . . . what are you going to do?" she asked quietly.

"I don't know," Zee said. "I don't know."

"Look. Let's just wait a couple days for Mr. Metos, okay? Just for a couple of days. We'll stay inside, and then they can't take any more shadows. So no one else can get hurt. And you can, you know . . . make sure they don't come for me."

That would have been a low blow if Charlotte hadn't actually meant it. As much as she wanted to keep her word to Mr. Metos, and thus save the world, she also didn't like the idea of having those men come for her in the middle of the night, taking her shadow or her blood, or quite possibly her entire self. She could close her eyes and feel the ground opening beneath her, feel herself being grabbed and dragged down. . . .

"All right," Zee said. "Two days. But then I'm going to go out and . . . I don't know. Follow the Footmen. I can't sit here and do nothing, Charlotte. I can't."

She nodded softly. "I know."

Charlotte had a hard time sleeping that night. Visions of nightmares danced behind her eyes, except the nightmares were real. Hideous man-like creatures made of clay clutched at her with their bird-claw hands, and she could not run, she could not move, she could not yell. Were they nightmares or visions? She had no idea—she would just find herself shuddering awake and looking at the clock and seeing only fifteen minutes had passed since the last time she had awoken.

So it was a refreshing change for Charlotte to wake up to the sound of a soft knock on her door. She opened her eyes, and her mother's head popped in the doorway.

"Charlotte?" she whispered. "Are you still awake? I saw the lights. . . ."

"Oh . . . I must have fallen asleep with the lights on." This was technically true—she did, in fact, fall asleep with the lights on; no need to mention that it was on purpose.

Her mother smiled. "Let me turn them off."

"No . . . no . . . I'm not sleeping well. I might read for a while." The words just popped out of her mouth, but really it sounded like an excellent plan. No nightmares when you are reading! There are many wonderful things about reading, but surely that is one of the most wonderful of all.

"It's pretty late, sweetie," Mrs. Mielswetzski said kindly. "Just a little, then try to get some sleep. Good night, my dear." And she disappeared.

"Mom?" Charlotte called quickly after her. "Will you tuck me in?"

Her mother reappeared in the doorway and smiled a motherly smile. "Of course, dear." Mrs. Mielswetzski sat on the edge of the bed and put her head on Charlotte's forehead. "I'm having trouble sleeping too. I just went down to drink some warm milk. It's *strange* tonight." She paused. "You know," she said, beginning to stroke Charlotte's hair, "you used to fall asleep with the lights on all the time when you were younger. You'd read into the night and just fall asleep. Your father and I would come in and find you clutching your book, and we'd tuck you in and turn out the lights. You never woke up, you were such a good sleeper."

Charlotte relaxed a little, letting her mother run her hands through her hair. Her eyes closed, her shoulders fell into her body, her bones sank into the bed. She exhaled.

"That's my girl."

"Do you know where Mew is?" Charlotte asked sleepily.

"She's prowling around downstairs." Mrs. Mielswetzski laughed a little. "She's strange tonight too! I don't know what it is. She keeps watching out the windows and growling."

Charlotte's eyes flew open. "Oh!" With a flash she remembered Mew's behavior earlier in the night, when they were leaving. She had not wanted them to leave. Almost as if she knew . . .

"Must be another cat out there or something," her mother said.

"Must be," Charlotte said weakly.

"Okay, honey, I'm going to try to sleep. You do the same, okay?" Mrs. Mielswetzski kissed her daughter on the forehead, tucked the blankets up, and headed to the hallway—leaving the lights on, which suited Charlotte just fine.

Charlotte had insisted on leaving her bedroom door ajar ever since she found Mew; it had been quite a change for her, as she had strictly been a sleep-with-the-door-closed kind of girl. But it was an adjustment she was happy to make, and it didn't take too much time to train her parents—who were also suddenly sleeping with their door ajar. And as she left, Mrs. Mielswetzski obediently left the door open a crack, and Charlotte was glad because if someone was coming to take her, she would at least hear them coming. . . .

Suddenly there was a loud crash downstairs. Charlotte jumped. Then she heard Mew let out a Mew yowl. Okay, she told herself. Just the cat. Must have knocked something over. A vase. Or something. Nothing to be afraid of.

Charlotte shivered in her bed. No, no, she could not read after all—all she could do was lie there thinking about all the things that might be coming and what they might sound like, and unfortunately, after an hour or so of this she did accidentally fall asleep. She fell asleep soundly this time, so soundly that when the footsteps came, she did not hear them. But anyway, the footsteps were not coming toward her, but rather heading through the hallway, down the stairs, through the front hall, and outside the door.

When she woke up, it was 2 A.M. and there was a cat standing on her face. The cat was looking in her eyes and yowling.

"Cat!" Charlotte said dumbly.

"Yowl," said the cat.

She willed herself to wake up. "What is it?"

"Yowl," said the cat.

Bartholomew started running to Charlotte's door and back to Charlotte. Charlotte got the point pretty quickly. She got up sleepily and followed Mew into the hallway.

Mew ran up to Zee's room. Charlotte followed. The door was wide open and the bed was empty. Charlotte gasped. Mew began to run back and forth up and down the stairs, then to the front door.

Charlotte looked at the cat, then at the door. She felt a lump in her throat. "We made a deal," she protested. "He wasn't going to go out. He was going to wait for two days. For Mr. Metos."

"Yowl," said the cat.

"Why did he go out? Did he go to find the Footmen? They'll take him! Why did he go out?"

"Yowl," said the cat.

"What should I do? Should I wake Mom and Dad? What should I do?"

"Yowl," said the cat.

"They won't believe me. And even if they did . . ." Charlotte shuddered. The Footmen took children's shadows. No one had mentioned what they would do to adults. She looked at Mew and gulped.

"I have to go out there, don't I? I have to find him. By myself."

Mew cocked her head.

"Not by myself?"

"Yowl," said the cat.

Charlotte felt tears in her eyes. She inhaled deeply. "Okay," she nodded. "Let's go."

Her cousin was in trouble and she was going to save him. She could do this. She could be brave. She could be the heroine. She could also be kidnapped by shadow-stealing goons and forced into the Underworld, but that's okay. Charlotte slipped on her sneakers, then opened the front door and, heart in her throat, gazed out into the cold, black night. There was nothing to see—just sleeping houses and dim streetlamps and empty streets. And darkness. And whatever lurked behind the darkness. She took a deep breath and stepped out into the night.

The wind blew past her, and her pink flannel pajamas seemed to quaver in its mighty presence. Charlotte hugged herself. She looked back toward the front door, behind which was her very thick, warm, cozy winter coat, and sighed. There was no time. She had to get to Zee before . . .

"Where to?" she asked Mew.

Mew stood on the front step, nose sniffing, ears

rotating like satellite dishes. Charlotte did not let herself wonder where Zee had gone or whom/what he had found, because then she would not be able to leave that spot. Courage, she decided, depended quite a bit on a failure of imagination.

And then, suddenly, Mew sprang into the night. Charlotte took off after her. Across the street the cat ran, into the neighbors' yard, through the fence, behind the garage, out into the alley, and then through another yard, and Charlotte followed, the whole way, ripping her pajamas on a bush. They emerged at the other side of the block, then went rushing down the street. The wind seemed to freeze Charlotte's cheeks, her breath chilled against her mouth, but all she concentrated on was the gray and white kitten who charged on ahead of her and who, occasionally, would stop and wait until Charlotte was in sight, before tearing off again.

And then, four blocks from her house, she saw her cousin. He was a block ahead of them, dressed only in his pajamas, barefoot, and walking as if he were taking a nice evening stroll. Relief sprang up in Charlotte, along with a sudden urge to throttle him. But there was no time; the Footmen could come any minute, and she did not think Mr. Metos could save them now.

"Zee!" Charlotte called. "Zee, wait up!"

Zee didn't even look behind him. He just kept going,

as if he didn't hear her—or at least wanted it to seem that way.

But he didn't alter his pace, either, and Charlotte ran until she caught up to him. "Zee!" she said. "What are you doing?"

And still he kept walking. Mew was running in circles around his legs.

"Zee! What are you doing? Zee, you said we were going to wait! You promised!" She grabbed on to his shoulder, and only then did he stop.

"What?" he said. He shook his head. He blinked. "Charlotte?"

"Zee?"

Zee looked at Charlotte, then at himself, then at the world. "Where are we? What's going on?"

Charlotte gaped. "What are you *doing*?"

He looked around helplessly. "I have no idea. . . ."

CHAPTER 16

Life Lessons From Charon

IF YOU ASKED CHARON—NOT THAT ANYONE EVER does—he'd tell you he gets a bad rap. The Ferryman for the Dead is widely considered, in both legend and life, to be rather, well, greedy. But really, if you look at all the facts, you can't blame him. He has a family to feed.

Everyone knows he has the worst job in the Underworld. He spends his days rowing back and forth along the Styx, listening to the Dead freak out because they're Dead and they had so much to live for, blah, blah, blah, and where in the heck are the Pearly Gates, anyway?

Actually, he kind of likes that last part.

But regardless, Charon has had his job since the beginning, the Very Beginning; when there first was an Underworld, there was Charon on the river Styx in his ferryboat. He doesn't remember anything before that.

In the Beginning it was a nice life. A few Dead here and there, and most of them knew enough to bring a little tip for the Ferryman. That's what civilized people do, you know. They tip. There's no such thing as a free ride.

But that is beside the point.

Which is:

That was the good old days, when it was just he, Thanatos, Hypnos, Hades, and the Erinyes. They'd pal around and drink wine and play cards, and Hades would tell lewd jokes. He knew so many! No one's ever known as many dirty jokes as Hades! Like, did you hear the one about Perseus and the Gorgon's head?

No?

Oh, anyway. Everything changed when Hades brought Persephone to the Underworld. He got all funny, the way men do. Started spending all his time in the Palace. Never hung out with the guys (or the winged she-demons) anymore. Stopped caring about the Kingdom. He gave Hypnos and Thanatos their fancy-dan titles, and suddenly ol' Charon was just a grunt, just a laborer, just the Ferryman.

Oh, and then the Dead kept coming. More and more. Charon barely got any time off. He had to get a bigger boat, which he paid for with his own hard-earned money, mind you. Did he mention he had a family to feed?

Oh, and *then* the Underworld just kept getting bigger and bigger, and Hades tried to lure more Staff so he could sit on his bony butt and pitch woo to the Ice Queen. And Hades promised prospective employees all these lovely perks but didn't bother to tend to those who'd been there since the Beginning. You know how it goes. In with the new, forget the old. At least the Erinyes got to torture people.

He used to be fun, Hades did. A riot! Did you hear the one about Jason and the Golden Fleece?

No?

The point is, Charon had a family to feed. And he didn't have any of those bonuses or benefits or personal holidays or vacation time or paternity leave or anything else that everyone and their Aunt Fanny seemed to have. He depended on fares. Not that they were enough. With the family to feed.

So Charon developed a little side business. A trade of his own. Hades liked entrepreneurs, so Charon became one. He traded in the most valuable commodity there was:

Information.

Information! Ah, how he loves having it! How everyone else wants it! You want to know what your implets do after school? You want to know what your minions say when you're out of earshot? You want to know who is building a shadow army to take over the Underworld?

Really, he's providing a service. And if he happens to make a profit, *to feed his family*, well . . . can you blame him? Can you?

Actually, he doesn't have a family. He's more the solitary type. Brooding. A loner. Plus, a wife and kids are *expensive.*

But he digresses.

So, say you're one of those Promethian descendants and you wander on down to the Underworld. (Because let's face it: Everyone knows how to get in and out. Hades thought his precious Decree would stop people, but really, he doesn't know a thing that happens outside his Palace walls. All he does is sit on his scrawny bottom and make goo-goo eyes at the Ice Queen.)

Say you're one of those descendants of Prometheus. And you're sworn to protect humans against the whims of the uncaring gods, blah, blah, blah. And you get wind of some nefarious Underworld scheme. And you want more information so you can save your precious humans. Whatever do you do?

Well, you go down and see Charon.

But bring cash.

Charon knows. He knows everything. And for the right price he'll tell you.

Okay, now. Say you are Charon. Say you give this guy all the information he wants. Say, in the process, because you are oh so subtle and clever, you get a little information from him. What do you do then?

Well, just follow these simple instructions:

Put a sign on your boat. BE BACK IN 15 MINUTES. It doesn't actually have to be fifteen minutes. The Dead have no sense of time. Let them wander around on the shores for a while. Builds character.

Find your subject. Approach him casually. You're buddies, right? Act like one.

Like this:

CHARON: Hey, how's it going?
SUBJECT: Good, good.

Excellent. Now tell a joke. Loosen him up.

CHARON: Hey, did you hear the one about
Heracles and the Cerynitian hind?

Like that. Now start asking questions. Be casual.

CHARON: How's that shadow army?

As if you really want to know, because you care. About *him*. Everyone likes to be listened to. People want to talk about their evil schemes. Just give them the chance.

SUBJECT: Just about done.
CHARON: Wow! That's amazing.

Flattery will get you everywhere.

SUBJECT: It truly is. The army, you should see them. They're so beautiful. I almost hate to send them out. . . .
CHARON: When are you going to?
SUBJECT: I just need to get my Zero down here to utter the final words of the spell.
CHARON: Oh.

Pause. Think for a moment. Ask innocently:

CHARON: And how are you going to do that?
SUBJECT: I've been sending him dreams. Vivid ones.
CHARON: [*Innocent. Wide eyed. Appreciative!*]

Wow! I thought only Hypnos could do that.

SUBJECT: I've learned a few skills here in Exile.
The boy will be down here soon. He may be
asleep, but he'll be here.

See? They brag! It's the most wonderful thing!
So you nod. You smile. You praise him some more.
You sidle up close to him. Your smile grows. You whisper
tantalizingly:

CHARON: I know something you don't know.
SUBJECT: You do?
CHARON: Yup.

Pause.

SUBJECT: What is it?
CHARON: It's gonna cost you.

Really, that's the best part. It's gonna cost you! It's
gonna cost you! And he, your subject, is waiting, hun-
gering, practically drooling for your information! And
he inevitably says:

SUBJECT: How much?
CHARON: This is pretty great information.

Shake your head. Like you can't believe how great it is. Like it's so great it's going to cost him *a lot*.

Your subject will sigh, reluctantly, and offer you a price. Double it. Triple it if he's a raging egomaniac with a freaky evil plan for taking over the Underworld. He'll refuse. Shake your head, sigh, nod like you understand, and walk away slowly. He will inevitably say:

SUBJECT: Wait!

Turn gently, slowly, casually.

CHARON: Yes?
SUBJECT: All right, I'll pay.

Ah, now you have him. Lean close and whisper in his ear.

CHARON: Have you ever heard of the descendants of Prometheus?

Tell your story. Watch his eyes bug out. It is, after all, very good information. When you are done, collect your sizable fee and head back to your boat. Later you will go to the Palace and visit the scrawny, bony, woo-pitching, goo-goo-eyed Hades and tell him you know something he does not.

CHAPTER 17

Waiting for Mr. Metos

Z EE'S DESIRE TO GO OUT AND CONFRONT THE
Footmen lessened significantly after his sleepwalking
adventure, or so he told Charlotte as they huddled up in
his room afterward. Charlotte thought that sounded
pretty sensible.

"Do you remember anything?" Charlotte asked.

"No," Zee said. "I was dreaming. I had to go somewhere . . . I had to open a door to get there, and I was
heading to that door. That's all I know."

"Do you know where the door was? Or what it
led to?"

Zee shook his head helplessly. Sighing heavily, he leaned back against the wall, then thumped his head against it for good measure. Charlotte raised her hand to the back of her head sympathetically.

After a minute or so Zee asked, "How did you find me?"

"Bartholomew!" Charlotte said. She told Zee the whole story, from waking up to find Mew on her face, to the cat's leading her right to Zee. Zee's face grew more and more incredulous, while Charlotte happily stroked the kitten, who was sleeping the sleep of the innocent.

When Charlotte had finished, Zee said quietly, "Doesn't that seem a little . . . weird?"

"Weird?" Charlotte said blankly.

"*Amazing*, even?" Zee studied her carefully. "Doesn't that seem like really *amazing* behavior for a cat?"

"Well, she's a great cat," Charlotte protested. Zee gave her a look, and she sighed. "Okay, yes. It is amazing behavior for a cat."

With that, Charlotte leaned against the wall. She and Zee alternated between casting sidelong looks at each other and staring off into space. She was always imagining people and things as supernatural somehow, but she was never really *serious*.

Finally Zee exhaled and asked, "So, are there any cats in Greek myths?"

"Not that I know of," Charlotte said. "There's an Egyptian cat. Bastet. I don't know anything about that, though." Elizabeth had a cat named Bastet, and Elizabeth said she was named after the Egyptian cat goddess, and that formed the beginning and the end of Charlotte's knowledge.

"Egyptian," Zee said dismissively.

"Yeah. No Greek. Maybe when Mr. Metos comes back, we can ask him?" She sneaked a look at Zee, who sneaked a look back at her. Both of them were thinking the same thing: *When* Mr. Metos comes back, or *if* he comes back? If those creeps could make a boy walk half a mile without even waking up, were they really going to be afraid of an English teacher? "Anyway, back to Mew."

"She—" Zee began, then stopped himself, blushing. "Well, Bartholomew," he continued, his voice dropping to a whisper, "I don't know how to say this, but . . ."

"What?"

He eyed the sleeping cat. "She's never, you know, *said* anything, has she?"

Charlotte's eyes popped out. Zee blushed again.

"Well," he protested, "weirder things have happened today." Charlotte could not argue with that. "Anyway. She doesn't talk . . . and she doesn't, you know, understand us?"

Charlotte considered. "I don't think so." She leaned

down and whispered in the kitten's ear, "Do you understand us, baby?"

Mew was mum. Charlotte stroked her for a while, then looked at Zee and shrugged. "One thing we know, though. . . ."

"What's that?" he asked.

Charlotte tilted her head. "Whoever she is, she's on our side."

Zee considered, then nodded slowly. "Yeah. Yeah, she is." He smiled a little, and Charlotte could not help but smile too. Zee put his hand on the kitten and started stroking her neck; she stretched and yawned and turned over for a belly rub. Charlotte yawned too. Perhaps she *could* sleep a little tonight—it was only 4 A.M., no school tomorrow, she could get lots of sleep still. And there were certainly no more adventures scheduled for the night. If any Charlotte/shadow-stealing freak wanted to break into her house, surely it would have happened by now. She stretched and was about to tell Zee when he suddenly muttered, "Hey, what's this?"

"What?"

Zee had been running his cupped hands along Mew's front legs (something that she quite liked), but he'd stopped and was holding her right leg in his hand. Mew was gazing at him with a distinctly perplexed look. "Here. On her paw."

Charlotte looked. The bottom of Mew's paw was covered in a chalky substance. Charlotte pressed on the paw to extend the claws, and they, too, were covered in what looked like dried white mud.

"From being outside?" Charlotte asked.

Zee wet his finger and rubbed the paw. He smelled his finger.

"I think it's . . . *clay*," he whispered. "And here, look!"

Trapped on her claws were a few black silk threads. Charlotte and Zee gazed at each other.

Charlotte gulped. "There was a crash earlier, and she was yowling. . . ." She sat up suddenly and grabbed Zee's hand. "Zee," she whispered urgently, "*they were trying to get in the house!*"

If, the next morning, Mr. and Mrs. Mielswetzski were surprised to find Zee sleeping on the floor of his room with pink bedding from Charlotte's bed, while Charlotte slept in Zee's bed, they did not say anything. (Charlotte had been perfectly happy to sleep on the floor, but Zee would have none of it. He went into Charlotte's room, got the comforter and the pillow, and made himself a nest on the floor. He would brook no argument; Zee was nothing but polite until you tried to infringe on his gentlemanliness.) If they were surprised that both of the children slept until eleven o'clock, they didn't mention it, either. Much to Zee and Charlotte's relief.

When the two both stumbled downstairs at about eleven fifteen, they found Mr. Mielswetzski at the kitchen table reading the paper.

"I drove to work this morning to find they'd cancelled school," Mr. Mielswetzski explained. He motioned to the paper—the headline read, MYSTERIOUS FLU STRIKES AREA YOUTH, CLOSES SCHOOLS. Charlotte gulped. "Some kids there are sick too," he added. "Of course, nobody bothered to call the teachers." He stood up and smiled. "So, sleepyheads. Nice to be off for a day, huh? Do you want pancakes?"

Charlotte's stomach turned, and she shook her head. "Thanks, but I'm not really hungry, Dad."

"No pancakes? Suit yourself. Zachary? . . . No? Okay! So, did you kids sleep well?"

Charlotte and Zee exchanged a look. "Not really," Charlotte said. "I had a really bad dream. I went downstairs for some water, and Zee was up too."

"I was!" Zee agreed.

"Yeah, and he let me sleep in his room." Her eyes grew wide. "It was a really, really bad dream."

"My poor girl," Mr. Mielswetzski clucked. "Sounds like everyone had trouble sleeping. I think Mew knocked something over, too, did you hear the crash? It scared the dickens out of me, I thought we were being robbed! Still can't figure out what she knocked over . . ."

"Uh-huh," Charlotte whimpered, pouring herself some orange juice.

"But then I went out like a light. I don't know what it was. Couldn't sleep, and then about one o'clock I was out like a baby! Your mother, too!"

"Uh-huh," Charlotte whimpered, pouring herself some cereal. She poured a bowl for Zee, too, who didn't seem very capable of doing much by himself that morning. He had slumped in a chair, and he looked as though some of his bones were on the verge of snapping in two. Charlotte poured him a nice big glass of juice, too.

She wasn't the only one to notice. "Are you all right, Zach?" her father asked. "You look a little frazzled this morning."

Zee paled—which was fairly impressive, as he had been pretty pale this morning to begin with. He looked at Charlotte helplessly.

"Probably from sleeping on the floor!" she said quickly. "Poor Zee, on the floor all night! . . . So, is Mom in her office?"

This Charlotte could do. She could come up with a convincing story in no time flat—yes, that Mr. Metos dinner had strained her powers a little bit, but she was under duress, okay? She could pour two bowls of cereal and a nice tall glass of orange juice for her freaked-out cousin and weave stories with a golden tongue. It was a small gift, a small space in the world that she could manage and call her own. It had nothing to do with staring down clay-made monsters or freaky, mind-controlling, power-hungry Underworld guys, but it was something, and in that moment she was safe.

"Well," Mr. Mielswetzski said, clapping his hands together. "We all have a day off! What shall we do?"

Charlotte sighed. "I don't know, Dad. I'm pretty tired. I think I'm going to read."

"Zachary?"

"Um, thank you, Uncle Mike," he said quietly. "I'm knack—beat, myself. I've got a pile of homework to do too."

"You kids are boring today!" Mr. Mielswetzski exclaimed. "Well . . . I'll go bother your mother."

And that he did.

For the rest of the day Charlotte and Zee sat in Zee's room, pretending to read/do homework, and waited for some sign of Mr. Metos. Charlotte occasionally checked her shadow to make sure it was still there. Bartholomew stayed with them, sometimes sleeping, sometimes running in circles around the room or batting around the plastic cap from Charlotte's soda.

"Good footwork," Zee muttered, watching Mew.

They could not deny that she seemed genuinely to be a cat. As opposed to something else—a demon or a god or a descendant of somebody or something. She was just a *cat*. An amazing (and incredibly cute) cat. Charlotte had heard that cats were able to sense ghosts; maybe her behavior was perfectly cat-like. She would have to ask Mr. Metos when . . .

"When do you think he'll come?"

"I don't know," Zee said, shaking his head. There was no need for him to ask whom she was referring to.

Charlotte looked back down at her book and stared at the words for a moment, then looked up. "He's going to come soon, right? Today or tomorrow?"

"I don't know," Zee said.

"I wonder how he's getting down there. And how he'll get back."

"I don't know," Zee said.

"I wonder what he's going to do."

"I don't know," Zee said.

"What if he doesn't come?"

"I don't know," Zee said quietly. "I don't know."

They sat through the afternoon, into the early evening. Charlotte kept wanting to ask questions, and Zee kept wanting to sit quietly and think in his Zee way, so they compromised; Charlotte asked questions, and

Zee stopped even trying to answer. Mrs. Mielswetzski popped in to say hello at one point. A few moments later Charlotte heard her say to Mr. Mielswetzski, "Those two are getting along so well! I was worried there for a while, but . . ."

They were called to dinner at six—turkey loaf with spinach and bread from the bread maker—and they ate quietly. Charlotte was conscious of her parents' eyes on the both of them. They were asking too-casual questions, and Charlotte parried the best she could. *We're just tired. We didn't sleep well. No, no, we're not sick. But it's hard, all of my friends. You know, we're worried. Maybe that's why we're not sleeping well.* They didn't even try with Zee.

After dinner was done and the plates were cleared, Charlotte and Zee went back upstairs. They sat for a while, watching dusk turn to night, and wondering what that night might bring.

"Mom and Dad are catching on," Charlotte muttered to Zee after a time. "They know something's up."

"You handled it well," Zee said. "You're good at that, you know?"

"Lying?" Charlotte said.

"No . . . no . . . just always knowing the right thing to say. I never do."

"Are you kidding?" Charlotte exclaimed. "You're,

like, Mr. Perfect. You're so polite and charming, and everyone loves you."

Zee raised his eyebrows.

"It's true. You're, like, the coolest guy in school. Ever since you got there, everyone's been following you around."

"Look, they like me because I'm the new guy. And I have a funny accent. It'd be the same if you came to my school. Of course . . . there are no girls in my school. But anyway, it doesn't mean anything. I don't have anything to say to them. And I can never talk my way through something. Not like you."

"You don't need to," Charlotte muttered. "Everyone just likes you."

"Well, they'd . . ." Suddenly he stopped himself, rather suspiciously Charlotte thought.

"What?"

"Nothing."

"What?"

He sighed. "Charlotte . . . do you actually . . . you know . . ." He trailed off and looked away.

"*What?*"

He swallowed. "Do you *want* to, you know, have people like you?"

Charlotte gaped. "What do you mean?"

Zee started to rub his face, looking rather like he

wanted to rub himself away. "It's just . . . well . . ."

"Zee!"

"You don't really seem like you, you know, are that interested in other people. . . ." Zee squeezed his eyes shut.

"*What?!*"

"I mean, everyone *would* like you. But they don't think you care one way or another . . . You can give off the impression of . . . oh . . . you know . . ."

Charlotte could not believe what she was hearing. Kids had been talking to Zee about her? Who? They'd said she was cold? That she was—what was the word her mother had used?—*prickly*? Charlotte was *prickly*? Charlotte wasn't prickly; she was, you know, careful.

"That's not true. I'm not like that!" She shook her head. "They're confusing me with Gretchen-the-goth-girl."

"Gretch?" said Zee. "Naw, man, she's brilliant. . . ." He caught himself and blushed furiously. "Charlotte, it's just . . . look . . ." But then he suddenly stopped, straightened, and turned his head toward the window. "Did you hear something?"

The expression on his face made Charlotte entirely forget their conversation. Anyway, she'd been down this road before. "What? Where?"

"At the window."

Charlotte listened. There was a rustling, like a branch. Or, no, a tapping.

"Something's tapping on the window," she whispered.

Zee and Charlotte stared at each other. Charlotte bit her lip. Zee swallowed. "I better go see," he said quietly.

And so, with Charlotte holding her breath, Zee walked slowly up to the window. It could be a branch, Charlotte thought. A tapping branch. Or just the wind. Or something stuck against the window. It could be anything, really. Any other night if something were tapping against the window, it wouldn't scare Charlotte at all—it would just be a normal, everyday thing. Still, Charlotte squeezed her eyes closed as Zee opened the blind. And then he made a strange noise, somewhere between a gasp and a gurgle.

On the windowsill was a large black bird, staring right at them. Large, as in gigantic. Gigantic, as in enormous. Ginormous. Ginormous, as in a big black eagle-size bird with black, beady eyes. Did I mention that the eyes were looking right at Charlotte? The bird flapped its wings and tapped against the window.

"More smart animals," Zee muttered.

The bird flapped again, then raised its leg. Something white fluttered in the breeze—it was a piece of paper, attached to the bird's leg.

"It's a note," Charlotte said.

Charlotte's heart went into her stomach, and her stomach went into her feet. Zee's mouth hung open uselessly. They looked back and forth at each other, then to the bird, which kept waving around the letter impatiently.

"I guess we should see what it says," Zee said, reaching over to open the window.

Journey to the Underworld

THE BLACK BIRD FLEW INTO THE ROOM WITH A
whoosh. It perched on Zee's dresser and let out an
emphatic squawk.

"Well, it doesn't *seem* evil," Charlotte said.

"Kind of friendly," Zee agreed.

"Squawk," said the bird. It raised its leg again, displaying the rolled-up note.

"That's a large bird," Charlotte said.

"Gigantic," Zee agreed.

"Squawk," said the bird, waggling its leg pointedly.

"I guess he wants us to take the note," Charlotte said.

"I guess so," Zee agreed.

"Squawk," said the bird, glaring at them. Charlotte was glad the door was closed.

Zee was closer, as Charlotte noted happily, so he approached the bird carefully and untied the note from his leg. The bird waited, holding his leg perfectly still. When Zee was done, the bird squawked again. He put his leg down and gazed at them from the dresser.

"He's waiting for something," Zee said.

"Maybe we're supposed to tip him?" Charlotte said.

"What do you tip a bird? Cheese?"

"I don't know," Charlotte said.

The bird tucked his head into his shoulder and proceeded to groom himself.

"Guess not," said Zee. "Well . . . should we read the note?"

"I guess so," said Charlotte.

Neither of them moved. If in every battle between evil, shadow-stealing geniuses, and good-hearted innocents there is a point of no return, this was that point, and they both knew it. Charlotte trembled a bit. The bird moved to his left shoulder and started to nibble.

"All right," Zee said heavily. And he unrolled the note. And he read. And he went green.

"What?" Charlotte said. "What?"

Zee shook his head wordlessly and passed her the note. Charlotte sucked in a breath and read:

> *Charlotte and Zachary—*
> *I have been captured. It is up to you now. There is no other choice. Follow the bird; he will show you where to go.*
> *—Metos*

"Oh," said Charlotte.

"Yeah," said Zee.

Without Charlotte's noticing it, someone had taken her bones and slow-cooked them, and suddenly, right at that moment, they became jelly. Bone jelly. Charlotte sank onto the bed.

"Oh," said Charlotte.

"Yeah," said Zee.

The bird looked up, shook his head, and began to nibble at something on his neck.

Zee, who apparently had also fallen victim to the evil bone-jelly plan, fell against the wall and sank to the ground.

Time passed. The bird nibbled. Bones hardened again, took shape and purpose. The world sharpened before them. And Charlotte shook her head and said meekly:

"It's up to us now. We have to save everyone."

And Zee nodded slowly.

Still they sat. The bird looked up, appraised the two of them for a moment, rolled his eyes, then starting working on his right wing, smacking a little as he did so.

"I guess it means . . . we're going down *there*," she said.

"I guess so," Zee said.

"Oh, goody," she said, putting her head in her hands and breathing in heavily. Zee leaned back and thumped his head against the wall.

"Okay, then," she said.

"All right, then," he said.

As one, they both sighed and stood up. The bird watched them carefully.

"Do you think we need anything?" Charlotte asked.

Zee shrugged. "Warm clothes?"

"I'll be right back." Charlotte went into her room and grabbed the warmest sweater she could find. She reached into her bottom drawer and took out her allowance, which she tucked into the front pocket of her backpack. She emptied her school things out of the backpack, then she tiptoed down into the kitchen and grabbed four water bottles, a pack of cereal bars, and a box of Fruit Roll-Ups, which she stuffed into the backpack.

She paused on the stairs. She could hear her

parents in the living room, the welcoming sounds of nighttime—the news on the television, coffee cups clinking against dishes, bursts of whispered conversation, Mew doing laps around the room. For a moment she thought she would go in and tell them everything, she would fall into their laps and they would hold her and tell her they were going to make it all right, she didn't have to worry about a thing. Charlotte closed her eyes and pictured doing that, tasted what it would be like, and then swallowed, and headed up to Zee and the black bird.

"I have to leave them a note," she whispered to Zee when she went into the room. "Mom and Dad. I don't know how long we'll be gone. They'll think . . ."

Zee nodded. "Yeah."

"What do I say?"

Zee shook his head, eyes wide.

Charlotte bit her lip. "May as well tell them the truth."

She wrote:

> *Dear Mom and Dad—*
>
> *We know what's making everyone sick. We had to go save the world.*
>
> *We'll be back as soon as we can. We love you.*
>
> *—Charlotte and Zee*

She pursed her lips, thought for a moment, then added:

P.S. Don't worry!!!!

"That's going to go over well," she muttered. "Now what?"

Zee looked at her, and they both looked at the bird, who raised his head imperiously.

"We can't go out the front door," Charlotte whispered. "They'll hear us."

The bird looked at the window, then looked back at them.

"Out . . . there?" she said. For a second she thought the bird was going to take them flying. The bird was big, but not that big.

Zee resolutely opened up the window, and the bird flew out and perched on the branch right outside. It squawked.

Zee and Charlotte got the message. They put on their sweaters; Charlotte left the note on Zee's bed, then slung her backpack on her shoulders and crawled out the window and onto the branch. Zee followed, closing the window behind him. They climbed down the tree and out into the street.

The leaves twitched, the branches itched, hearts

pounded, and breaths sounded, so neither Charlotte nor
Zee noticed Bartholomew, who had just run up the stairs
at full speed, standing on the windowsill howling with all
her might.

They crept silently through the street, the bird hovering
just ahead of them. Charlotte could not help but note
that they were going in the same direction that Zee had
been heading the night before. Which, she supposed,
made sense.

The streets were empty, and houses were tucking
themselves in for the night, so nobody noticed the two
children and the enormous black bird. Or if they did,
they weren't telling.

The trio walked for twenty minutes, and then the
bird suddenly circled around and perched on the back of
a bus stop bench.

"What? Are we here?" Charlotte asked.

The bird hopped up and down on the bench.

"You want us to sit?" asked Charlotte.

"Squawk," said the bird.

Charlotte looked at Zee. "I think we're supposed
to . . . wait for a bus?"

Zee threw up his hands, as if nothing would surprise
him anymore.

So they sat. And they waited. It was late, and buses

were few this time of night. After about twenty minutes one finally pulled up, and Charlotte and Zee stood, but the bird started squawking madly, flew around their heads (awfully close, if you asked Charlotte), and perched on the bench again.

So they waited. And waited some more. Charlotte took out a Fruit Roll-Up from her backpack. She offered one to Zee, who shook his head. Another bus pulled up, and still the bird sat. Then when the third bus came into view, the bird sprang from his perch, landing on the sidewalk. Charlotte and Zee stood up, and when the bus pulled up and the doors opened, the bird flew right in.

"How's that going to go over?" Charlotte muttered, counting her change.

But the bus driver didn't say a thing about the unusual passenger; he just watched Charlotte put her money in the till and waved them through.

The bird had made himself comfortable on one of the seats toward the back of the bus and was proceeding to have another nice bath. Charlotte and Zee sat down next to him.

"Where does this go?" Zee whispered.

"I don't know," Charlotte said. "I didn't even look. . . ." She leaned up to check the bus number, then looked at the map. "It just goes into the southwest suburbs," she said. "Near the airport? Oh, great. I can just see taking the bird on a plane."

Zee let out a little laugh. Just a little.

A few stops down a man got on. He looked like one of the reasons Charlotte's mother didn't like her to take the bus at night. He was scruffy and thin, with a shabby trench coat (and honestly, if you're a creepy man on the bus, shouldn't you wear something besides a shabby trench coat? Really, it's so typical. Let's break form, shall we, people? Strive for originality!), and was carrying a plastic cup the size of Charlotte's head, from which he slurped very noisily through a straw. The contents did not look like soda to Charlotte. Though the bus was empty, he sat opposite Charlotte and Zee and stared directly at them. Charlotte looked away, but she felt the man's watery gaze still on her. Zee moved closer to Charlotte.

The man cleared his throat. "Nice bird," he rasped.

Charlotte drew herself up. "Thank you," she said formally. "He's a messenger from the Underworld. . . . He bites!"

The man started, muttered something, and got up and moved to the front of the bus. Charlotte wasn't sure, but she thought she saw Zee smiling to himself a little. Just a little.

They were in the suburbs now, first passing small row houses, then large retail buildings. Charlotte and

Zee watched out the window, looking for some sign of . . . something, while the bird kept on grooming himself. And then, after they had been on the bus for what seemed like eons, the bus approached the biggest retail center of them all.

The Mall.

The bird hopped up, flew up to the signal cord, and landed on it, then flew down the aisle.

"You have got to be kidding," Charlotte said.

Zee was staring out the window and shaking his head. "What in the . . ."

The Mielswetzskis had not taken Zee to the Mall. There hadn't really been time, and Aunt Suzanne had been so horrified when she went years ago. Apparently the British don't really have malls, and especially not megamalls. It was better to break Zee in slowly, they all thought. So he'd never seen it.

The Mall was Big. It was Huge. It was Mega. As the bus pulled into the parking lot and began to circle around the driveway in front of the Mall, into the six-story parking garage where the bus stops were, Zee's eyes grew bigger and bigger, until they threatened to take over his head. After this, Charlotte thought grimly, the Underworld will be easy for him.

Then the bus doors opened, the bird squawked at them, and Zee and Charlotte—both extremely perplexed for entirely different reasons—followed.

The bus driver, who didn't seem at all curious about why two thirteen-year-olds and a large black bird would be going to the Mall well after it had closed, waved at them. "Have a nice night."

Charlotte swallowed.

The bird led them up to the front door. Charlotte could see that the Mall was completely shut down for the night. "It's going to be locked," she said.

"Squawk," said the bird.

"What in the . . ." said Zee.

Charlotte pulled the door, which was, of course, wide open. They walked (or flew) in, and she cringed a little, but no alarm sounded.

Zee kept muttering to himself as the bird led them down the passageway into the main Mall corridors. They went through the middle of the Mall, through the LEGO land, past the Ferris wheel and the roller coaster and the water ride thingy. Empty carts decorated with pictures of peanuts and cotton candy, and booths hawking ice cream and soda dotted their path. Zee seemed to have entirely forgotten about the purpose of the journey and was simply gawking at all the awful, beautiful excess.

Charlotte hadn't forgotten. She couldn't help notice how quiet everything was. It's after hours, of course it's quiet, but shouldn't there be security guards? Alarms? Something? She followed the bird resolutely as they wound their way out of the amusement park and to the other end of the Mall. They walked past stores, sleeping behind their gates, then turned down a small, dark corridor that Charlotte—despite her many, many visits to this particular Mall—had never noticed before. Next to her, Zee inhaled sharply.

The bird disappeared into the corridor. Slowly the cousins walked down together, letting the darkness wash over them.

They reached the end, their eyes adjusted, and they saw in front of them a very plain door, on which there was a very plain sign, which read, very plainly: NO ADMITTANCE.

Zee gasped. His hand reached out suddenly for the doorknob as if by instinct, and he quickly pulled it back.

The bird landed on the floor right in front of the door and danced and squawked.

Zee reached for the door again, more slowly. Charlotte closed her eyes. A simple twisting sound, and the door was creaking open.

A musty smell washed over them; cold, wet air blew at them; and in front of them there was nothing but black.

"I guess we should go in," Charlotte said.

"Let's go," Zee said.

The two grabbed hands, and together they walked into the blackness.

PART FOUR

———•———

The Beginning of the End

CHAPTER 19

Descent

Dɪᴅ I sᴀʏ ʙʟᴀᴄᴋɴᴇss?

Yes, blackness.

Cold blackness. Wet blackness. Slimy, icky blackness. The sort of blackness that would make you want to turn around, run home, and hide under your covers, never to get out again.

But, with trembling hands and brave hearts, Charlotte and Zee stepped into the cold, wet, slimy, icky blackness—for sometimes, as scared as you are, as much as you would like to run, you really have no choice but to go forward—and the door slammed shut behind them with a certain finality that Charlotte did not like one single bit.

They were in a very narrow tunnel made of rock, that much they could tell. The air possessed a certain chilly hollowness that gave Charlotte the feeling that the tunnel wasn't going to end any time soon. When they stepped forward, their footsteps made muffled clunks against the hard stone floor.

"At least we have the bird," said Charlotte.

"Squawk," said the bird, who suddenly flew off ahead of them, his flight stirring up the dust of the ages. He disappeared into the blackness, but they could hear the beating of his wings. It went on and on and on for what seemed like miles, getting quieter and quieter, until it faded away. Charlotte and Zee stopped and waited, but the sound did not return.

"Or not," said Charlotte.

"I guess we're on our own," Zee murmured.

They moved on, the light from Zee's watch the only thing keeping them from perfect blackness. The cave quickly became too narrow for them to walk side by side, so Zee, ever the gentleman martyr, took the lead. Charlotte held on to the back of his sweater.

Oh, it was cold. The type of cold that travels through your warm sweaters, your shirts, your undershirts, your skin, your muscles, and hits you right in the bone. The type of cold that makes you shiver from your inside, the one that goes beyond chilling your body into freezing your very essence.

"Wow, it's cold," Charlotte muttered.

"Yeah," said Zee, his voice shaking a bit. He stopped and turned to glance at Charlotte, who was trembling. "Maybe . . . well . . . here." Tentatively he reached out toward her, putting his hands on her arms. He began to rub them up and down, with a strange combination of chivalry and uncertainty, but all Charlotte could feel was the warmth in his hands. She leaned into him, and he wrapped his arms around her and warmed her back.

"Better?" he said.

"Yeah," said Charlotte.

"Okay, let's keep going."

And they did. On and on, through the darkness, stopping occasionally to warm each other, forgetting their awkwardness in the need to stop trembling. Every once in a while something flittered by them on the walls, on the ground, or in the air, but Charlotte opted not to think about that too much. Their eyes adjusted a bit over time, and they could see a few feet in front of them, but the view was always the same—craggy rock, slanting down, leading them deeper and deeper into the earth.

And deeper they were going. Charlotte could feel the pressure changing, as if the weight of the earth were above them, which in fact, it probably was. Her breath felt labored. She noticed Zee seemed to be just fine, which, she supposed, happened when you spent your afternoons running back and forth on a soccer field. She'll suggest that to the gym teacher as a slogan when they get back—Get in shape! You never know when you'll have to descend into the Underworld! It's a looong way down!

Though as they continued to make their way downward, even Zee seemed to labor a bit. As one, they stopped and leaned against a rather slimy wall to rest.

"Oh, man," said Zee, catching his breath.

"Yeah," said Charlotte, catching hers.

He nodded toward Charlotte's backpack. "Do you have any water in that magic bag of yours?"

"Oh!" Charlotte slung her pack off her back and unzipped it, bringing out one of the bottles. They each took a few sips. Charlotte wanted to drink the whole thing down, but she had a feeling it might be a wise idea to conserve. Which reminded her:

"Hey, Zee . . . when we're down there? Don't eat anything. Like fruit from the trees or whatever."

Zee made a sound through his nose. "I assure you," he said, "that I will not."

Charlotte grinned. "I suppose that was pretty obvi-ous. Persephone did it, though. She ate some pome-granate seeds, and that's why she had to stay."

Zee shook his head. "Next you're going to tell me not to drink the water."

"Well, yeah," she smiled. "Don't do that, either." She took a sip from her bottle. "You know . . . you can be funny when you put your mind to it."

Zee gaped at her. "Can I?" Was Charlotte mistaken, or did he sound just a mite sarcastic? Really, she was just trying to help.

"Yeah!" Charlotte said. "Once you've, you know, relaxed."

Zee let out something between a cough and a snort, then grabbed Charlotte's hands, looked into her eyes, and said, "Charlotte, I promise you on my life that once we get out of the Underworld alive, I will be the funni-est person you've ever met."

Charlotte blushed. "Okay, okay. It's just . . . you know. What you said before. About not knowing what to say. I mean, all the girls at school are totally crushed out on you."

Zee dropped her hands. "They are?"

Charlotte nodded. "Most of them, anyway. Ashley and Audrey asked me if you had a girlfriend."

"They did?"

"Yup."

Charlotte watched as Zee contemplated this for a while. Then something seemed to come over him. He looked away and muttered, "Well, I don't. Have a girl-friend."

His tone seemed to end the conversation. Charlotte offered him a last sip of water, then screwed the top back on and put the bottle in her backpack. Zee was still staring at something indefinable off at the other end of the tunnel. He exhaled and then said quietly, "There was a girl, though. In London . . . Samantha . . ."

Charlotte looked up. "Oh! What was she like?" Some sort of large, spiderlike thing crawled right by her foot. She glared at it. She was finally getting something personal out of her cousin; no Underworld spider was going to make her shriek.

"I don't really know," Zee shrugged. "But I wanted to find out." He shook his head. "She was one of the first to . . . you know—they took her shadow."

"Oh."

"Yeah, so . . ."

"So." Charlotte looked at Zee, and Zee looked at Charlotte, and they both nodded and proceeded on their way.

It was about a half hour later, when they were just beginning to despair of ever reaching the end, that they noticed the change. Something had opened up, the air moved more freely, and off in the distance—in the very great distance—they could see something that looked very much like light.

Charlotte's heart started throbbing, and not from the exertion. Her grip on Zee's sweater tightened. He reached back, grabbed her hand, and squeezed it (Charlotte noticed his palms were as clammy as hers), and together they moved toward the light.

A few paces on, Zee stopped and started to look around carefully. He leaned back and whispered, "Did you hear something?"

"You know," Charlotte whispered back, "I really hate it when you ask that." She listened. Yes, she did hear something. Wings! She heard wings! Their bird was coming toward them! Well, good, that would be a big help. . . .

No, no, wait—not their bird. Too big to be their bird. Really, those wings sounded awfully large—very, very large. . . .

"Duck!" Zee hissed.

"Du—? Oh!" And Charlotte ducked.

A huge mass of a thing flew by them, a thing that was definitely not a duck, a thing that made their bird look like a chickadee. The thing was the size of a bear—a *flying* bear—with vast wings like those of an eagle. It was an eagle, a bear-size eagle, or it would have been, had its face not been that of an old woman. A nasty old woman, like the one who sat in the ice cream aisle of Charlotte's grocery store shouting mean things at whoever passed her by. The thing (the ugly bird, not the ugly ice-cream-aisle woman) had claws the size of sickles, the tips of which seemed to gleam.

The Harpy—for that is what the woman-faced, eagle-bodied, impossibly enormous, and, while we're at it, quite bad-smelling creature was—was singing a little song to herself. If it could be called singing, if singing were a tuneless, phlegmy, cackling, screeching sort of endeavor, which it's really not. But anyway. The song went something like this:

> "I'm a little Harpy, short and stout.
> Here is my handle, here is my spout.
> I'll be back soon, so start ta shiver,
> Cuz I'm coming to gnaw on yer liver."
> [*Repeat*]

Charlotte and Zee remained as still as they could possibly be, long after the sounds of the flapping wings and the raspy song had faded into the air.

"Is it gone?" Zee whispered after a time.

Charlotte checked behind her. "I think so."

"Man," said Zee. "I hope there are no more where she came from."

But as they continued on, they found that there were at least two more where she had come from, or so they learned as a pair of them swooped in from behind them, heading toward the light. Charlotte and Zee ducked again, but the Harpies had no interest in them, they were too busy singing, in a round, this song:

"Twinkle, twinkle, little man,
I wonder how you'd taste with jam,
Chained above the world so high,
Like a lamb chop in the sky.
Twinkle, twinkle, little man . . ."
[*And so on*]

The Harpies weren't the only creatures Charlotte and Zee encountered. There was more flapping, more scurrying, more crawling, and a great deal more creeping. Two-headed bats flew by; rats with fire for eyes and a squadron of fist-size beetles scurried past as if they had somewhere very important to be.

And then, suddenly, they were out. The cave ended and launched them into . . . not light, exactly, but not blackness, either. Grayness, maybe—a strange, glowing grayness that seemed to flicker as if lit by fire.

They stood at the mouth of the cave, looking out at what lay before them. It was a world made of rock—a deep red rock that looked like nothing on Earth, craggy and cliffy and endless. Perpetual fog rolled in front of them. And there was not a creature in sight. Charlotte felt suddenly a distinct and terrible sense of loneliness, as if she were the only person in the world, as if she would never see anyone again, never hear another voice, never feel another touch. Her very bones were lonely. Next to her she felt Zee shudder—and the cousins stepped closer together.

Charlotte gulped. They had better get moving. "I don't think . . . I don't think," she started. "I don't think we're really there yet. There's a river we have to cross. . . ."

Zee nodded slowly. "Okay, let's keep going."

They exchanged a look, then began to move forward.

"The Outer Banks are where people, um, line up and wait after they've died," Charlotte said after a few moments. "And I guess Charon—that's the Ferryman—won't take you over unless you've got a coin. And if you haven't been buried, well, you can't go into the Underworld for, like, a hundred years, so you wait on the Outer Banks."

Charlotte realized Zee probably knew most of this and was simply too polite to tell her to shut up already;

he'd seemed pretty caught up with the whole Greek myths unit. (And . . . hey! Wasn't it funny that Mr. Metos had started with a Greek myths unit? It was like he was trying to prepare them. Which he probably was. Wow . . . cool.) Anyway, it was reassuring for Charlotte to say it. As if she had some idea what in the heck they were in for. As if.

It didn't matter. Zee didn't seem to be listening anyway. He was off in Zee land again, staring at something that wasn't there.

"Hey, um, Charlotte?" he said quietly. But then he pursed his lips and shook his head.

Charlotte stared at him. "What?"

"Well . . . I'm just wondering . . . ," he muttered, looking down at his feet. "Do you think we might be able to, you know, find people who have died?"

"Oh!" she gulped. "I . . . I don't know." She bit her lip and looked at the ground.

"Okay," he said. "Okay. So anyway, to the Styx . . ."

They walked up a small hill and looked down. A valley stretched before them, long and dark, filled with that strange, glowing fog. Rock formations were everywhere, cliffs rose from the ground, and at the end of the valley, just beyond the cliffs, they could see the river. Which seemed to be, by the way, steaming.

And there was nothing else. Just . . . nothing.

"Shouldn't there be, you know . . ." Zee trailed off.

"People?" Charlotte said. Yes, there should be. People . . . or whatever they were now. She hadn't known what to expect in the Underworld, but she certainly didn't think it would be empty.

"Maybe they're all . . . somewhere else," Zee said weakly.

"Yeah," agreed Charlotte, gulping. Not that she actually wanted to encounter any Dead, now or in the rest of her life, but she'd at least like to know where they all were.

Slowly they began to climb down the rocky hill. Charlotte gasped as her foot hit a small rock and she started to skid. Then Zee reached out and grabbed her arm before she fell down completely.

"Thanks," she muttered.

"We better be . . ."

Zee stopped. He was staring at something just beyond, looking as if he had seen a . . . well, you know. Charlotte turned. Just ahead of them hovered a bright, ghost-like form, and before Charlotte could really process that, another appeared before them. And then another. And then another. The cousins stood, wide-eyed and trembling.

"I guess those are the Dead," Charlotte said, nearly inaudibly.

"I guess so."

And then the cousins realized that these ghosts were everywhere, had been everywhere the entire time— what they had thought was fog was a great mass of Dead. Charlotte and Zee were surrounded. Hundreds, thousands, of ghosts floated about. They were indistinct, faceless, like shadows without a body—but these shadows were made not of darkness, but of an eerie, pale kind of light. Charlotte felt tears rise to her eyes, chills wracked her body, and somehow despite herself she could not help but feel that there was something oddly beautiful about them, these creatures of light illuminating this dark, dark place.

There were more Dead, and more, and soon the cousins realized that they were at the center of a great crowd of them, that the crowd was reaching toward them, pushing toward them, trying to get a glimpse of Life. The Dead were everywhere. They crowded, thicker and thicker, until they became indistinct from one another. The Dead were the air, and the air was the Dead, and the cousins were surrounded. Never had Charlotte been so cold.

"How do we . . . how do we tell them apart?" Zee asked quietly.

"I don't know," Charlotte whispered, casting a glance at him. He looked overwhelmed, strangely desperate, and achingly sad. Charlotte had an urge to put her arm around him and lead him away from all this, but she could not. And she knew, anyway, that right now he would not go. And maybe now, with the world at stake, she wouldn't go either. Yes, Charlotte Mielswetzski was going to try harder. Though, right now, she would rather not meet new people.

"Do you think we can talk to them?" Zee asked. "Maybe they can help us."

Charlotte shook her head. "I have no idea," she whispered. She was sort of hoping the answer was no.

Zee turned his head a little toward one part of the crowd. Sucking his breath in, he took a step toward them. "Um . . . hello?"

A great shudder seemed to pass through the Dead, and Zee shuddered in concert. Charlotte hung back, hugging herself tightly.

"Hello?" Zee said again, nearly in a whisper. The Dead trembled, but they did not respond. "Uh . . . can you talk?"

Nothing.

"Hello?" he whispered. He kept getting quieter and quieter, and soon it seemed he would not be able to make any sound at all. He looked around desperately, and Charlotte caught a glimpse of tears in his eyes. She inhaled and, taking a step toward him, put her hand gently on his arm.

"Your grandma wouldn't be here, you know," she said softly. "She'd be on the other side."

Zee turned his gaze from the Dead toward Charlotte. He sighed and nodded slowly. "We better just keep moving," he said. "Come on." He tugged at her arm, and they went, through the light, through the Dead, toward the Styx.

They climbed their way through the craggy Outer Banks, now ignoring the great fog of Dead that huddled around them. The rocks grew and grew, and great cliffs rose from the landscape ahead of them. They reached a small passageway in the cliffs, exchanged a glance, and stepped in. At that point the Dead stopped following them, and Charlotte tried not to wonder why. Was it worse to have the Dead following you, or for them not to want to go where you were going?

Zee seemed to have calmed a little; he was looking ahead, not back, and he'd stopped trembling. Charlotte understood. They couldn't talk to the Dead, they couldn't think about his grandmother, they couldn't focus on the task ahead of them (for they had no idea what they were supposed to do), all they could do was keep walking.

Slowly they began to hear noises again, strange to their ears after all the deathly quiet. They could hear distant, scratchy, singsongy voices that sounded all too much like the Harpies for Charlotte's taste. From somewhere far away came a few sudden cries, which exploded, then were extinguished—whether from an animal or a human, Charlotte could not tell. As they passed deeper into the rock passage, a twittering began to accompany them, a hollow whistle that sounded like the death of spring. Charlotte looked up and saw what seemed to be the skeletons of small birds flying above their heads. She inhaled sharply. There were small holes in the rock face, and little bird skulls were peering out from them here and there. Some skeletal bodies sprang from the rock and joined the pack. The songs multiplied; the pack of birds thickened. There were more and then more, and soon Charlotte's ears were ready to burst with all the sound. There were packs, droves, and as Charlotte looked up to see the sky darkening with them, the bird skeletons looked down and noticed her. One came swooping down from the sky, then another, then the whole pack of the deathly creatures dived right toward Charlotte and Zee. Charlotte screamed, and the cousins covered their eyes with their hands as they dropped to the ground. They felt the birds coming closer, closer, barreling right toward them, until, as one, they turned and flew off through the passageway. While Charlotte and Zee crouched on the ground, a group passed inches from their heads, bone wings making strange creaking noises in the air.

And then they were gone, they had flown off into the distance, and the cousins got up, trembling, and walked forward again. Soon all other sounds became drowned out by the rushing of the river—strong, fierce, and near.

They emerged to find themselves on flat land. In front of them stood a smaller white boulder, and up ahead in the distance flowed the waters of the Styx, which were—Charlotte's eyes had not been deceiving her—in fact, steaming. Well. They were certainly not going to swim across. Charlotte was eyeing the river nervously when suddenly she heard a strangled noise come from Zee.

"Charlotte! Look up!" He had turned around and was pointing to the top of the cliff they had just passed through.

A man was chained to the cliff, a shirtless man dangling against the rock face, with blood all over his stomach. Three Harpies were circling around his head. And even though she could not really see his face, Charlotte knew.

"Mr. Metos!" she exclaimed.

"Oh my god," said Zee.

"Oh my god," said Charlotte. She cupped her hands and shouted, "Mr. Metos? We're here! We came!"

The man started and looked down. His eyes popped. "What are you doing here?" he yelled fiercely.

Charlotte and Zee exchanged a glance. "We got your message!"

"I didn't send you a message! I told you the last thing we wanted was for you to be down here. Do you think I'd then send you a message telling you to come down here?"

Charlotte stumbled back. "You didn't send the message?"

"No," said a silky voice behind them. "*I* did."

CHAPTER 20

Oops

THE COUSINS WHIRLED AROUND. A MAN WAS STRIDING toward them, or something like a man—really, he was too tall to be a man, and, frankly, too evil looking. He wore a black tuxedo topped with a white cravat and had a black cape. Black, spiky hair framed a thin, cruel gray face, and red eyes matched red lips that seemed to stretch on for miles. The lips smiled; large, bony hands clapped; and a voice oozed, "Hello, my sweets!"

Mr. Metos bellowed, "Run!"

No need to tell them twice. Charlotte and Zee turned and ran—in their minds they traveled back through the passage, back through the fog of Dead, back through the rocks and the cave, through the end- less tunnel, through the very plain door, through the Mall, on the bus, and back home.

But in reality they made it about three steps. The man's voice sang out, "Oh, lads?" and just like that, the Footmen appeared from the shadows. Two, four, six . . . twelve of them surrounded Charlotte and Zee in a per- fect circle. The cousins looked around wildly, but there was nowhere to go.

Oh, they were hideous. It was one thing to see two of them hovering over you in a neighborhood street— okay, that was a big thing, but still—it was quite another to see twelve of them surrounding you in the rocky plains of the Stygian banks, their lips cracking, their yellow eyes glowing, their white faces flickering in the strange, unsteady light of the Underworld. Charlotte and Zee drew toward each other and grabbed hands. Zee urgently whispered something to Charlotte, but she could not hear over the sound of her heart pounding in her ears. She shook her head at him, and he whispered again, "If I can—"

But Philonecron loudly cleared his throat, then with a flourish of his cape the demon-like man glided into the circle next to Charlotte and Zee, and Charlotte could not catch the rest of Zee's words.

"I've been so rude! I haven't introduced myself," the demon-like man said. "I am Philonecron." He bowed deeply and then surveyed them, smiling strangely. "Oh my darlings, I'm so glad you are here!" he enthused. "It's been quite a challenge to get you down here, you know. I tried kidnapping, I tried seducing you through your dreams. . . ." He clucked, staring at Zee. "Fortunately, when your meddling friend came down here"—he pointed up at Mr. Metos—"it gave me an idea."

From his unfortunate position on the cliff, Mr. Metos started yelling something at Philonecron in a language that Charlotte did not understand, but one thing she could tell: The words did not sound like nice words.

"Really, Metos, such language," Philonecron chided, looking up at him. "Why don't you be quiet so my Harpies can enjoy their dinner? Liver is their favorite."

From up in the air, where the Harpies circled around her English teacher, Charlotte could hear the very distinct sound of raspy nursery rhymes. She whirled toward Philonecron.

"You can't do that to him!" she yelled. Zee clenched her hand.

"Oh, can't I?" Philonecron smiled haughtily.

"He's mortal," she protested, ignoring Zee. "His liver won't regenerate . . . he'll die!" There were tears in her eyes, which she tried to will away. I will be brave, she thought. I will be brave.

"Ah, I see you know your history, my dear girl. Do not worry, I would not let Metos get out of his due punishment so easily. I've cast a spell—his liver will regenerate every night so my Harpies can feed on it anew in the morning." He clapped his hands together and smiled brightly. "Feel better? Now, what else . . . you've met my men. Lads?"

As one, the twelve Footmen bowed. Charlotte noticed that one of them was wearing a bandage around his ankle, and his pant leg was frayed. Philonecron followed her gaze.

"Yes, your little hellcat destroyed a perfectly good pair of tuxedo pants," he growled, shaking his head tragically, "not to mention an ankle. Poor Epsilon! Poor, beautiful trousers!" Philonecron sighed. "Now, where was I? Oh, yes. My children. Do you know how long I've waited to meet you? Not you so much"—he glared at Charlotte—"but you, my precious, my sweet, my little Zero."

Zee gasped involuntarily and took a step back.

"Oh, no, no, no . . . don't be scared! Don't be," Philonecron said softly, creeping closer to Zee. "Don't you see? You're *home* now!" He put his arms out and gazed lovingly at Zee. "My dear, I know. I know you've never felt comfortable anywhere. I know that." He nodded earnestly. "I'm *just like you*. I never had a place in the world either, until now. But here"—he twirled, arms wide—"with me, my little Zero, you belong."

Charlotte moved in front of her cousin, stomping her foot on the ground. "Stay away from him!"

"My, aren't you saucy," Philonecron smirked, reaching down and patting her on the head. "Now, be quiet. Zero and I have much to discuss."

Charlotte opened her mouth, but Zee moved in front of her, as if she weren't even there. "Why are you calling me that?" he whispered urgently.

"Why," Philonecron wrapped his hands around Zee's cheeks, "that's who you are, my sweet. My Patient Zero. Brave and strong and handsome and clever. Oh so clever! You are going to start an army. A revolution!" He tapped Zee on the nose with one finger and smiled kindly.

That was the last straw. It was one thing to insult her, but another to abuse Zee. Zee was sensitive. Charlotte found herself starting toward Philonecron—surprising even herself—and, in a blink, three of the Footmen moved to her, one grabbing her by the shoulders. She squirmed. From his perch Mr. Metos started yelling again.

"Why do you think I'm going to help you?" Zee

asked dully. He looked so strange, Charlotte thought. Not struggling at all, not defiant, just staring up at Philonecron, sounding like he really wanted to know the answer to the question. She didn't understand. He'd been fighting all this time, the whole way—he was the brave one. Why was he stopping now?

"Because you are my precious Zero," Philonecron said. "And because you will see it's . . . for the best." He nodded menacingly toward Charlotte. She shuddered, and the Footman tightened his grip. "And if you do not, I can simply hypnotize you, make you say the spell, then leave you at the mercy of the Harpies." From above, the Harpies let out a little cheer.

"I have your blood, my boy," he purred. "I know you. I know your blood. I know what makes it sing, what makes it flow, what makes it boil. Remember your little sleepwalking trip?" He leaned down to Zee and looked him in the eyes, his voice growing soft and dreamy. "Zachary," he sang, "lift up your left arm."

And before Charlotte's eyes Zee's left arm went up. Something inside Charlotte screamed.

Zee gasped and slammed his arm down at his side, then balled up his hands as if he were going to start punching Philonecron—who didn't seem at all concerned.

"Now, Zachary," he murmured, looking back and

forth from Charlotte to Zee, "take those lovely fists and go punch your little cousin in the stomach."

"Hey!" Charlotte yelled.

But Zee said nothing. He just turned toward Charlotte. His face was contorted, his eyes burning, his every muscle clenching. Yet he began to move to her stiffly, slowly, painfully, looking like a very uncomfortable zombie. Mr. Metos kept shouting from above, and Philonecron let out a merry laugh. Charlotte could only stare as her cousin stopped right in front of her. He looked at her helplessly, then closed his eyes. Charlotte squirmed again, and the Footman held her tightly.

"Zee!" Charlotte screamed.

"No cheating!" Philonecron sang. "Punch her as hard as you can."

Well, maybe he was just pretending, Charlotte thought. Maybe Zee was pretending to be under Philonecron's control to trick him, and—

And then suddenly a truck ran into Charlotte's stomach, and everything went black for a moment. She tried to gasp, to take in air, but she couldn't breathe. She was completely empty, hollow, and her body sang with the pain of it. She tried to take in air again and again—she was going to die, right there, her ears were buzzing with death—and then finally her lungs filled. Breathe. Deep. Breathe. Her legs had given out and tears were streaming down her face. Breathe. Breathe. Come on, Charlotte, you can breathe. Philonecron was laughing, and in front of her, tears dripped from her cousin's eyes. Charlotte stared at him plaintively.

"Charlotte, I'm so sorry," he whispered desperately, "I'm so, so, so sorry. . . ."

"Come back, Zero," Philonecron said. And Zee turned and walked back, tears silently flowing. "Now, stay still. That's my boy. Yes, you see"—he smiled brightly to the whole group—"I can make Zero do whatever I want . . . but that's not as much fun, is it?" He turned to Zee and held his arms out to him. "Wouldn't it be better to do this together, my Zero? Yes, I really thought . . ." He looked down at the ground, shaking his head, gathering himself. "I really thought this would be something we could do together."

Zee's whole body was trembling with rage. The tears had stopped running, and now his face was twisted over with hatred. He stared at Philonecron as if he were the devil. One breath, two, three . . . something seemed to pass over Zee, and he closed his eyes and was still a few moments.

Charlotte stared, still gasping. Philonecron stroked Zee's face with a bone-like finger, and then Zee opened his eyes and turned to look at Charlotte. The Footman grinned, put his arm around Charlotte's waist, and lifted her in the air. Charlotte tried to kick, to fight back, but her muscles just wouldn't work. Zee shook his head and looked at the ground.

Charlotte knew that look by now. That was the *This is all my fault* look. That was Zee's *My grandmother is dead* look. That was his *I don't want anyone else to suffer* look. Charlotte gasped, "Zee!" The Footman clamped his other hand around her mouth. She bit down, but he did not let go. She got the worse end of that deal; his hand tasted like mold.

And then Zee spoke. "I'll do it," he said quietly, "if you let Charlotte and Mr. Metos go."

"Zachary, no!" Mr. Metos shouted.

"No!" screeched the Harpies as one.

"Ah, my boy." Philonecron clasped his hands together, his eyes filling. "You're so noble! I knew you would be. You're a wonderful, wonderful boy." He nodded affectionately at Zee. "But, alas . . . we all have our destinies. Metos is destined to be on the menu at my little restaurant for all eternity. A house specialty, as it were. You can't fight destiny, my boy. You'll learn that. But your little friend, well, why not?"

"You'll let Charlotte go?" Zee stared at Philonecron.

"Zee!" Charlotte yelled.

Zee turned to glare at her. "Would you let me do the talking for *once*?" he snapped.

Charlotte gaped. Yes, the circumstances were extreme, but there was no need to be rude.

"I will," Philonecron said. "For you, Zero, I will let her go. Now, come with me."

He held out his hand and Zee took it. Charlotte didn't know if he had done so out of force or will. Mr. Metos was still shouting things that Charlotte, by this point, was beginning to understand. Philonecron led Zee to one of the Footmen, who bowed. "Now, you go with Alpha here, and he'll take you to the shadows, all right? I'll meet you there." He smiled giddily. "Oh my boy, we'll remake the world! What a grand thing! What a great day it is!"

The two walked off, Zee shooting looks at Charlotte all the while, as if he was trying to communicate something. But what?

Philonecron stood on his tiptoes, watching them go off into one of the caves. "Bye!" he waved.

He turned to Charlotte. The Footman still held her by the stomach, and Charlotte winced when he squeezed. Philonecron walked up to her, chucked her on the chin, and kneeled in front of her, grabbing her hands.

"My dear," he smiled earnestly. "I'd like to let you go. I really would. I don't want to deceive the poor boy just as he and I are developing an interpersonal trust. But my Zero, he is, well, naive. An idealist. You know how he is. You and I, we're realists, we know how the world works. And you know I can't just let you go." He grinned menacingly. As he talked, something in Charlotte's mind began to soften, as if someone had turned the dimmer switch down a bit. She shook her head back and forth.

"Oh, I know you, little girl," he continued. "I was the one who found you, you know . . . Zero's blood led me to you. You helped us find so many wonderful shadows. But still, your blood is weak. I've tried to speak to it, but it's just not the same. You just don't have enough Zero in you . . . he's twice the person you are. You're really just a mongrel. An unfortunate, meddling mongrel with a rather unpleasant complexion. You'll go scampering off to Hades and warn him, in some futile attempt to save the world. We can't have that, can we?"

He stood up, brushed his hands off, and turned to the Footman who was holding her. "Throw her in the Styx."

Charlotte was being carried in the arms of the Footman, like a damsel over a mud puddle, heading down the clearing toward the Styx. She could still hear Mr. Metos's invectives echoing behind them, but the Footman did not stop. A Harpy flew overhead, looked down at them, screeched, "Freckle face!" and went on her way.

Charlotte tried to keep herself from struggling. She had to think. She kept hearing Zee's whisper in her ear, whatever he had been trying to tell her when Philonecron confronted them. *If I can—*

If I can *what*?

She could hear the sounds of the words, she could almost make them out, but not quite. For surely Zee had a plan, surely he did not mean just to give in, surely he had a way out of this.

Of course, she thought, it was just like him to give in to save her. Always so polite and generous all the time. Hiding behind his chivalry. So brave when it came to protecting Charlotte. Sure, evil guy, you can corrupt me, I'll destroy the world, just to save Charlotte. Come on, now—don't hurt my little cousin, she's very fragile and can't do anything by herself. Except for mouth off, maybe.

That's a laugh. Charlotte was doing things by herself long before Zee got there. And if Zee didn't have a plan, if he really was being such a stupidhead and sacrificing himself to save her, well, then . . . it was all up to Charlotte.

All up to Charlotte.

She had to do something. She couldn't just walk

away from this. It was time for Charlotte to act, time for her to take charge. Time for Charlotte to save the world. Once upon a time there was a girl named Charlotte who was not good for anything, until she saved the world.

But how?

And then she realized: Philonecron had told her exactly what to do. In his evil speech. "You'll go scampering off to Hades and warn him," he had said. Charlotte almost laughed out loud. Really, people should stop making evil speeches, because they always give themselves away.

And he had. He had given himself away, for that was exactly what Charlotte needed to do. She couldn't fight off Philonecron, but Hades certainly could. He was a god. One of the biggies. One of the Big Twelve—really, the Big Three! And he surely had, you know, monsters working for him. Centaurs and Minotaurs and Gorgons (oh, my!). And stuff. All she'd have to do was make her way through the Underworld, find Hades, and convince him he was in danger. And that she could do, for she was Charlotte Mielswetzski, and she could talk.

But first she had to get free, as she was about to be in some very hot water—and she meant that quite literally.

The Footman was walking along slowly, stiffly, bearing her like a prize. As they went along and she didn't fight back, he seemed to relax his grip on her a little, as if he'd forgotten she was animate, and Charlotte closed her eyes and tried to figure out how to get out of this. They really hadn't covered this one in their self-defense unit in gym.

It was hard to think calmly. She did not want to die. Not ever, really, but not now, not here. She had to save the world. And then she had to go back and take care of Mew and write Caitlin and be nice to her mom and maybe try out for the gymnastics team again.

And then the Footman stopped suddenly. Charlotte felt a great heat near her, and her eyes popped open. They were on the banks of the Styx now, and the Footman was studying the river, as if to determine the proper trajectory in which to throw her. Charlotte's heart raced, and she had to bite back the fear that was threatening to overwhelm her.

Come on, Charlotte. It's now or never. This is your chance. You are a heroine, and it is time to start acting like it. What does a heroine do?

The Footman stepped forward and death was before Charlotte, and something surged through her veins. She exploded into action. Quick as she could, she leaned over, bit the Footman on the shoulder (gross), kneed him in the stomach (payback), and elbowed him in the neck (for good measure). With a soundless cry of surprise the Footman dropped her. She felt steam hit her face—she was looking over the river now; one wrong move and she'd be in, but there was no time to think about that, she had to fight—and she sprang up, back toward the bank, scrambling up against the loose rocks. She looked around frantically—she could run, but where? She needed to get across the river, and she needed to stop the Footman from killing her. Actually, the latter was more pressing. The Footman had righted himself, and he bowed his head and smiled at her, then made a grab for her. Instinctively she ducked out of the way. She was small but quick; he was big but slow, and he tumbled forward. And there Charlotte saw her chance. She lunged behind him, and with a great breath she pushed, with all her might she pushed, his feet slipped on the rocks, and the Footman went headlong into the Styx.

Splash! The river roiled. The current began to carry him off, even as he bobbed up and tried to claw his way back to shore. The steam seemed to come up to him, it surrounded him, and before Charlotte's eyes his face began to melt. Clay dripped and rolled, splashing into the bubbling water, until there was nothing left but a very tall, very narrow tuxedo floating off into the distance.

She had done it. She beat the Footman. She had lived. Better, she had *survived*.

But instead of feeling elated, she felt spent. Charlotte collapsed on the bank. Closing her eyes, she put her head in her hands and began to cry.

She cried for Mr. Metos, getting his liver pecked out. She cried for her gentlemanly cousin, who had punched her in the stomach, who thought he was saving her and was now in very great trouble. She cried for all the children who had lost their shadows. And, most of all, she cried for herself and what she had already done and how much she still had left to do.

That was enough bravery, enough heroism for one day. She had stopped the Footman from killing her. Charlotte Mielswetzski had acted, had seized life, had become everything everyone wanted her to be. Wasn't that enough?

It wasn't. She knew it wasn't. She wasn't done yet.

So then Charlotte Mielswetzski did the bravest thing she had ever done. She wiped her tears away and began to get up.

"That was impressive," a nasal voice said.

Charlotte looked around. A few feet upstream was a small, thin, very old, and rather skuzzy-looking man sitting on a small wooden boat, chewing his cuticles. On the bank next to the boat was a great line of Dead. The line, formed by a vast network of velvet ropes and giant brass pedestals, wound and stretched as far as

Charlotte could see. The man didn't seem interested in the line at all. She turned back toward him.

"Thanks for your help," she muttered, nodding to the spot where the Footman had fallen.

"Philonecron will be mad about the tux, though," he continued. "A shame." He smiled, revealing a toothless mouth, and climbed out of the boat onto the shore. "I won't tell him who did it . . . if you make it worth my while."

"You must be Charon," Charlotte said.

"Yup," said Charon. Charlotte eyed him. Boy, he was gross. His clothes were ragged and filthy, he was streaked with dirt, and he had a little greasy, gray, stringy beard. He made the creepy man on the bus look like a movie star. And after the events of the day, Charon—eternal Ferryman of the Underworld— looked like just another creepy man on a bus.

She sighed, got up, brushed herself off, and approached him. "Can you take me across?"

He frowned and sniffed her, then shook his head emphatically. "I don't take living mortals over. Big trouble. It's always trouble."

"I can pay." Charlotte reached into her backpack and pulled out her allowance. "You can use the money to buy a new shirt," she added.

Ignoring the last remark, Charon grabbed the money from her and counted it.

"Not enough," he said. "What else you got?"

"Well . . ." Biting her lip, she reached into her back-pack. "I have Fruit Roll-Ups. . . ." She took out the box—as Charon watched carefully—opened it, grabbed a package, unwrapped it, and began to unroll. "They're grape," she said, peeling off a piece from the wax paper backing. "They're really, really good!" She smiled brightly and tried to look convincing. Charon took the piece from her hands and licked it, then grabbed the whole Roll-Up and ate it, wax paper and all.

"Delicious!" he said, and grabbed the box. "So fruity! And so portable! . . . Okay, I'll take you"—he squinted at her—"For the *whole box*."

Charlotte sighed as if this were a great sacrifice. "All right, you win. But"—Charlotte turned to look at the lines of Dead—"what about them?"

"They have all the time in the world," he smiled greasily. "Shall we?"

And Charlotte stepped carefully into the boat, and he began to row across the great river, through to the Land of the Dead.

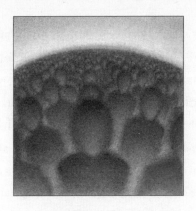

CHAPTER 21

Zero

ZEE WANTED TO KILL PHILONECRON. NOT LIKE WHEN you're really angry at someone and you say, "I'm gonna kill that guy," but you don't really mean *kill* kill. Zee meant *kill* kill. Zee meant a long, slow, painful death for Philonecron, effected by him, Zachary John Miller.

Never in his life had he felt hatred before. Real, pure hatred. It started in his chest and worked its way throughout his body. He could taste it in his throat, hear it in his ears, feel it rumble in his arms and tingle in his feet. Zee was a new person now—he knew what it was to hate.

Zee was sitting on a rock in a small, shallow cave, with one of the Footmen standing watch over him. The Footman had led him off, away from Charlotte and the banks of the Styx, through another passageway in the high rocks, and then tucked him into this cave, where he sat burning with hatred and thinking about just how he might go about killing an Immortal. Or at least causing him a lot of pain. Or at least—yes, that's what he wanted—making Philonecron feel utterly helpless, utterly alone, utterly lost, just the way he had made Zee feel.

Can you imagine? Can you imagine being under the control of someone else? Can you imagine hurting your family because of it? Can you imagine feeling your body do things you never wanted it to do?

All of his life Zee had been master of himself. He had made his own choices and suffered the consequences for them. Now he no longer was. So who, then, was he? What became of someone who was utterly under the control of someone else? What became of someone who had no will? He was a robot, a cipher. He was nobody. He was Zero.

And he had punched Charlotte. He had hurt Charlotte. He would never ever, ever forget the way she had looked at him. At least she was safe now. He could do that for her. She was probably on her way back home, where she belonged. This wasn't her battle. This was all his fault—his shadow, his blood—and it was up to him to make it all right.

He had had a plan, too. Or at the very least it was an idea. He came up with it when they were going down to the Underworld. There was only one way he could think of for an ordinary kid (him, specifically) to defeat someone like Philonecron. And if the shadows started their march, it seemed like the only option. But his plan required him. Zee. Not automaton Zee, but real Zee.

But he wouldn't be able to do it. Because he could not fight off Philonecron, and that meant he was going to fail. He was going to fail and everyone was going to suffer for it.

And do you want to know the worst part? The worst part was that there was part of him that didn't even care about everyone anymore—not about the kids, the shadows, the world—for all he wanted was to make Philonecron pay.

Zee picked up a rock and threw it as hard as he could against the wall of the cave. The Footman gazed down at him imperiously, arching an eyebrow. Zee wanted to tell him off, but he couldn't quite find the words. Charlotte would have told him off. Charlotte would have had just the right thing to say.

But Zee was not Charlotte. He was not even himself anymore. He was nobody.

Zee kicked the ground in front of him, and dust flew everywhere. The Footman's other eyebrow went up, and Zee glared at him. Boy, that would show him!

"Zero!"

He turned. At the mouth of the cave was Philonecron, beaming and holding his arms out. Zee gulped down his hatred. "Charlotte's safe?"

Philonecron clasped his hands together. "Oh my boy, I find your concern so touching. That's the problem with the modern world; people just don't care anymore. You care. It's such a beautiful thing."

"Is she *safe*?" Zee asked. He could feel his mind fogging over a little at the sound of Philonecron's voice. *Yes, I care, yes, it is beautiful.* He squeezed his eyes shut.

"Would I go back on my word to you? I assure you, your little cousin is completely out of danger."

Zee inhaled once, twice. He wanted to run to Philonecron and start pounding on him, but he couldn't. Even if he could, he shouldn't. Zee didn't have anything else to do but try his plan, even though he knew it would fail. And that plan depended on Philonecron's believing Zee was on his side.

"Zero, my boy!" Philonecron stepped forward. "Is something troubling you? You don't seem yourself!"

Don't seem myself. As Philonecron got closer, Zee's head fogged more, and soon Philonecron's voice seemed to be ingratiating itself with Zee's very veins. Zee shuddered and tried to move back a little.

"No!" Philonecron said quickly. "No! Don't retreat from me! Oh, Zero. Don't you see? We're going to have so much fun together, you and I." He got down on his knees, grabbed Zee's hands, and stared into his eyes. Zee was helpless to resist.

"My precious boy. We're really going to change things! We'll clear this place of bureaucrats, throw the Shades into Tartarus, and make a new world! Don't you see? There's nothing to be frightened of. You must be happy. Don't look back anymore—look ahead! It's going to be a bright, new day. Do you see?"

Bright, new day. Look ahead!

"Now, my Zero. What would you like to do first? Do you want to talk awhile? I could read to you. Would you like me to play the violin? . . . Or would you like to see your army?"

Zee sat up. Suddenly his mind was perfectly clear. "I would like to see the army," he said.

Philonecron beamed and clapped his hands together. "Oh, how grand! How grand! The army it is, then! Oh, boys?"

Philonecron snapped his fingers, and two more Footmen entered the cave. There was barely room for them, and they had to sidle around Philonecron to get behind him. Not that there was anything behind them to get to—just a craggy cave wall.

Or so Zee thought. The Footmen stood on either side of the back wall of the cave, looked at each other, nodded, and in perfect synchronicity pressed down on two rocks that jutted out from the wall.

And then the wall evaporated. Just like that. *Poof!* Zee gasped. Their cave was not shallow at all, rather, it was the doorway of an enormous expanse, of a great cavern the size of several football pitches, lit by countless burning braziers. Zee's eyes could not take it all in; it went on and on—but he knew the cavern was far, far bigger than the rock that housed it.

And the shadows were there. Thousands, tens of thousands, of four-foot-high figures—all lined up in perfect formation, waiting to be brought to life.

They were in the vague shape of people, yet without any real definition. They looked like, well, like shadows—black, flat, faceless, opaque, each one identical to the next. They had bodies that seemed to grow out of the ground, thick and shapeless at the bottom, narrowing up through the torso, with ovular bulges where the arms should have been and heads like candle flames. And they were all perfectly, eerily still—objects forever stuck in space, an endless series of black paper dolls, like crosses in a military graveyard. The shadows stretched as far as Zee could see, and beyond, and still beyond that. They looked like a great ghost army frozen in time. Zee shuddered.

"Impressive, isn't it?" said Philonecron. "If I do say so myself."

Zee could only nod.

"Would you like to examine the troops?"

He nodded again. He hated to give Philonecron the satisfaction, but he did want to look more closely at the wonder before him. He needed to know what he was dealing with. So, willingly, he followed the creature who had taught him to hate into the room with the vast legions of shadows.

"See, my darling?" Philonecron said, holding his hands out. "This is what you have done."

Slowly, carefully—aware of his heart beating too fast and the dry taste of fear in his mouth—Zee walked along the front row of the army, examining the soldiers.

As Zee studied the shadows, he tried to keep himself calm. He could look through one and see the foggy forms of those behind it, on and on. He reached out to touch one, slowly, and his hand passed through, as if through smoke.

"Oh, do not worry, my dear Zero!" Philonecron said. "As soon as you enchant them, they will be able to gain substance at will—or become as insubstantial as fog. It's going to be quite devastating!" He cackled.

As Zee walked, he noticed that the farther away from Philonecron he was, the clearer his mind was. Philonecron was talking to him, but the words were just words—they stayed out of his head, out of his blood.

But what use was it? The army was too big. Once launched, it could never be stopped. The shadows were insubstantial, could not be hurt—and vested with Philonecron's power, who knew what they could do?

It occurred to Zee then that there was another plan, a far simpler plan. Philonecron needed Zee to enchant the shadows. If Zee were dead, he couldn't utter the words of the spell. All he would have to do was run, run as fast as he could. If he could get to the Styx before the Footmen got to him, he could jump in and save the world. Easy.

It was the best way. The best way for everyone. His other plan was far too complicated, and he could easily mess it up, and what if it didn't work and what if Philonecron stopped him and what if he then doomed humanity because he was just too weak-minded to resist?

Zee's heart pounded. He was on fire, every part of him. This would do it. This would humiliate Philonecron, leave him just as helpless as he made Zee feel. This would solve all Zee's problems. All he had to do was keep away from Philonecron, get free, run, and then jump—and then it would all be over.

He walked behind a row of shadows, trying not to attract attention. If he could just get past the small cave, he'd be home free. Slowly, resolutely, he made his way toward the door of the vast room, trying to quell something that was rising in his chest and throat. No, no, this was the right thing. He was almost there, he was ready to make his break, and then—

And then he felt Philonecron's hand on his shoulder and his voice whispering in his ear. "Shall we get started?" he murmured. And that's when everything went black.

The next thing Zee knew, he was standing on a large platform, supported by four of the Footmen, holding a hollowed-out horn of some beast or another, shouting something in a language he'd never heard before:

"*Ek skotou es to phaos!*"

The enchantment had begun.

Philonecron was standing right behind him, telling him what to say—and the words, whatever they meant, were coming right out of his mouth.

"*Ek thanatou es to sden!*"

He still felt so foggy, as if he were half there—but he was aware enough to know that he had completely failed. He couldn't even kill himself. He wanted to sob, to run, to die—but he couldn't move from where he was. And now it was too late, and it was all his fault.

In front of him were fifty thousand shadows, in perfect rows, still and stiff. From where he stood, they looked even more like headstones towering up into the night.

Zee could hear his words booming through the hall over them—he barely recognized his own voice, sounding so strong and sure through the bullhorn.

"Ek skotou es to phaos! Ek thanatou es to sden!"

And the shadows heard him too. Suddenly he was not addressing paper dolls anymore. The shadows were coming to life.

"Ek skotou es to phaos! Ek thanatou es to sden!"

It was as if the whole room had taken a breath. Zee could feel the air change. Where once there had been six living creatures in the vast room (if the Footmen could be described as living), suddenly there were fifty thousand. The shadows twitched and stirred, stretched and shook.

They were alive.

"Ek skotou es to phaos! Ek thanatou es to sden!"

They were alive, the shadows were alive—because of him. It was as if the room had held thousands of pictures of fire, and then before his eyes the fire had become real. The shadows drank up his words, thrived on them; they stretched, grew, upward and outward. They were five feet tall, then six. They thickened, too, gained depth and substance—the paper dolls were now three-dimensional creatures with life and will. They bent and swayed and stretched and flickered, shaping themselves arms, then hands and fingers, stretching the fingers out to impossible lengths, reaching their heads up to the sky, then molding it all back into their bodies again. They were animate spirits, ones with intelligence and desire—and what they desired was Zee's words.

"Ek skotou es to phaos! Ek thanatou es to sden!"

The more he repeated the incantation, the stronger they became, the more alive they were. And suddenly all the despair, all the helplessness he had been feeling went away. The hatred for Philonecron was gone too—or at least it had moved aside, made way for something much more intoxicating. Because Zee was feeling something he had never felt before in his entire life: power.

Zee had power. It welled up inside of him, his heart sang with it, his chest filled with it. He had power, and he could use it. He did not have to kill himself. He could still save everyone. He had power, he had a plan—a good plan. And he could do it, he could make it happen, because he was Zachary John Miller, enchanter of shadows.

"Ek skotou es to phaos! Ek thanatou es to sden!"

They were alive! They were rustling, rumbling, waiting. Fifty thousand spirits waiting to destroy a world.

"My boy! Zero! We did it!" Philonecron hooted. "We did it!" He clapped Zee on the back and then corrected himself. "No, no . . . *you* did it. My perfect, wonderful Zero."

Everything happened quickly after that. The Footmen lowered Zee to the ground, then picked up Philonecron, who started shouting commands to the shadows. They were an army now, erect and attentive, waiting for their orders.

"My army!" Philonecron shouted. "We are going to bring down Hades! We are going to march through the Underworld and tear his City to bits! And then we will bring down his Palace! We will conquer the Underworld!"

And then, as one, the shadows lowered themselves to the ground, their bottom halves disappearing into the earth. And, as one again, they stretched back up toward the sky, and when they rose from the ground, it was apparent they had given themselves long, strong legs.

Then they began to march. They marched in place at first, their footfalls eerily silent on the cold stone floor. Then, at a word from Philonecron, they started to move.

Oh, it was an army, all right. They stepped in perfect precision, moving in exact formation, regiment by regiment. They looked as if they'd been training for years. They kept coming and coming. Surely there didn't need to be so many. Surely a few thousand would have been enough. As the shadows marched by him out into the world, soundless and precise, eerie and intangible, Zee shook off the feeling that he was witnessing an army of Death.

In his head Zee saw images of every battle he had ever seen, every army marching through a city, every war march throughout history. He couldn't get a good breath; he couldn't calm his heart; he couldn't stop the sweat dripping from his brow.

It didn't matter, Zee was ready. As soon as they got to the Palace, he would act. He would need Hades to take care of Philonecron—and that Zee wanted to see.

But then Philonecron turned to Zee. "Now, you rest up! I'll be back soon!"

Zee's eyes widened. "I'm staying here?"

"Yes. Of course you are! I'll be back for you soon, fret not."

"No!" Zee said. "I want to come with you!"

"Oh, of course you do!" Philonecron chucked him under the chin. "My brave boy. But I fear some things are not meant to be seen by your eyes. You're so innocent, so pure. I don't want you to lose that. You've done your part, my boy. You rest now. You must be exhausted! You stay here and dream of the world we'll make."

Stay here, yes. Rest and dream.

"Don't worry, I'll bring you back something from the Palace!" Philonecron squeezed Zee's cheeks, gazed into his eyes for a moment, and then turned and left the cave.

Zee closed his eyes and exhaled, getting his mind back. It's okay, he told himself. He could follow behind them, no one would notice. It would be better this way; he could stay out of range of Philonecron's brain waves, or whatever they were. He would just wait a few minutes, then sneak over the bridge and follow them all the way to Hades.

"Oh, and Zero?" Philonecron's head popped back in. "If you need anything, I'll leave Beta and Theta to watch over you." He smiled. "They'll be right outside the cave!"

The two Footmen turned and stared at Zee ominously. Philonecron waved and left.

Zee kicked the dirt and put his head in his hands.

CHAPTER 22

Into the Land of the Dead

As soon as they landed on the other bank of the Styx, Charlotte hurried out of Charon's boat. To Charlotte, Charon seemed like the type who might change his mind, and she was out of Fruit Roll-Ups. She scurried up the bank without looking back—because Charlotte knew of two good rules for navigating the Underworld: 1. Don't Eat the Food and 2. Don't Look Back.

As she was crawling up the bank, Charon shouted after her in his grim, grizzly voice, "Give my love to Cerberus!"

Charlotte shuddered. She had forgotten entirely about Cerberus. The Hound of Hades, the three-headed watchdog of the Underworld, who permitted the Dead to enter but never let them leave.

So when she heard a very canine growling and bounding heading toward her, she panicked. Quickly she ran through everything she knew about Cerberus — Heracles kidnapped the dog after a great struggle, Orpheus sang him to sleep, and Aeneas drugged him. And Charlotte? What did Charlotte do?

Charlotte squeezed her eyes shut and pretended she was invisible. It wasn't the best plan, but it was the best she could do on short notice.

It did not work. The strange, feral noises moved closer, and she cringed, took a deep breath, and opened her eyes.

Before her was a cub-size three-headed dog with three pairs of sad brown eyes that were looking at her plaintively. He was brown, black, and white, with floppy ears and a mass of shiny fur. He cocked his heads. Charlotte cocked hers.

"Why, you're cute!" Charlotte said. "Even with the three heads!"

The dog tipped his heads the other way.

"You're a good doggy!"

The dog wagged his serpent-like tail.

"Good doggy!" she cooed, reaching over and rubbing him under one of his right ears.

Cerberus rolled over on his back, and Charlotte sat down and gave him a good, long scratch.

"Well," she whispered, "I'd like to stay here and scratch you, but I have to save the world." She stood up, and so did Cerberus. He gave her a fond bark, then headed off down the bank.

She sighed and turned to survey the world ahead of her. Before her was an endless, grim, rocky, reddish gray plain, punctuated with little lakes and small, steaming pits here and there. And of course, the Dead were everywhere, innumerable Dead, like stars in the sky, sand on the beach. They stretched off with the horizon, becoming specks of light, becoming fog. They were right next to her, phantoms of light, hovering, still and aimless, against the dark landscape.

It all seemed to stretch on forever. There were rocky hills on the very distant horizon that seemed to mirror the place she had just come from. In front of the hills she could see a great, black, prison-like wall. A permanent black cloud hung over it, and she could just make out winged beasts flying in and out of the smoke. Suddenly she took a step back—that was Tartarus, the place of punishment, an endless pit in the ground where history's greatest sinners met their fate. And where Philonecron wanted to send the Dead.

Charlotte looked quickly away.

To the right the view was much less ominous. On the other side of the horizon, rising out of the plain, was a great city. She saw a jumble of spires and buildings and towers, and in the center of it all, soaring up over the Kingdom, were the looming black domes of the Palace.

"Well," Charlotte muttered, stepping forward, "follow the yellow brick road."

Sensing the presence of Charlotte, the Dead began to stir. From the crowd around her distinct groupings began to form—little circles of Dead huddling together. It was as if they were whispering to one another, yet no sound came from them. Charlotte looked straight ahead and kept walking. Finally about a dozen broke off from the groups and floated up to Charlotte, resting right in front of her eyes. She stopped.

"Hi," she said weakly.

They nodded their heads, a bow. Charlotte noticed that when she looked at them directly, all she saw was shape and light, but when she looked away, looked at them out of the corner of her eye, she could almost see the imprint of the long-gone faces of the people they once were.

"I'm, um, going to see Hades," she told them. "I

need to warn him. There's a man, an evil man. . . ." She paused, chewing on her lips. "Can you help me?"

The Dead did not answer, they simply watched her.

"This man, he's very nasty. He wants to overthrow Hades. . . ."

Still they did not move. Charlotte, remembering what Mr. Metos had said about the Lord of the Dead, wondered if perhaps they thought overthrowing Hades was not such a bad idea.

"He has my cousin. He wants to throw the Dead in Tartarus!" She gestured to the gigantic, smoking pit to the left, and the Dead shrank back abruptly.

"I-I need to warn Hades. Can you take me to the City?" She pointed to the towers ahead. But again the Dead stepped back. Charlotte didn't understand. "You should come to the City with me. This is so grim. It looks much nicer there."

She pointed again, and as one, the group of Dead hurried away.

"Ooo-kay," Charlotte breathed.

She moved on, cutting a swath through the oceans of Dead. She had to step carefully; the plain was littered with small rocks, and she could just see herself twisting her ankle. That would be great.

The landscape was awful. It smelled like Harpy, it was treacherous, and it was deathly boring, like one of those long car trips through states that never end. At least in Tartarus something happened.

She moved on, slowly, carefully, the Dead falling in line behind her. One by one they joined her—they kept their distance, but she could sense a growing column of them weaving behind her as she walked—not leading her, but following.

They are drawn to Life, Charlotte thought sadly.

There weren't just Dead, of course. On the ground scurried those fist-size spiders, while cobra-size nine-headed Hydras slithered after them. In the air flew gaggles of black birds of the type that had brought the note to Charlotte and Zee, and in the background she could hear the sound of the Harpies singing, their voices magnified by the great silence of the Dead. The very sound of those voices made Charlotte shudder.

But singing wasn't all they did. They kept flying right over the Dead, shouting insults at them, and the Dead cowered in their path. Off to the right one of them buzzed directly into a crowd of Dead, cackling as it chased them away. Next to Charlotte, another hovered right over a group of Dead and threw a ball of purple green slime at them, screeching, "Here's a present for you!"

Charlotte did not want to think what that was. She looked up and shouted, "Now, that's just mean!"

The Harpy turned to her. "Carrot top! Big mouth!"

"Smelly old hag!" Charlotte yelled.

"Underachiever!" the Harpy yelled back.

An ear-shattering screech sounded from the air, and in swooped another gigantic flying creature—not a Harpy, but a Griffin, with head and wings of an eagle, body of a lion, and scaly tail of a snake. The Griffin soared into the Harpy's path and lunged at it, and the Harpy lunged back.

"Lion butt!" screamed the Harpy.

Feathers flew everywhere, and screams filled the air, not to mention some insults that Charlotte really could not repeat. Green blood dripped from the sky; a few drops landed on Charlotte's backpack and burned a hole through it. The pair of hideous, bird-like birds tumbled and pecked and screeched in the sky, and Charlotte was relieved that at least there was someone protecting the Dead—until the Griffin spit Harpy feathers at them.

This was awful, Charlotte thought. Was this what Death held? Barren landscapes and mean monsters and eternal quiet and all this boredom? Why didn't Hades do something about it? Mr. Metos had said that Prometheus believed Zeus wasn't worthy of being a god because he didn't help humans. Hades, then, seemed hardly worthy of being Lord of the Dead, but it didn't look like anyone was asking Charlotte. Maybe she could say something to him after he, you know, stopped Philonecron and saved Zee and didn't eat her or turn her into a ferret.

Charlotte walked for an hour, passing such lovely sights as Harpies dining on the carcass of one of their own, a Cyclops picking his substantial nose, and piles of steaming evidence of Hades's legendary herd of night black cattle. She didn't know which smelled worse, the piles or the Harpies. Too close to call.

The City grew closer and closer, and Charlotte was soon able to make out details. It seemed a bizarre place to find in the Underworld—its elegant stone structures and spires looked like something out of a Dickens book. But there were no jet-black palaces in Dickens, at least Charlotte did not think so.

Then, suddenly, there was movement in the silent column of Dead, a rustling, a sense of chaos, where once there had been quiet order. Charlotte turned to look at them.

"What?"

They were all staring at something off in the direction of the City. Charlotte gazed over and she started.

There was someone hurrying toward them. Someone who looked very, very much like a person. Like a boy.

He couldn't really be a boy, of course—and certainly when he got closer, Charlotte would see that he had red eyes or hands made of birds or a snake's head for a tongue. Or he spit fire or had five noses or had a hideously long tail. Or something.

But he came closer, and closer still, and Charlotte saw no deformities whatsoever. In fact . . . well . . . in fact, the boy was quite handsome. Really quite handsome. He was wearing jeans and a black T-shirt, and he had dark chocolate brown eyes and wavy black hair; he would have looked like he belonged in the halls of Charlotte's school if he hadn't been far, far more attractive than anyone who had ever graced the hallways of Hartnett Prep.

Charlotte stared. Who was he? What was he doing down here? And, um, however did he get so cute?

Charlotte stood where she was, while around her the Dead backed away slowly. She didn't really notice; her eyes were locked on the boy's chocolaty orbs. Charlotte did so like chocolate.

The boy sauntered up to her.

"Hey," he said.

Charlotte stared. "Um, *hey*." The boy was acting like he was, in fact, encountering her at the halls of Hartnett instead of the deathly terrain of the Underworld. Which was kind of cute, actually, in its own weird way.

"I'm Joshua."

Charlotte bit her lip. That was her favorite name.

"Charlotte."

The boy grinned. "I love that name! It's my favorite."

Charlotte's heart raced. Who knew that she'd come to the Underworld and find love? What a magical, wondrous place the universe was!

"So, where are you going?" he asked, staring at her as if he might have a better idea.

"Um . . ." Charlotte gulped. She couldn't say she was going to Hades to save the world, how dorky was that? What a grade-A loser she would sound like! "To the City," she said vaguely.

"Cool," The boy nodded. "Hey, though, I've got a better idea."

"You do?" Charlotte's knees seemed to be melting. She had always thought that was a figure of speech, but no, her knees were actually melting. Well, figuratively.

"Yeah. I've got great tickets to Tartarus. Have you ever been there?"

Charlotte drew back a bit. "Huh?"

"To Tartarus. It's awesome. You really can see some great stuff. We could sit and make fun of everyone. It'll be a blast."

Charlotte blinked. "Well, I have to be somewhere," she said vaguely.

"Aw, hell, it can wait. We'll have fun. I have a private box." He stared at her meaningfully.

"Oh!" Charlotte said. There was something going off in her mind, some kind of high-pitched beeping noise like the one that used to wake her up in the morning back in her old life, where she didn't spend her time talking to really cute boys.

"What's the point of saving the world, anyway? Someone else will do it. It's not really your problem."

Something inside Charlotte snapped. What was she doing?

"Yes!" she said loudly. "Yes, it is my problem!" It *was* her problem. She wasn't going to sit on the sidelines of Tartarus and make fun of people, no matter how bad they had been in Life. She had to act. She had to save everyone, she was the only one who could. And, hey, how did he know—

"Okay!" He held up his hands. "Don't have a Nemean lion!" He sighed heavily. "If you'd rather 'save the world' . . . Do you want to make out first?"

"What?"

He stepped closer and put his hand on her shoulder. The hand was strangely cold. "I said, do you want to make out? You're really beautiful."

And that's when Charlotte got suspicious. The boy looked soulfully at her, and oh, he had such nice eyes, but those same nice eyes seemed to be focused on her . . . neck. . . .

Charlotte wrenched away and then kicked the boy as hard as she could in a place you are absolutely not supposed to kick boys, unless they are really mind-reading vampiric demons trying to suck your blood. She reached into her backpack, pulled out some of her bottled water, and threw it all over the boy, who was rolling around on the ground wincing, and then she turned and ran.

It wasn't holy water, of course; it was bottled in California. But it seemed to have some effect. Charlotte heard a loud, inhuman squeal, and she turned her head to see the boy transform into a flame-haired demon with the top of a woman, bronze horse-like legs, hooves, and, yes, a hideously long tail. The demon rolled around and howled, revealing two rather sharp-looking fangs, and Charlotte turned her head away and ran as fast as she could toward the City.

Charlotte had never been a particularly fast runner; she always finished in the middle of the pack in school fitness exams. But never during the exams had they used vampires to motivate Charlotte, and if they had, Charlotte would have been tops in the whole nation. It's amazing the things you can do when you're really motivated.

After she'd run for what seemed like hours but was probably minutes, Charlotte allowed herself a glance over her shoulder. There was no sign of the demon. She stopped and looked all around but didn't see the creature anywhere. The Dead, too, had begun to re-form around her, solemnly, silently following in her path.

"Thanks for warning me," she muttered.

The Dead said nothing. Charlotte exhaled. "Yeah, I guess I could have figured that one out on my own."

Charlotte sighed and brushed some sweat off of her forehead. A night black centaur galloped past her, kicking dirt in her face. Her eyes stung and she tried to wipe them out as best she could.

Charlotte was tired. You couldn't blame her; it had been a really, really, really long day. She'd been tired back in the passage to the Underworld, and that was several attempts to murder her ago. She'd been awake . . . oh, she didn't even know how long. Time didn't seem to have the same meaning in the Underworld. But her whole body felt ready to sink into the ground at any moment; she had to fight the urge just to curl up beside a nice rock and rest.

But she couldn't. She had a job to do, and she would do it bravely and well, even if she didn't have her gentlemanly cousin to go first all the time. And what of Zee? She hadn't been able to give him any food, any water. What were they doing to him now? Would Philonecron hurt him? Had he done his part, and were the shadows now on the march?

Her muscles protested, her bones rebelled, but Charlotte kept moving. If she could just get to Hades, she could stop all this. If she could just get to Hades, everything would be all right.

And then finally, *finally*, she reached the gates to the City—imposing gates of intricately wrought iron framed by black stone. The archway was inscribed with words Charlotte could not read.

She turned to the column of the Dead. "Shall we go in?"

The Dead froze.

"What?"

They began to back away. Charlotte's heart flipped, and she looked wildly around.

"More vampires?"

They backed away still farther. Charlotte looked to the gates and then back at them.

"You're stopping here? You don't want to come in?"

No, it appeared not. The truth began to dawn on Charlotte.

"You *can't* go into the City, can you? . . . You're not allowed? . . . Well, who's it for, then?"

Silent, the Dead faded off into the distance. As they did, the gates creaked open for Charlotte. She took a final look behind her and then stepped into the City of Death.

CHAPTER 23

The All-Seeing One

CHARLOTTE DIDN'T KNOW WHAT SHE HAD BEEN expecting—something sort of medieval, sort of evil. Creepy, haunted-looking buildings, demons swooping in and out, lots of fire and skulls and people being tortured here and there. But it wasn't that at all. The City was bustling with activity. Official-looking buildings made of stone lined the roads, gaslights lit the streets, and pairs of ox-size black horses pulled carriages and carts with signs like PEGASUS DELIVERY SERVICE or AJAX AND SONS' GROCERY.

It would have looked like a picture of Victorian

London, except for the strange reddish gray of the sky, the odd smell of burned leaves in the air, and the fact that the creatures on the street were decidedly not British. There were many who looked like men, like Philonecron—extremely tall, with four limbs and human faces, and dressed in bowler hats and frock coats. Others flew, crawled, or slithered—winged blue women, trotting centaurs, giant slugs, half-fish-half-men who carried tanks of water over their heads, hundred-eyed creatures, hundred-eared creatures, snake-haired women, and woman-haired snakes. All of them looked like they had very important places to be.

Many stared at Charlotte as she passed; some stopped right where they were and gaped. Each time Charlotte took a deep breath and snapped, "I'm going to the Palace."

Which made them stare all the harder, but no one tried to stop her. Or, for that matter, eat her.

Through the winding, gaslit streets Charlotte went, heading always toward the Palace at the City center—past office buildings with signs like DEPARTMENT OF MORALE PROMOTION and INTERNAL OPERATIONS AGENCY and the like. A giant, mausoleum-like building proved to be a school, and what seemed to be a cemetery next to it was a playground. Vast neighborhoods of stone houses stretched off like a network of tombs. She went past restaurants and clubs, in which strode men that could be Philonecron's brothers, and in the middle of the City, just before the Palace, there was a park.

Not an Underworld park, rocky and bare, with pools of blood for community swimming. An Upperworld park, with a pretty gate and green grass and flowers and trees and benches and a giant, sparkling, crystal clear lake that looked like summertime and safety and warmth and life. The Palace loomed up ahead, waiting for her—but Charlotte couldn't help it; she stepped into the park.

As soon as she crossed the gate, the rest of the Underworld disappeared. Gone was the Palace, the City, the musty, horrid smell. Gone was the ever present awareness of terror and Death and loneliness. Charlotte was back in the Upperworld, in a vast green park on the most beautiful day ever made. The sun shone warmly overhead, and puffy white clouds floated through the air. The wind carried the scent of lilacs. She walked up to a great elm tree, on which hung strange, wrinkled brown fruit like large, shriveled-up eggplants, the sun beaming down through the leaves. The lake sparkled and gleamed and seemed to beckon to Charlotte. She walked up to it and stared. She wanted to drink from it, dive in it, bathe herself and then swim off into forever—but she was pretty sure she shouldn't. A small black-and-white bird burst from the lake and up into the sky, splashing water in his wake, then a yellow one followed, then a purple and orange bird, then an all white one. They soared off into the distance, into the vastness of the blue sky. Charlotte's heart leaped with joy—she couldn't stay, she had to go, but oh, she never wanted to leave. She walked over to a bench and sat down for a minute, closing her eyes and lifting her face in the air, basking in the warmth of the sun.

Her eyes popped open. Was that a noise? She turned her head back to the lake. There was a small, skinny old man in overalls, scattering birdseed along the banks, who had not been there before. He had pure white skin, with eyes like the lake in front of him. His face was gaunt and wrinkled, and wavy white hair hung past his shoulders. He looked up and started.

"Hello?" his gravelly voice rang through the air.

"Um, hi," Charlotte said, taking a step back and checking his mouth for fangs.

"I'm sorry, but . . ."—he stared at her, blinking—"Are you mortal?"

Charlotte nodded slowly.

"Oh my!" he said. "Oh my!"

Charlotte looked around uncomfortably. It was just her luck to have some creepy guy ruin paradise for her.

"Listen . . ." He took a step toward her. "Could you

do me a favor? Could you look into the lake for me?"

"What?"

"Just stand on the bank and look at the lake. I just want you to tell me what you see."

Charlotte stared at him suspiciously.

He held up his hands and smiled kindly. "I'm not going to play any tricks or push you in or anything. I'll stand back here. I just want to know what you see. Please?"

Actually, the old guy wasn't so creepy. He seemed fairly nice, really. But . . .

"Wait," Charlotte said. "Where are we?" She shook her head. The whole place had the feel of a dream, but she knew she was awake. "I have to go. I have to get back to the Underworld. I have to hurry."

The man nodded. "We're still in the City. I just like it better this way." He gestured around him. Charlotte didn't blame him. "You don't have to worry, time doesn't pass here, not like it does in the rest of the Underworld."

Charlotte bit her lip. She couldn't help it; she was a little curious about what was going on. And the lake was just so peaceful—she'd seen so many ugly, horrible, awful, deathly things today, she couldn't help wanting a little beauty. Another small bird broke through the water and flew up to the sky.

Charlotte took a deep breath, stepped forward,

casting a glance back at the man to make sure he was not, indeed, going to push her in, and then gazed down at the lake.

As she looked down at the lake's surface, something flickered in front of her—not quite a reflection, just the idea of one—and then disappeared. And then Charlotte saw nothing reflected in the lake, nothing at all. She shivered a little. Was she a vampire now too? She looked up at the old man. "Nothing," she said. "Nothing there."

"Not your own reflection?"

"At first, maybe," Charlotte said. "But then nothing."

"Fascinating!" He peered at her. "Would you describe yourself as unformed?"

Charlotte took a step back. This was getting a little personal.

"I'm sorry," he said gently. "I should have explained. This is the lake where dreams come from."

"Dreams?"

"Dreams," he nodded. "Night visions? You know. This park belongs to Hypnos; he's a big shot for Hades. Dreams and sleep are supposed to be his domain, but he's too busy now hiring and firing people and creating Divisions and the like. I watch over things for him, take care of the grass and the birds." A black bird burst from the lake and flew up into the sky. "Oooh, that one looked nasty." He shook his head. "The dreams fly up on their own, or else someone down here comes on in and conjures one up to send to somebody up there."

With a flash Charlotte remembered her dream—the ground cracking around her, the Footmen coming up to grab her. Had someone sent that to her? Why? To warn her? But who?

A rustling came from the towering tree next to Charlotte. She looked up. One of the shriveled brown fruits had begun to wiggle around just above her head. Then the fruit leaped from the branch into the air—no, it wasn't a fruit at all, but a bat, a horrid, sickly looking bat stretching out its wings. No, not a bat—the creature spread its wings out and, before Charlotte's eyes, transformed into a great, beautiful bird—like a mix between a swan and a peacock, but colored in pure gold. Its feathers gleamed. The bird let out a cry that sounded like the singing of a harp, and went off into the sun.

"So beautiful!" Charlotte said.

The man grunted. "No, it's not. That's the Elm Where False Dreams Cling. There's nothing beautiful about it. Remember that, mortal, it's the most beautiful dreams that are false."

"Oh," Charlotte said. She looked back at the lake. "Why can't I see myself?"

The man shook his head. "Supposedly, when mortals look into the lake, they see, well, not themselves, really.

But a dream of themselves. Something they want to be or something they are becoming. I would guess you don't know yet."

"Oh," Charlotte said. "Oh."

"It's okay," the man said. "I bet in a couple years you'll come back here and see something for sure."

Charlotte shuddered. One thing she knew, she was not coming back here.

"I have to go," she said. "I have to go."

"All right," he said. "Thanks for coming by."

Charlotte nodded at the old man and headed back toward the gate. She didn't see that as she turned, her reflection shone in the lake, clear and strong.

Stepping back into the City, Charlotte felt loneliness and exhaustion wash over her again. The rotting, moldy, smoky smell hit her with full force, darkness surrounded her, and cold seemed to seep into her veins. Unwittingly she felt tears spring to her eyes, and she shivered.

The park was behind her now, the Palace ahead. She was so close to being done; she would talk to Hades, and then he would stop Philonecron and free Zee, and they could go back home and leave this horrible place behind.

There was no bustling on the Palace grounds, and no

bowler hats either. The Palace stood right in the center of the City, yet seemed strangely apart from it too. It stood six stories high and was made entirely of black marble. Three onion-shaped domes of various sizes reached up into the sky. The walls were perfectly plain, except for two stately columns (Ionic, Charlotte noted. Her art teacher would be so proud!), which framed the front door. All else was shiny, smooth blackness.

Surrounding the Palace was a great, three-story iron gate. Charlotte inhaled, then pushed on the gate, which squeaked like a very large bat. There was a long path paved in gold, and framing it were thin, bowing trees with small red fruit clinging to the branches.

Charlotte walked up to the massive black door, stood on her very tippy toes, and knocked.

No answer.

She tried again, louder, loud enough to wake the . . . Dead.

She stood back and studied the front door, arms crossed. It would be just her luck to come all this way and not be able to get in.

Stepping back, she cupped her hands to her mouth. "Helloooo?" she called. "Anyone there?"

Before her eyes one of the front columns seemed to stir. Two eyes popped open sleepily, then a mouth appeared, which let out a great yawn. Charlotte stared.

"Yeesssss?" the column asked in a rather dusty voice.

"Um, hi," Charlotte said.

"Hello," said the column. "May I help you?"

"Um, yes," Charlotte said, more squeakily than she would have liked. "I'm here to see Hades. It's extremely urgent—"

"You are? Really!" The column stared at her.

"Yes . . ."

"Most curious," he said. "Don't see your kind much here . . . don't see anyone, really. Well, I should get someone to open the door for you, shouldn't I?"

"That would be great, um . . . sir?"

"One moment, please," he said politely.

The eyes and mouth disappeared—Charlotte didn't want to think where to—and a few moments later reappeared.

"Someone will be right with you."

"Thank you," Charlotte said. "Um, I don't want to be rude, but are you, you know, trapped in there?" She'd read about people in Greek myths getting punished by being trapped in trees. Columns were another story, but . . .

The column laughed. "No, no. I'm a spell, lovey. An awfully good one, if I do say so myself. Unfortunately, no one gets to see it much these days. Not too many people come to the front door requesting an audience with the

King, you know? It's my cross to bear. Well, anyway"—
he yawned again—"I think it's time for a nap."

And with that, the eyes and mouth disappeared. A
few moments later the enormous door creaked open,
and Charlotte found herself staring at a man in a tail-
coat, with stark white skin and no face at all. He bowed
deeply.

"Mademoiselle," he said in a voice that sounded like
smoke. "Come in."

"Um, okay," she whispered.

Before her was a long hallway, impossibly long,
really, with an impossibly high ceiling. The walls, floor,
and ceiling were all in black. Black doors lined the hall
in perfect symmetry, candle sconces lit the walls, and
an eternally long Persian rug rolled off into the distance.

"Wow," Charlotte whispered under her breath.

"It's hand knotted," said the butler rather ominously.
Charlotte did not stop to wonder how he talked with no
mouth.

"The Palace doesn't look this big from the outside. . . ." she said faintly.

The butler laughed a knowing laugh. "No, it doesn't,
does it? Come this way."

He led Charlotte through the hallway into a small
sitting room, which looked like it belonged in that

railroad baron's house she'd been to on many years' worth of field trips. Ornate furniture, rich fabrics, opulent art, and even some lace doilies dotted the room. The only sign that this was not an ordinary room in an ordinary manor was the size of the furniture—clearly built for those many feet taller than she.

"Wait here, please," the butler said, bowing. "I'll come get you when the King is ready to receive you."

Charlotte nodded, feeling a little like a dwarf.

"Would you like anything?" he continued. "Tea? Our chef makes an excellent scone. Light as air."

"No. Thank you," Charlotte said firmly.

"As you wish." The butler left. This all seemed surprisingly easy to Charlotte. She suspected that you couldn't just waltz into most palaces, ask for an audience, and be shown right to the king. Shouldn't Hades have a bit more security? This did not seem to bode well.

Charlotte sat in the room, her legs swinging in the giant chair, hugging herself, thinking of all the things that did not bode well, and practicing what she would say to the King of the Underworld. *Coup . . . army . . . shadows . . . danger.* And when that was done and settled, when he had sent out his army to squash Philonecron, she could ask him why he didn't treat the Dead better. At least let them into the City! Not that the City was that great, but, you know, it's not nice not to let them in. It's the principle of the thing.

Then she could go back and get Zee and Mr. Metos, and they could go home. Wouldn't that be nice?

Soon the butler returned and led Charlotte back down the endless hallway. The butler knocked on one of the black doors, and a voice boomed, "Bring her in."

An involuntary shiver ran through Charlotte. The voice seemed to penetrate her body, resonating straight through to her heart. It was as if she had been thrown into a bath filled with ice water, as if her blood had suddenly changed to ice. She gulped and followed the butler inside.

She entered a vast throne room, which appeared, in itself, to be as big as the Palace walls. Two giant ebony thrones loomed at the end of the room, and the black marble floor gleamed. On either wall two large sets of glass doors led onto balconies—which Charlotte hadn't seen from the outside, and for that matter, one of the balconies was where the hall should be. The walls were lined with intricate tapestries. (The tapestries portrayed the formation of the earth and the ascendancy of the Olympian gods, though Charlotte didn't notice—and could you blame her? When you are in the presence of the Lord of the Dead, you don't stop to look at the art.)

And there was said Lord of the Dead, lording over the cavernous room. As Charlotte approached, the room seemed to shrink, while Hades seemed to grow.

With a face of shadow and bone, he looked as though he had been carved out of a tree. A black beard hung gloomily on his thin face. He had at least a foot of height on Philonecron, though he seemed to stretch before her eyes. He wore a plain crown, wielded a scepter, and was cloaked in blackness. Next to Hades stood an angular figure with pitch-black skin, white eyes, and a shiny, bald head, but Charlotte barely noticed him—she only had eyes for Hades.

She reached the thrones and kneeled, for that is what one does in the presence of a king.

"Charlotte Ruth Mielswetzski," Hades intoned.

She started. "How . . . how . . . do you know my name?"

"I know everyone's name," he said. "You all belong to me, after all."

Well, that was one of the creepiest things Charlotte had heard all day—and it was a long list.

"But," he continued, peering at her, "you're *mortal*. What are you doing here? How did you get here?"

Charlotte gulped. "Your Highness. I'll tell you later. There isn't time. I'm here because you're in danger. The Kingdom is in danger. . . ." In a rush she spilled out everything she could about Philonecron and the shadows, ending with a plaintive, "They'll be here soon!"

"Oh, yes, Philonecron." Hades waved his hand.

"Assistant Manager of Sanitation. Charon told me all about it. He'll never be able do it. He needs that boy to enchant the shadows, and he'll never be able to get him down here. It's impossible." Hades nodded importantly at Charlotte and the black-skinned man. "I made a Decree!"

"But," Charlotte said, bewildered. "The boy *is* down here. I mean, *I'm* down here."

"Yes, you are!" He tilted his head. "How did you get down here?"

"I took a bus to the Mall. And there was a door, and we opened it."

Hades leaned in. "Just like that?"

Charlotte nodded.

"Impossible," he declared.

This was not going well. Charlotte stood up, brushed off her knees, and said quietly, "Sir, Zee—the boy—is here. I'm here. We opened the door, and we came down, and the Harpies made fun of me, and now Philonecron has Zee. Please believe me."

"Hmmm . . ." Hades looked at the black-skinned man, who was, of course, Thanatos, Chief of Staff. "I see this Philonecron's power is growing. Banish him, will you?"

"My Lord . . ." Thanatos bowed. "Um, he is already banished."

"Oh," Hades said. "Clever of me . . ." He looked off somewhere in the direction of the window. "Where is my wife?"

"I don't know." Thanatos bowed again. "Probably in her garden."

"Yes, yes, probably . . . I'm sure she'll be back for supper."

"Excuse me? Your Highness?" Charlotte inhaled and stepped forward. Underneath Hades's cloak she could see the faint outline of a potbelly. "The shadows are coming. They could be here any minute. They're coming to overthrow you. You have to do something! Do you have an army?"

Hades blinked at her. "Army?"

"To defend the Kingdom?"

He glanced at Thanatos, then shook his head. "Why would I need an army? This is the Underworld. No one else wants it."

"Well," Charlotte said, "someone does now."

Hades sat back in his chair and stared at Charlotte. At that moment the marble floor seemed to shake. Something in the distance rumbled.

Hades tilted his head. "Did you hear something?"

"Oh no," Charlotte moaned.

CHAPTER 24

A Surprise

ZEE PACED BACK AND FORTH IN THE SMALL CAVE. THE
Footmen had shut the secret door to the shadows cavern behind them, and he found himself in a ten-foot-by-
ten-foot prison with nothing but a flat rock on the floor
to keep him company and the dank smell of the
Underworld sneaking in from the cave entrance. Zee
kicked the walls a few times, until it started to hurt a lot,
and then he kicked up some dust and then threw around
some pebbles and then chastised himself for kicking
and/or throwing things when he should be doing *something* to save humanity.

But what?

Everything had depended on his being with Philonecron. It would have been all right to enchant the shadows as long as he'd been able to follow them; now everyone was doomed.

Zee sighed and sat down on the rock. The two Footmen stood right in front of his doorway, their garish faces peeking in every once in a while. They seemed to be quite delighted with his predicament. Zee wanted to hurl rocks at them, but he had a feeling they'd be more than happy to come in and break his neck or choke him with clay or something.

He could try to disable the Footmen—hit one over the head, maybe, and just try to outrun the other one. Then he could still make it to the Palace. Then he'd still have a chance. Of course, when he and Charlotte had tried that when the Footmen attacked them in the Upperworld, they had stopped time and frozen him in place. (He hadn't thought of that when he was considering killing himself. That was dumb.)

Zee sat and he thought. He thought about everything that had happened so far, about how terribly wrong it had gone, and about the chances he had had to make it right, and about all the ways he had made things worse. He thought about all the Dead, and all the Dead that were to come, and how unless he thought of something fast, they were going to spend eternity in torment.

And he found himself thinking of his grandmother. What would she think of him now, sitting here? Would she be ashamed of him? Ashamed of him for letting Philonecron control him like that, ashamed of him for running to the States and leading the shadow thieves there, ashamed of him for falling for Philonecron's trick, ashamed of him for enchanting the shadows, ashamed of him for not doing something now—now when there was nothing left to do?

Zee sighed. The sad part, the really sad part, was that she would probably not be. She would probably love him and be proud of him anyway. That was just the way of Grandmother Winter.

She was down here . . . somewhere. He would never be able to find her, he knew that now, but she was here. She was near him. She had promised him she would watch over him, and now when it mattered most, she was close by. Grandmother Winter had a way of getting what she wanted. He wanted to see her, to give her a hug, to tell her how much he missed her, how much he needed the strength she gave him. But he couldn't. He would simply have to get the strength from the idea of Grandmother Winter—the sweet, soft, strong idea of her.

And with that strength he would have to do

something. He would have to try. He would have to try to get past the Footmen, even if it was impossible, even if it meant his death. Which it probably did. Because at least he could say he had tried. At least he would not have let the world go without a fight.

Zee closed his eyes and he pictured his grandmother. He remembered the floury, talcum powdery, lotiony scent of her, he held it in his mind, he breathed it in.

Then suddenly he sensed something in the cave with him. Something small and not quite human. He'd seen enough creatures that day to know they tended to pop up everywhere in the Underworld—and it wouldn't do him any good to be killed by a vampiric lizard right now, so he opened his eyes, expecting to see such a beast, or maybe a four-headed rat or a mucus-spewing mole.

But what he saw was a cat.

Not a demon cat. Or a skeleton cat. A regular cat. Almost, well, a kitten.

The cat had darted into the cave and was making its way slowly toward him, eyes set on him. Zee stared. Upon looking closer at the cat, he thought it looked a great deal like Charlotte's cat, Mew.

In fact, Zee couldn't be sure, but if he had to bet, well, he'd bet the cat *was* Mew.

"Mew?" he whispered.

The cat leaped toward him and frantically rubbed against his legs. Zee felt tears springing to his eyes; he couldn't help it. "What are you *doing* here? How did you get here?" He picked up Mew and squeezed her. "You really are an extraordinary cat."

He shot a glance at the doorway, but the Footmen didn't seem to have noticed a thing. They were standing a few feet away from the door, stock-still now—they looked like wax statues.

Mew bonked her head against his a few times, then leaped out of his arms and dashed to the left wall of the cave.

"What is it?" Zee asked.

Mew began to scratch violently against the wall. Zee got up. "What are you doing?" he whispered, walking over to her. He stood between Mew and the doorway and stared at her. She looked at him and kept scratching.

Zee examined the wall. It didn't look different from any of the others—ragged, with bits of rock jutting out. . . .

Oh!

Zee put his hands on two of the rocks and pulled down. Nothing. He tried two more. And then he saw a small, round rock just to the right of his head. He put his hand on it, pressed down—and the wall evaporated.

In front of him was a slightly larger room, maybe four times the size of the little cave. It was quite clearly a laboratory—Philonecron's laboratory. It was filled with test tubes, beakers, strange contraptions, and jars of unidentifiable substances. Cabinets and shelves lined the walls. Hanging against one wall was a very long white lab coat, and there was a bookshelf filled with quite ancient-looking texts, and on top, a box of scrolls. And there was a whole wall containing small jars of what looked very, very much like blood. The markings on them were in Greek, and so Zee couldn't tell which jar was which, but he knew his blood was somewhere in there. He grimaced.

Mew had run over to a corner and was squawking madly at Zee. He got the point. She was standing right in front of what looked like a trash bin, and Zee hurried over, raised the lid, and gasped.

The bin was filled with shadows.

They were piled on top of one another carelessly, like old towels. They looked thin, used, torn. Zee tried to pick one up, but he couldn't get hold of it—his hands just passed right through.

Zee looked at Mew, who stared pointedly back at him.

"I have to enchant these, don't I?" he said.

Mew simply looked at him.

"Then they can take care of the Footmen, and I can get to Philonecron."

Mew stared.

"I should hurry, shouldn't I?"

More staring.

"All right, then."

Zee knew what he had to do. He went over to Philonecron's cupboards and searched until he found what he needed. With a deep breath he went back over to the shadow bin and stood over it.

"Here goes . . ." He took the knife and sliced open his arm. Pain shot through him, and he winced. He felt tears leap to his eyes, and he exhaled deeply, then held his arm over the pile of shadows and squeezed, watching the blood as it dripped down.

He nodded at Mew, then toward the doorway. "Go check on them, will you? I'm going to make some noise."

Mew turned her head toward the door and crept off.

He closed his eyes. He had no idea if this would work. His words were supposed to be the final step, so whatever needed to be done to these shadows, he hoped Philonecron had already done it.

And the words—Zee had repeated them over and over again earlier today. Did he still know them? He exhaled and tried to clear his head.

Ek . . .

Ek skotou . . .

Yes, that was it. *Ek skotou es to phaos!* That was the

first sentence. *Ek skotou es to phaos!* The next was much the same.

Ek thanatou . . .

Ek thanatou es to . . .

Es to what? *Si* something. *Si* something?

Argh!

Ek skotou es to phaos. Ek thanatou es to . . .

Es to . . .

Sden!

Zee leaned into the bin of shadows and whispered, *"Ek skotou es to phaos, ek thanatou es to sden! Ek skotou es to phaos, ek thanatou es to sden! Ek skotou es to phaos, ek thanatou es to sden!"*

There was movement in the bin. A stirring. The shadows were coming alive.

"Ek skotou es to phaos, ek thanatou es to sden!"

The pile began to thicken, the shadows were growing. The pile wrenched and pulsed, and then a shadow jumped from the bin and stretched its arms out. Then another. Then another.

"Ek skotou es to phaos, ek thanatou es to sden!"

The shadows were leaping out—or were being tossed out by the other shadows. Some lay limp on the ground, others stretched and writhed until they, too, popped up and stood in front of Zee.

He had two dozen, then three, standing at attention

in front of him. A few others roamed around the room aimlessly, and others still lay lifeless in the bin.

He stared warily at his strange new soldiers, these spirits cut out of darkness. They twitched and shimmered as they stood, seemingly eager to try out the profits of life. Would they really obey? Would they turn on him? How alive were they—did they think, did they want? They were smoky and indistinct, vague creatures with stumps for arms, and they looked as if they could haunt Zee for the rest of time. There was something so . . . negative about them; they seemed to be cast from Nothing, like animate black holes, and Zee could not help but feel that if they got too close to him, they would take his soul.

He had to command them now. He had to be strong and sure. If only he were Charlotte, he could do this. But he wasn't. So he had to channel all the Charlotte-ness inside him. Zee took a deep breath.

Suddenly he heard a loud squawk behind him. Mew! He whirled around. The Footmen were approaching the lab, grinning broadly and viciously, Mew running behind them. Mew leaped from the ground and began clawing feverishly at one of the Footmen's thighs, and he reached down and threw her aside. She hit the ground and yelped.

"Shadows!" Zee yelled. "Attack them!"

His heart went into his throat. He had no idea what would happen—it all had been a good plan in theory, but in theory shadows could not come to life.

The shadows flickered, expanded into the air, stretched up and out as if they were letting out a silent roar.

Zee stepped back. The Footmen sneered and took long, sure steps toward Zee. He suddenly doubted Philonecron, doubted the shadows, doubted the whole plan, doubted everything but the Footmen, who were going to tear him to pieces.

And then the shadows sprang. They moved like shot fire, hurling through the air, trailing darkness behind them. They were on the Footmen in a blink, swarming over them, and the Footmen seemed swallowed by darkness.

They didn't have a chance. Some shadows stretched out like snakes and slithered over them, cutting swaths through their bodies. Others grew themselves long legs, which they used to wrap around the Footmen's waists, and long arms, which they used to pull the Footmen's arms from their shoulders and smash them to the ground. Others wrapped themselves around the Footmen's legs and squeezed until the legs fell off. The Footmen flailed around, trying to toss shadows aside, but they couldn't get hold of them. Some of the shadows dived right into the Footmen and then burst out again, spewing dust everywhere as Zee watched, wide-eyed, shuddering. Still the Footmen struggled and flailed, large bits missing from their bodies, while their body parts fell off and shattered on the ground. Their heads toppled and fell, eerie grins frozen on their faces, then smashed against the ground too. Soon there was nothing left of them but shredded tuxedo and chunks of clay.

Zee could barely breathe. His whole body was wracked with shivers. The shadows retreated, retracted, slid over to him calmly, and stood at attention again—waiting for their next target. Zee imagined them tunneling inside his own body, bursting out, sending chunks of Zee everywhere while he watched himself being eaten from the inside out. What on earth had he done?

Zee closed his eyes and tried to calm himself, then suddenly remembered Mew. He hurried over to the corner where she was lying on her side whimpering. He crouched down next to her.

"Dear cat, are you all right?" he whispered gently.

He carefully ran his hands over her rib cage, her hips, her spine, her back legs, then her front. She let out a little yelp and hopped up. Her left front leg dangled in the air, crooked.

"Oh, Mew!" Zee said. "They broke your leg. Does it

hurt too badly?" She cocked her head and looked at him sadly. "Oh, Mew . . ." He looked around the room, then grabbed a piece of tuxedo and gently wrapped up the kitten's leg. "You know," he murmured, scratching her chin, "you really are an extraordinary cat."

Then he gasped. Mew was covered in blood.

Oh, he realized slowly, it was his blood, from his arm. It wasn't gushing or anything—more of a steady dribble, really. Zee ripped off another strip of tuxedo, wrapped it around the wound, picked Mew up delicately, motioned to the shadows, and made his way out of the cave.

Zee had to hurry. Philonecron had left ages ago; it could already be too late. He'd stumbled at every turn since they'd come down to the Underworld. It would be just his luck to arrive at the Palace after Hades had been overthrown. Carrying Mew gently in his arms, Zee turned back into the passageway in the cliffs through which the Footman had led him before. The shadows floated behind him. He kept glancing back at them to make sure they were still in place, still contained—in a second they could leap at him and tear him to pieces.

But no, they were calm still—floating gently just above the ground. They were perfectly silent and utterly attentive to Zee. There was no indication that they had just ripped two creatures to bits. Zee felt like Dr.

Frankenstein, only his monsters were truly capable of evil. They had no conscience, no heart, no remorse—and they were devastatingly fast, utterly malleable, and, it seemed, supremely powerful.

And they obeyed his every word.

Zee shivered again.

Mew was perched in his arms, peering ahead to the light at the end of the passageway. A few of the skeleton birds flew above them, and Mew stared up at them and hissed loudly. She was talking tough, but Zee could feel her trembling against his body, and her eyes were dull and sad.

"What am I going to do with you?" he whispered to her. "I can't take you to the Palace like this."

She turned and glared at him.

"You've got a broken leg, cat, and I have to hurry. We could be too late already. You can't limp to the Palace."

She narrowed her eyes and let out a small grunt.

"Of course, I need someone to protect me from these guys," he murmured, motioning behind him at his small shadow regiment. They still followed loyally, bodylike puffs of smoke moving silently through the air.

Finally they emerged from the cliff into a clearing, the same rocky clearing where they had first encountered

Philonecron, where everything had gone so terribly wrong. And that's when Zee remembered . . .

Mr. Metos!

Zee whirled around and looked up at the cliff face. Mr. Metos was still there (where, exactly, would he have gone?), now hanging limply from his chains. Zee's heart froze. Was he still alive? Philonecron had said he had made Mr. Metos's liver immortal, but not the rest of him. Could he truly survive?

Zee heard singing in the distance and he shuddered. He couldn't leave Mr. Metos up there. He cast a glance toward the steaming river in the distance. Beyond it lay the Land of the Dead, the Palace, Hades—and somewhere, Philonecron and the shadows. Had they reached the Palace? Had they reached Hades? How much time would it take for Zee to get across? Too much. There was no time, he knew that.

And he looked back up at Mr. Metos—bloody and limp. Somehow Grandmother Winter had known him, or known about him. She had been trying to tell Zee to find him, he knew that now. Grandmother Winter had chosen Mr. Metos for a reason; she believed in him. And now Zee had to save him.

He turned to the shadows, who were standing in formation behind him. "Shadows! That man is chained to the cliff." Zee pointed toward Mr. Metos, his stomach twisting.

Was he condemning humanity to save one man? He had no choice. There are people in the world who have the constitution to sacrifice one for many. Zee was not one of those people. "He's been injured. I want you to unchain him and bring him down to me. Be very careful with him."

In a moment two of the shadows sprang from the group. Long arms and legs flickered out from their bodies like flames from a fire, and in a blink they were swimming up the rock face, their arms and legs treading air as they moved swiftly upward. Zee's stomach turned; he'd rather expected them to go the normal way, like walking up a path. They were inhuman, unreal; they were shadowy monsters who moved like night. Were their counterparts swarming up the walls of the Palace even now?

Soon—frighteningly soon—the two of them had reached Mr. Metos. Zee watched as, in perfect synchronicity, they each stretched an arm out into the iron manacles that held him. In the next moment the manacles exploded—bits of iron flew everywhere. Zee hugged himself.

And then Mr. Metos began to fall. A gargled scream escaped from Zee's throat as he watched the man plunge toward the ground. Zee tried to yell something to the shadows—anything—but his words choked in his mouth. Mr. Metos's arms went out into the air, thrashing, a drowning man trying desperately to swim in sky.

It was as though the Footmen were there, slowing time down—but they were not; there was only a helpless Zee, a flailing, plummeting Mr. Metos, and the murderous shadows.

Zee closed his eyes and clutched Mew to him, waiting to hear the sickly thump of man against ground.

But the sound never came. His eyes opened and he saw a thicket of shadows in front of him, arms raised into the sky, holding Mr. Metos up in the air as if he were a virgin to be sacrificed. The shadows walked Mr. Metos over to Zee and deposited him gently at his feet, then stood at attention again. Mew let out a squeak, burst out of Zee's arms, and limped her way toward Mr. Metos, while aftershocks of horror rippled through Zee's body.

Mr. Metos lay on the ground, clutching his stomach, grimacing at the shadows, and muttering to himself. Zee sprang over to him.

"Mr. Metos, are you all right?"

Mr. Metos looked at Zee darkly and shook his head. "Zachary, you fool! There was no time for this. You should have—" Suddenly he stopped talking; Mew had started bonking her head lightly against Mr. Metos's arm, and he was staring at her, wide eyed. "Is that a *cat?*"

"Yes," Zee said. "It's Charlotte's cat. . . ." He paused, then asked carefully, "You don't . . . *know* her, do you?" If she were some sort of Greek somebody, it would explain a lot.

But Mr. Metos just looked at Zee oddly. "The cat? No!" He shook his head quickly. "What is she *doing* down here?"

Zee shrugged. "Saving us?"

Mr. Metos tried to prop himself up and then winced abruptly. He sighed and laid his head back. "I must admit, Zachary," he said softly, "I do appreciate your getting me down. . . ."

Zee regarded Mr. Metos. His eyes had lost their sharpness, his skin was deathly pale, and his mouth was set with strain. Blood slowly seeped from his stomach.

"Here," Zee said, taking off his T-shirt. "Use this." He placed the shirt against Mr. Metos's stomach, and Mr. Metos nodded and pressed his hand lightly against the shirt. "Mr. Metos, what happened?"

Mr. Metos closed his eyes. "They knew I was coming. The Footmen were waiting for me. Charon must have told them. I was a fool." He shook his head and broke off in a fit of some very nasty-sounding coughing. "Oh . . ."

"I thought I could just sneak down here and free the shadows. This is all my fault." He blinked and stared at Zee intently. "Zachary, you have to go. You have to go now. They're already in the City." He smiled grimly. "I'm afraid I had quite a good view."

"What do I do?"

"You enchanted these shadows, Zachary." He motioned around him. "You know what to do."

Zee nodded. He did know what to do. He had known all along.

"Zachary," he continued, "when you get to the Styx, there's a bridge. The shadows built it, I saw them. Just cross it." Zee looked at him questioningly. "Don't worry about Charon, you'll find him lying unconscious in his boat with a nice lump on his head." He closed his eyes and took in a labored breath, then looked at Zee again. "And then head straight for the City, as fast as you can. You'll know where to go . . . Charlotte certainly did."

Zee stopped. "Charlotte?"

"Zachary," he said, and coughed again, "you'll learn that there are some people in the world you can't make deals with. A Footman tried to drown her, but she turned the tables on him." Mr. Metos allowed himself another grim smile. "That's a tough cousin you have. She made her way all the way to the City, and that's the last

I saw of her. Now, go. Go as fast as you can. It may already be too late."

Zee nodded. He regarded Mew, who stared at him earnestly, her bound leg dangling in the air. "You stay with Mr. Metos, okay?" She narrowed her eyes and glared at him. He leaned over and scratched her on the head, and she mewed softly. "You can come save me if I get into trouble." He turned to the shadows and motioned to the injured pair. "Protect them. If I don't come back"—he gulped—"take them to the Upperworld. Listen to Mr. Metos, he will tell you what to do. Follow his orders as if they were mine."

Mr. Metos nodded. Zee nodded back, and with a last glance at the bleeding man, the injured cat, and the lurking shadows, Zee made his way to the Styx.

CHAPTER 25

The Shadows Come

Yes, Charlotte did hear something. Very definitely. Some sort of rumbling thing, some sort of stomping thing, some sort of banging and thumping thing. Something was coming.

The shadows were coming. The shadows were coming, and they were coming loudly and they were coming soon. In the throne room the two gods and the girl froze, listening to the approach of their doom.

So this is what it sounds like: Gentle at first, a thunderstorm off in the distance. It grows louder, and louder still; the sound begins to overtake the pounding of your heart. There is fire, there is destruction, and there is this—this relentless approach. You are still, you are aware, and there is nothing you can do but wait.

Hades stood up and swept to one of the pairs of glass doors, and Thanatos quickly followed, with Charlotte—heart in throat—following right behind.

From the balcony one could look over the entire Kingdom. Charlotte could not help but think Hades did not do that very often. On a given day, standing on this balcony, he could see his bustling City; he could see his languishing Dead; he could see the great, smoking blackness of Tartarus; the steaming, snakelike form of the Styx, with Charon on his boat and the unending line of Dead waiting patiently in the rope lines to cross into his Kingdom.

Now, though, now Hades looked down upon a vast and unending column of dark marchers bursting into his City. The shadows were alive now; they were tall and dark and fierce, like creatures of night black flame moving inexorably through the Kingdom. And there were so many. They stretched on from the inside of the City through the plains back to the shore. The City's iron gates lay twisted and useless on the ground.

"Impossible," he said. "How did they get over the river?"

To Charlotte that didn't seem the best question to

ask at that moment. However they had gotten over the river, well, they had gotten over the river, and the point was pretty much moot. The Dead throughout the Kingdom had flown away from the wide path of the marchers and were cowering in the distance, so clustered together that they looked like great masses of light.

"How did they take down the gates?" Hades asked.

The marchers carried fire, they carried smoke, and they were working their way through the City toward the Palace. The Immortals, unprepared and untrained, were fleeing in droves. A few were fighting back—some threw small lightning bolts, some spit acid, some breathed fire or ice. But the shadows, they kept on marching. Smoke rose up in the City, stones tumbled everywhere.

"Why is everyone running?" Hades asked.

The shadows threw bits of themselves at buildings, the bits pierced the stone, and the stone burst into pieces. Sometimes the shadows walked right into buildings, seeping into the mortar, and the bricks tumbled down around them. Unharmed, they moved on.

"How can they do that?" Hades asked.

Harpies flew in and out of the chaos, cackling merrily, some throwing bits of building at the fleeing Immortals, some dive-bombing the crowd of shadows. The shadows threw their fire at the Harpies—a bit of shadow hit a

Harpy and exploded her from the inside out—and, screeching, the rest flew away. Griffins soared in from the horizon, pecking and clasping, but to no effect. Their claws went right through the shadows.

"How is that possible?" Hades asked.

They moved so steadily, determinedly. They moved like fire, like wind, leaving ashes and rubble in their wake. And they were entering the Palace grounds. *Crash!* The iron gates went down, and the shadows began marching through the breech. They circled all the way around the grounds, turned to face the Palace, and stopped. The rest filed in, lining up beside them. Fifty thousand shadows stood in a perfect circle around the Palace, staring toward it, ready to attack.

Charlotte desperately scanned the shadows, but nowhere did she see the thin, mortal form of her cousin.

"Zee," she whispered, "where are you?"

His words rang in her head again. *If I can—*

If I can—

They were all on the grounds now, filling in around the Palace, a great moat of shadow. Charlotte expected them to throw their flames, their magic, but they were perfectly still. Waiting. But for what?

"This is ridiculous," Hades said. He picked up his scepter, muttered a few words, and aimed it down at a regiment of shadows.

Charlotte gasped. "Wait!" she said, grabbing his robes.

He looked down at her. "What?"

"What are you doing?"

"Well, now . . . I'm not sure, you understand, because I've never done this to a shadow army before. It doesn't work on everyone. But I believe I am going to shoot a ray of interminable fire at them out of my scepter. The fire, you might be interested to know, is blue." He turned back and began to aim.

"You can't!" Charlotte jumped up and yanked on his scepter arm. "Those belong to children. You'll kill them!"

Hades tilted his head. "And?"

"They're just *kids*!"

He turned to Charlotte, smiled slightly, and patted her on the head. "Everybody dies eventually. Trust me." He picked up the scepter again.

"No! There's got to be another way! Anyway, you can't get them all at once, they'll tear down the Palace! Look what they did to those buildings! Look, they're just enchanted. If you can break the spell, if you can get Philonecron—"

Hades said matter-of-factly, "Philonecron is not here. I banished him." He looked over at Thanatos. "Right?"

Thanatos nodded.

"See?" He began to aim again.

Just then the faceless butler appeared in the doorway. "Excuse me, my Lord. . . ." Charlotte thought he looked a little nervous. She didn't blame him, she thought, checking on the army of shadows.

Hades turned. "Yes?"

"A Philonecron to see you, my Lord. He says it's quite urgent."

"Impossible!"

The butler paused, then bowed. "Nonetheless . . ."

"Oh, show him in!"

At least, Charlotte thought, hugging herself, with Philonecron in the Palace, the shadows probably wouldn't burn it down. That was nice.

Hades swept back into the throne room, Thanatos followed, and Charlotte crept in behind them. She did not exactly want to see Philonecron again—he was probably laboring under the impression that she was sleeping with the Styx fish—but she needed to find out about Zee. She hid herself behind one of the thrones.

The butler went to the door, bowed, and opened it an inch. "Philonecron, my Lord. Assistant Manager of Sani—"

But before he could finish his words, the door swung

open, hitting the butler in the face. Hades muttered something to himself.

Through the door marched two Footmen, carrying something carefully on their shoulders. They moved forward, revealing two other Footmen behind them. The four were carrying a great litter, like the kind in which they carry princesses in fairy tales, but inside was no princess.

The Footmen gently set the litter down. With a flourish one of them pulled off the fabric that covered the litter to reveal Philonecron, sitting in a very high chair made of bone and smiling like he had never smiled before. His legs were crossed and his feet dangled in the air. From her perch behind the throne, Charlotte shuddered.

Hades strode forward. "How . . . how did you get in here? I banished you!"

Philonecron nodded his head and waved his hand in the air, as if to bow. "My Liege." He cleared his throat. "If I recall correctly, on the occasion of my banishment you told me that I could not set foot in the Kingdom." He wiggled his feet. "You said nothing about being *carried* in. Really, though, this is most inconvenient." He sighed. "As soon as you have transferred power to me, all your spells will be broken, and I can walk again. I do look forward to that. I am a great walker. It's very good for the body. And the mind."

Hades slammed his scepter on the ground. "How dare you? I will never—"

"Oh, really?"

In a flash Hades aimed the scepter at Philonecron. A great blue fiery light rushed from it, heading straight for Philonecron's head. But Philonecron, just like that, stuck his hand up in the air. The fire hit his hand, bounced off, and went charging toward Hades's throne—the one Charlotte was hiding behind. She leaped out of the way, and the chair burst into flame and then disappeared into a pile of ash. Thanatos, who was lingering by the window, shrieked.

Hades looked to the scepter, then to Philonecron. "Part demon, are we?" he muttered. "I should have known."

But Philonecron was no longer looking at Hades. His eyes had followed Charlotte as she emerged from behind the throne, and he was staring at her with a brilliant hatred. His lips curled up in a sneer. "Oh, *you*," he said.

"Oh, hi!" she said. "Missing a Footman?"

"You! You little . . ." He almost stood up, but then one of the Footmen rushed toward him, and he jerked himself down in the chair. He put out his hands, as if he were trying to steady himself on an invisible rail. "You are trying to come between Zero and me. I will not let you."

"Where is he?" Charlotte stomped her foot. "Where's Zee?"

"Zero is home. He is resting; he's had a very trying day. Besides, there may be violence. I did not want him to see that."

"Is he okay?"

"I assure you, my dear, I would never harm your cousin. You, on the other hand . . ." He eyed her. "I should have personally dumped you in Tartarus. They've never had a living mortal to punish before. Well"—he tilted his head and smiled cruelly—"it does not matter. You escaped, you came all this way, but all your efforts were for naught. You came to warn Hades, and what happened? Did he offer to appoint a committee? Did he refer you to a Manager? Did he try to show you pictures of his wife?"

Charlotte gulped and looked at the ground.

"No, no, my saucy friend, you cannot stop me. Hades could have stopped me, but now it's too late." He looked around the room. "Where is the Ice Queen, anyway? I haven't seen her."

"Do not call her that," Hades breathed.

"What, the Ice Queen? It's just, she's not in her throne and she's not in the garden. I don't believe she's in the Palace at all. Do you know where she is? No? Hmm. Really, you should keep better track of your wife."

"Leave her out of this," Hades spit.

"I wonder if perhaps, when this is all done, she'd like to marry me. She makes such a lovely queen. Funny, you don't have any heirs, but I'm sure she'll give me some. After all, *I* never kidnapped her from the earth. She'll view me as her liberator. . . ."

Hades let out a fierce growl and aimed his scepter again.

"My Lord!" Thanatos shrieked, running up to him. "No!"

Exhaling heavily, Hades put the scepter down. He glared at Philonecron. "Well, perhaps I should be more precise in my language this time. Philonecron, grandson of Poseidon, Assistant Manager of Sanitation, I ban—"

"Wait!" Philonecron threw up his hand. Thanatos cringed. "I wouldn't do that if I were you. You're being watched, you know. And if I am banished, those shadows out there—have you seen them? Yes? Impressive, aren't they?—will tear this Palace down bit by bit."

Hades was visibly shaking with rage. Philonecron still smiled placidly. Hades closed his eyes, put a hand on his mouth, and squished his face in thought. Suddenly his eyes popped open, and he leaned over to Thanatos and whispered, "Can I banish the shadows?"

"My Lord." Thanatos bowed his head. "Um . . . I don't believe the shadows are citizens of the Kingdom."

Thanatos's voice was unusually high. "You have no control over them."

With that, Hades let out a *yeeeaarrgh!* that shook the whole room. Philonecron continued to smile. Charlotte slunk back toward the walls.

"Now." Philonecron clapped his hands together. "My Lord, in the spirit of reconciliation, generosity, and general bonhomie, I am giving you a choice. As you have seen"—he gestured broadly—"I have an army surrounding your Palace. You have no army. You have no defenses. You have nothing. Even a god cannot fend the shadows off forever; there are simply too many. At a signal from me they will start beating, burning, boring, busting, and generally wreaking havoc. They will continue until they get to you, my Lord, and when they find you, they will do the same to you until you surrender.

"After your surrender we will take you to Tartarus. You remember Tartarus, don't you? I'm sure all the people you've been punishing relentlessly for millennia will be very happy to see you. Not to mention all the Dead you've been mistreating, whom I'm going to throw in to keep you company.

"Or," he continued, spreading his arms out magnanimously, "you can just turn your crown and scepter and Kingdom over to me. I'll banish you—and I assure you, I am always very precise in my language—and we can save the Palace. Really," he said, looking around the room, "it has a lot of potential. Awfully plain on the outside, though. Mine will have a bit more . . . panache. Some cast-gold bas-relief ornamentation portraying the story of my great conquest over the indolent, uxorious tyrant—"

"Get out!" Hades spit.

"You get out," Philonecron declared.

"No, you get out!"

"No . . ."

Charlotte sighed heavily. This was going nowhere. Hades was going to do nothing, and the shadows were going to burn the place down. Charlotte would die and get thrown into Tartarus, the kids would all die and join her, Mr. Metos would have his liver eaten for all eternity, and Zee would have to spend the rest of his life with Philonecron.

She hurried over to the balcony to check on the shadow army. They still stood, quiet and waiting. It was so quiet outside suddenly—without the echoing approach of the army, with the great stillness of the shadows, the whole world before her seemed cast in perfect silence.

Except, of course, for sounds coming from inside the Palace. Philonecron and Hades were still yelling uselessly at each other. Charlotte crept over, closed the door, and began to listen to the great silence around her.

The shadows stared at her, without movement, almost without life. How strange it was. Maddy's shadow was out there, Elizabeth's, Ashley's, Audrey's, Angie's, and Zee's friends too—the kids from soccer, the kids from school, and that Samantha girl who made him blush. They were just things, just reflections of light, enchanted with blood and with her cousin's own words. . . .

If I can—

If I can—

The whispers reverberated in her mind, but she couldn't make out the words. She closed her eyes and pictured her cousin—on the first day, when her parents had thrust them together in the living room; at school with a crowd of kids surrounding him; on the soccer field, showing everyone how it's done; lying on the couch after his concussion, helplessly trying to deflect her mother's concerns; stopping to warm her as they went down to the Underworld; looking at her urgently as the Footmen led him away. She pictured him there, standing next to her, leaning down, whispering in her ear.

"What did you *say*, Zee?"

And then suddenly she could hear him—as if he were there, now, right next to her.

If I can—

If I can enchant them . . .

But before she could make out the rest, one of the Footmen came bursting through the door. He reached into his pocket, pulled out a small black horn, and blew—the commanding sound went through the Kingdom. The shadows started moving again then, stamping their feet, brandishing their fire and their bits of darkness. The whole Palace seemed to shake. Charlotte screamed. From inside the room came Philonecron's booming voice:

"Shadows!" he cried. "Bring the Palace down!"

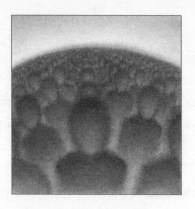

CHAPTER 26

Battle of the Shadows

THE SHADOWS SPREAD OUT ALONG THE GROUNDS, shaking their torches in the air. They lit trees on fire, surrounding the Palace in small bursts of flame. Charlotte could not move. In the blink of an eye Hades strode out onto the balcony, eyed a crowd of shadows that was bringing down one of the remaining trees, aimed his scepter, and fired a stream of blue flame.

Charlotte screamed, "Noooooo!" and ran to the balcony wall—but when the smoke cleared, the shadows were still there, though a nearby cypress had exploded in blue fire.

Cursing loudly, Hades fired the scepter again, but still to no avail. Smoke rose from the grounds below, and Charlotte began to cough uncontrollably.

A group of the eerie warriors reached into their chests, plucked out black balls of shadow, and began to hurl them at the Palace walls. The walls burst on contact. Shadowy bits flew through the air, like fireballs, destroying whatever they hit.

Some of the shadows dived into the walls themselves, and blocks of marble began to fall to the ground. Charlotte turned to Hades and yelled, "We have to go!"

He turned to her and shook his head firmly. "I am not leaving my Palace."

"It's too dangerous!" Charlotte yelled as a bit of marble burst around her.

"I'm Immortal," said Hades.

"Well, I'm not!" said Charlotte, and she turned and ran back into the throne room.

There she found that Philonecron and the Footmen were gone. The second throne had been turned into a pile of ash. Behind one of the tapestries stood the trembling form of Thanatos, and Charlotte shouted, "Let's go!" Another crash—the balcony doors exploded, and glass just missed Charlotte's head. Smoke filled the room, and the floor shook. She took off, her heart pounding in her ears, passing through the throne room doors, down the endless hallway, and out the Palace door.

The world was on fire, the world was breaking to pieces. Bits of marble and chunks of wood fell from the sky. The columns flanking the front door had large cracks running through them, and something welled up in Charlotte's throat. The column was just a spell, not real, not alive, but he had been nice to her—and kindness was hard to come by in the Underworld.

A chunk of wall came crashing down in front of her, and she took off again, running down the gold-paved front walk, through the line of flaming cypresses, with her sleeve to her nose and mouth so she could breath.

At least if I die down here, she thought, I won't have to wait in line at the Styx.

The shadows were everywhere, but all their attention was focused on the Palace, and they didn't seem to notice Charlotte at all. She darted in and around groups of the great black creatures on her way to . . .

On her way to where?

What, was she going to run away? Run back to the park, run back home, hide under the bed, while everything here collapsed? She couldn't leave the scene. She had to see this through, whatever it was. She had to do whatever she could to stop it, because no one else was going to. And if she did not stop it, at least she would not have run away. She could say to herself that when the time came—when the fate of humanity was in the balance—she, Charlotte Ruth Mielswetzski, stayed to see it through.

(Of course, she would be saying that to herself as her soul was being tortured in the eternal hell of Tartarus. You can't have everything.)

Charlotte skirted around the chaos, out of reach of falling chunks of marble and billows of smoke. She found her way to the Palace gates, now a tumble of iron and stone. A great pile of rubble lay just beyond the outline of the gates—the remains of some once-grand building—and slowly, carefully, she climbed up to the top and looked out at the destruction around her.

The Palace was full of gaping holes, and fire licked up all around it. The smallest of the onion-shaped domes was teetering precariously. The shadows went on throwing bits of darkness; they were relentless, mindless of all the falling stone and the smoke. It did not hurt them. It did not stop them. It didn't even slow them. The Palace would be nothing but rubble in minutes, and then what would Hades do?

The Palace was emptying out. Immortal or not, the Palace staff had decided to vacate the premises, and quickly. Shadowy butlers were trotting out as fast as their dignity would carry them. An ogre cook and spritelike maids came scurrying through the doors, followed by ghoulish creatures in business suits clutching papers in their hands. Thanatos came too, holding hands with his identical twin brother, Hypnos. They, and the whole crowd of Palace denizens, followed Charlotte's tracks through the smoky trees, by the remnants of the front gate, and out into the City.

Hades, though, did not leave. Charlotte could see him, still on the balcony, shouting and waving his scepter maniacally.

It didn't take Charlotte long to see what he was yelling at.

Over to Charlotte's left, in a spot just beyond the fracas, stood Philonecron. He seemed impossibly high up in the air, but when a crowd of shadows moved, Charlotte saw he was standing on the chair of the litter, which was being held up by the four Footmen.

Philonecron was holding his arms out majestically, framing the chaos below him. His grin stretched to his ears. Every once in a while he shouted commands at the shadows. "A little to the left!" or "Yes, yes, splendid shot!" or "Oooh, how wonderfully destructive!"

The Footmen were perfectly still and stiff, proper as posts, holding up their master. Charlotte wondered if she could hurt them somehow, run over and push them into the flames—maybe that would do *something*. Slow everything down, maybe. But it would never work; Philonecron would call the shadows to her, and she would last a lot less long than the Palace.

And the Palace was not lasting. The small dome came crashing down, bringing with it much of the roof. Philonecron let out a cheer, and the group of shadows right in front of Charlotte turned their attention to the other two domes. A wall-size chunk fell from the back of the Palace, another from just below the balcony, and Hades fell backward inside the building.

"Bring it down!" Philonecron shouted gleefully. "Bring it all down!"

Two stories of the Palace collapsed with a gigantic crash that shook the entire Kingdom. Charlotte went tumbling off her rubble pile, scraping her hands and legs on the way down.

She crawled halfway up again, dirty and bleeding, tears and sweat streaking lines down the dust on her face. The shadows in front of her toppled another dome, and Charlotte watched, small and helpless, as the Palace of Hades began to tumble down.

As the walls fell to the earth, a cry came from deep inside her. "Stop!" she shouted weakly. "Stop!"

And suddenly the group of shadows in front of her turned to look, rocks clenched in their hands.

She froze. But they did not fire. They were looking at her, waiting, as if . . .

As if waiting for her to tell them what to do.

"Stop!" she said again, and a few more stopped, turned to her, and waited.

She bit her lip. Her body trembling, she crawled all the way up to the top of the pile of rubble and shouted at the top of her lungs:

"STOP!"

And that's when she heard Zee's voice in her head, as clear as day.

If I can enchant them . . .

I can also stop them.

If I can enchant them, I can also stop them.

That's what Zee had been trying to tell her. That's why he had gone along with Philonecron. He thought he could stop them. If they were enchanted with his blood, with his voice, he could stop them.

But he wasn't here.

She was here.

What had Mr. Metos said? The Footmen had used Zee's blood to find her and steal shadows from her friends. She and Zee were blood relatives. The shadows were enchanted with Zee's blood, with Zee's commands, so surely . . .

"STOP!" she called again. All around her shadows

froze. Their attention was uncertain, wavering—she could feel it; she knew she could lose them at any moment. She channeled all the Zee blood inside her, all the Zee-ness, and she cupped her hands around her mouth, took the biggest breath she ever had in her life, and shouted, "STOP!"

A rush of power went through Charlotte. No one had ever listened to her at all before, and now an entire regiment of shadows was obeying her commands.

All around Charlotte the destruction had ceased, and Philonecron—shouting commands and cackling on the other side of the Palace—hadn't noticed a thing. *"Find him!"* he shouted. *"Find him and tear him apart."*

Her shadows were still, frozen, waiting—but, she realized with a sinking heart, it wasn't enough. She'd stopped a thousand, maybe two, but there were so many more. And the Palace was on its last legs, and then the shadows would go for Hades.

There was no time. She couldn't get to them all. . . .

But her regiment could.

"Go to the other shadows," she yelled at the group before her. *"Make them stop! Everyone must stop!"* She looked around frantically. *"Quickly!"* she added.

Her regiment peeled out in front of her, weaving their way in and out of the other platoons, blackness coiling around blackness. One shadow reached out and touched another, and that one stopped what it was doing and reached out and touched the one next to it, on and on down the line. One stopped, then the next, then the next—like very creepy dominoes. One regiment, then the next, then the next—they stopped in waves, putting down their fire and their smoke and their bits of shadow and looking up at Charlotte. That was enough to get Philonecron's attention.

"*Shadows,*" she heard him cry, "*what are you doing? Don't stop! Keep going!*" The shadows all twitched and rumbled, looking from one master to the other. Some picked up their weapons again uncertainly.

Philonecron looked around frantically, yelping as he saw Charlotte over the wreckage of the Palace. "*You!*" he screamed. "You worthless child! You can't command the shadows!" He paused and raised up his hands. "*Shadows, get her!*"

The squadron of shadows closest to Philonecron began to move—they rushed around their comrades, moving like raging fire. A flood of darkness swarmed toward her, a giant black wave coming to drown her, a great rush of spirits shooting through the air right toward her soul—and Charlotte froze with horror.

"*Get her! Kill her!*" Philonecron pointed at Charlotte and spit, "How dare you? How dare you try to command them? You're not Zero!"

And then a voice rang out, "No, but I am."

Zee?

Charlotte whirled toward the voice. And there he was, Zee, shirtless and with a bandaged arm, standing on top of one of the fallen domes, shouting through some kind of animal horn.

"Shadows! Stop! Stop at once!"

And just like that, the flood of shadows froze. *"All of you, stop! Put your weapons down!"*

Charlotte felt tears pouring down her cheeks as her cousin's voice moved over the whole Palace grounds. *"Come to me!"*

"Go to Zee!" Charlotte shouted. *"Put down your weapons and go!"*

A piercing scream hit the air—the shadows trembled, the ground shook, and Charlotte spun around.

"No!" Philonecron yelled.

Zee didn't move. *"Put down your weapons,"* he bellowed. *"Come to me!"*

"Go to Zee!" Charlotte yelled joyfully. *"Go to your master!"*

On top of his litter Philonecron was the very picture of horror. His hands clasped tight to his face, his mouth frozen in a scream, his red eyes popping out of his head. The four Footmen were watching him warily.

"Zero!" Philonecron shouted. "Zero, my boy! What are you *doing?*"

But Zee did not turn. He was magnificent. He was regal. He was a force. He kept shouting commands to the shadows, who were lining up in front of him obediently, like good little soldiers. Philonecron screeched again and yelled down to his Footmen, *"Take me to him! Hurry! Zero, stop!"*

But whatever control Philonecron had over Zee wasn't working from that distance, and Charlotte wasn't going to let him get much closer, if she could help it. She broke into a run, heading for Philonecron, heading for her cousin. Philonecron, wobbling as he was moved, was yelling, "Why are you doing this? Zero, why are you betraying me?"

"Go back to the Outer Banks!" Zee shouted to the army of shadows. *"Go back home! Wait for me there! Wait for my commands!"*

And, as one, the legions of shadows turned and began to march through the rubble, through the gates, back into the remnants of the City.

"Noooo!" yelled Philonecron to the marchers. "Come back! Come back! I am your master! Not him! Come back! We're so close!"

But the shadows paid him no mind; their true master had spoken. They were marching back home.

Charlotte cut around the great column of marchers, past the rubble of the Palace—which, by the way, seemed to be moving, as if something was digging itself out from the inside—and crept toward the duo.

For the Footmen had reached Zee and were carefully lowering the litter down while Philonecron stood balancing himself on the chair and shouted instructions. "Hurry up!" he yelled. "Steady, now! Don't drop me! Watch the *feet!*" Zee was standing his ground on top of the dome, staring down Philonecron.

Charlotte was close to them now, but Philonecron had not noticed her; his whole world was Zee. She crept through the rubble behind the Footmen, behind Philonecron and his litter. Zee saw her and winked— and at that moment she thought a wink was the best way ever to say hello.

As for Philonecron, he looked as if he very much wanted to get up off his perch, despite the whole banishment thing. He stared at Zee, shaking his head, his mouth opening and closing.

"You . . . you *betrayed* me," he emoted. "After all I did for you!" He paused dramatically, and a great tear ran down his cheek. "You were nothing, nothing, before me. I made you great. I made you the father of an army. You were my Zero!"

Zee was not moved. He picked up his horn, aimed it in Philonecron's face, and, articulating every word very carefully, shouted, *"Stop. Calling. Me. Zero!"*

Charlotte could not help but think that Zee had found the perfect thing to say.

Wincing, Philonecron closed his eyes until Zee had finished. Then he drew himself up, twisting with rage. "I made you, and I can break you, my boy. Don't forget, I know everything about you. I know what makes your blood crawl." He leaned forward as best he could on his perch in the chair, lifted up a hand, and whispered, "Zero. Come to me. Come. . . ."

And as Charlotte watched helplessly, Zee's arm fell and his eyes lost their focus. Philonecron's voice sounded so familiar, so beautiful, and part of Charlotte wanted just to close her eyes and do whatever he said. . . .

But just part. The Mielswetzski part roared inside of her, and she shook herself. *Come on, Zee. We're so close now.* She willed her cousin's attention to her. *Come on, Zee; focus on me.* She waved her arms in the air. *Look at this, Zee,* she willed him. *Not at him.*

But Zee's gaze did not waver. "Come to me, my boy," Philonecron hissed, "and I will rip out your thro—"

Just then a crashing sound came from the remnants of the Palace, and Zee, Charlotte, and Philonecron turned to look. A long, black-cloaked arm emerged from under a rock. The rock began to shift back and forth, back and forth, and finally it rolled off. A shoulder came out. And then a head. Which was wearing a perfectly intact, simple black crown.

Philonecron let out a roar of rage. "Get him!" he shouted to the Footmen, pointing at Hades, who was casually crawling out of the pieces of marble. The Footmen exchanged glances, then took a step toward the Lord of the Dead.

Philonecron turned back to Zee. "Look at me!" he whispered. "Look!" He raised his hands to Zee's eye level. "Come on, my boy. That's right." Zee seemed to slump a little bit. Charlotte fought hard against Philonecron's voice in her head; she had to now, it was all up to her. Otherwise he could kill them both, get the shadows back, and it would all be over.

"That's right, you worthless thing. Come to me, and I will rip out your throat. I will feed you to the Harpies. Finally you'll be of some use in your worthless little life—"

Charlotte ran at Philonecron, not knowing what she was going to do, knowing she had to do something. "Leave him alone!" she shouted. Philonecron whirled around on his litter and glared at her, and suddenly Charlotte had an idea. She wasn't positive, but it seemed like a rather good one. In the space of a breath Charlotte reached down, picked up the largest rock she could find, held it above her head, and crashed it down as hard as she could on the chair under his feet.

A great *crack* splintered through the air—Philonecron's mouth opened, his eyes bugged, and the chair broke into pieces underneath him. Philonecron went tumbling backward, his bottom hitting the ground, followed by his hands, followed by his feet.

A hissing noise emanated from the ground. Philonecron yelled and pushed himself up in the air, ready to dive back onto the litter, but he was too late. His feet started smoking, then they burst into a blood-red flame. The fire traveled up to his legs, and, screaming, he propelled himself onto the litter—leaving a pile of ash where his legs had once been.

Suddenly, from behind them, Zee and Charlotte heard a sizzling noise and then saw a great blue light. They turned—Hades, a little dusty but looking no worse for wear, was standing on top of the rubble, pointing his scepter at four bursts of blue fire. The flames grew into the air and then quickly extinguished.

On the ground were four piles of debris consisting of cracked clay and bits of fabric, drizzled with puddles of thick brown blood. The Footmen were gone. And then slowly, quietly, the debris shifted a little, and the four Unburied from whom the

Footmen had been made emerged mistily from the rubble. They looked around at the scene before them, brushed themselves off, and floated into the night.

Hades turned and strode up to Philonecron, who was writhing, legless, on his litter. He grinned, flipped his scepter, and proclaimed cheerfully, "Works on clay!"

CHAPTER 27

Daylight

THE LORD OF THE DEAD STOOD TOWERING OVER THE prone form of Philonecron, who was twisting in agony on his litter. Charlotte and Zee—who were covered in grime and smoke and dust and blood, who were panting and sweating and trembling, who were exhausted and exhilarated—stood in the background, shoulder to shoulder, and watched Hades savor the moment.

"Stop whining," Hades spit. "Your legs will regenerate."

"That's right, they will!" Philonecron looked up threateningly and raised his fist in the air. It really wasn't very intimidating. "I'll have my legs. I still have my Footmen. They will serve me until the end. There are seven Footmen—"

"Five, actually," Zee muttered.

Charlotte shot him an impressed look. Zee shrugged modestly.

"Ah, but Philonecron," Hades interjected, "this *is* the end. I will find your Footmen, do not worry about that." He flipped his scepter again. "And as for you . . ." He snapped his fingers in the air, and two Griffins came soaring in from the horizon. (Fat lot of help they were, Charlotte thought.) Hades beckoned them to him. "Now," he continued, pacing back and forth in front of the litter, "whatever shall we do with you? I banished you once to the Outer Banks, but that was clearly too good for you. Hmmm. I think I have an idea. Philonecron, Assistant Manager of Sanitation, I banish you to the Upperworld—"

"No," Philonecron shrieked. "No! I'll never survive."

"That is not my concern."

"I can't breathe up there," Philonecron protested. "And everyone wears polyester!"

Charlotte and Zee exchanged a look. They weren't ecstatic about the idea of Philonecron in the Upperworld. But Hades didn't seem to notice.

Hades continued, "You are banished to the

Upperworld, Philonecron. You may never set f—you may never enter the Underworld again. Griffins?" He held his hand up. "Take him away."

With that, the two Griffins swooped down, claws at the ready, grasped Philonecron—one by the neck and one by the bottom—and proceeded to fly away. The air reverberated with Philonecron's cries. "Nooooo!" Charlotte and Zee heard. And then, just as the trio was fading off in the distance, a cry shot out, "Zerrrrooooo!"

Hades, looking extremely pleased with himself, turned his attention to the cousins.

"That should take care of him," he said. He nodded at Charlotte. "That was very impressive, with the chair. You are quite resourceful."

Charlotte blushed. Hades might be creepy, but he was a Greek god, and they probably didn't give compliments lightly.

"And," he said, turning to Zee, "Zachary John Miller, your timing is excellent, as was your leadership."

Zee muttered to Charlotte, "How does he know my name?"

"Don't ask," Charlotte whispered back.

"Now, I thank you both for what you have done for my Kingdom." He reached into his pocket and pulled out a small, round red object, which he offered to them. "Pomegranate?"

Quickly Charlotte and Zee shook their heads.

"Worth a try. Well, you will find the door open for you on the way out. I shall see you again."

At this Charlotte and Zee shuddered, and before they could say anything else, the Lord of the Dead turned and walked away, calling, "Has anyone seen my wife?"

The cousins stood among the ruins of the Palace of Hades. More Griffins began to sweep through the air, and the Immortal residents of the Palace were beginning to emerge from the distance. Charlotte looked at Zee, and Zee looked at Charlotte.

"Let's go home," Charlotte said quietly. "Let's go home."

There were so many questions to ask, so much to discuss. Worlds had moved since Charlotte and Zee had last seen each other. They'd enchanted shadows, met the Lord of the Dead, seen a Palace fall, escaped from Footmen (twice), led an army, outwitted an evil genius, saved the world, saved each other. They should have been chattering away, their voices should have overlapped each other as they tried to tell their stories, their exuberance should have carried them up into the skies. But as they walked back through the Underworld, Charlotte and Zee were strangely quiet.

Behind them Immortals were filing (and slithering) back into the City, putting out fires, climbing around rubble, cleaning up. And in front of them—really, everywhere around them—the Dead were beginning to fill in the landscape again, and soon the air was crowded with them. Eerie and beautiful, silent and cramped, nervous and bored, the Dead reemerged to take their places in their perpetual sea of rocky dullness.

Charlotte whispered, "It's hard to feel really good about helping Hades, you know?"

Zee nodded as if he had been thinking the same thing. "I guess we helped them, though. Out here is a lot better than in there." He gestured toward the steaming structure on the horizon.

Charlotte started chewing on her lip. "I know, but . . . I thought maybe he'd ask us, you know, if there was something he could do for us. And we could, like, tell him to build a city for the Dead. Or something. And he would have been like, 'Okay.' And it all would have been better. We could have helped them all."

Zee nodded slowly.

"But he didn't ask," Charlotte continued. "He didn't. And I didn't say anything. We had him right there, and I didn't say anything."

Zee turned to her and put his hand on her arm. "He wouldn't have listened anyway, Charlotte. You know that."

The Dead, drawn to these two walking memories of Life, crowded, clamored, and clustered, but just as Charlotte began to wonder how they would get through, the great crowd in front of them split in two, marking a path for the cousins to walk.

The cousins stopped short.

"Oh," said Charlotte.

"Oh," said Zee.

They could see their path all the way to the Styx, but on either side of the path stood countless bodies of light, all stopped to watch them pass, an ethereal, glowing honor guard making way.

Eyes filling, they grabbed hands and began to walk on, through the watchful Dead.

"You know," Zee said, smiling a little, "there aren't any Dead on the Outer Banks anymore. The shadows built a bridge over the Styx to get across, and all of the Dead just poured over the bridge. All of them!"

"Wow!"

"Yeah."

"Charon's going to be real pleased about that!" Charlotte said.

Zee grinned. "When he wakes up. One of the Footmen clunked him on the head."

"Oh!" Charlotte thought that sounded like a good idea. She should have tried it herself instead of giving up a month's allowance and her Fruit Roll-Ups. "Hey, is that how you got across? The bridge?"

"Yeah. He didn't bother to take it down. Mr. Metos said—"

Charlotte stopped. "Mr. Metos!" Blushing, she realized she'd forgotten all about him.

"He's okay," Zee said. "We got him down. He's in a bad way, but he's resting, and—"

"We?"

Zee smiled. "Philonecron left a few shadows behind. And you'll never guess who showed me where they were."

Charlotte shook her head. "Who?"

"Mew."

"*What?*"

And then they began to tell their stories. Zee told Charlotte about enchanting the shadows, about the vast army he created, about Philonecron putting him to rest in his cave, about the two Footmen standing guard, about his surprise visitor, about the secret lab and the discarded shadows, about the Footmen's violent end, about getting down Mr. Metos, about running as fast as he could all the way to the Palace, about feeling Philonecron's voice inside his head, about losing his will, and about hearing his cousin's voice, clear as day, yelling to save him, and finally believing they might get through this.

And Charlotte told Zee about fighting the Footman,

about pushing him in the Styx, about Charon and Cerberus, about the vampire demon and the park, about the City and the Palace, about trying to convince Hades to act, about dodging blasts of fire, about Philonecron and his litter, about the shadows coming and the fires starting, about her accidental discovery, about commanding the shadows, about their swarming toward her, and about hearing her cousin's voice, clear as day, and finally believing they might get through this.

"You were pretty great, you know," Charlotte said. "With the shadows. You say you don't like to talk, but . . ."

"I wouldn't have been in time if it hadn't been for you commanding them," he said. "And with the chair. That was pretty great. I would have been a goner."

They were chattering now, voices and hearts light, the world seeming like a great, bright place where two cousins could work together to save it—even in that dark home of the Dead. They crossed the great expanse of the Plains, reached the bridge made of bone, and began to cross.

Suddenly, in the middle of the bridge, Charlotte stopped and turned around. Zee followed suit. Legions of Dead were behind them, watching and waiting, but for what? The cousins stared helplessly. For moments they stared at each other, the Living and the Dead, unable to move.

"Zee . . . ," Charlotte said. "Your grandmother . . . we never . . ."

"It's okay," he said. "When I was in the cave, well, I thought . . . I knew . . ." He trailed off, touching his chest, smiling a secret smile, the smile of someone who knew he was being watched over. Zee squeezed Charlotte's hand, and they turned their backs on the Dead and made their way to the Outer Banks.

They arrived at Philonecron's little clearing to find Mr. Metos on the ground, surrounded by about five hundred shadows, with Mew sitting watchfully on his leg. When he saw them, Mr. Metos looked as happy as it was probably possible for him to look—which was fairly impressive, considering half his liver had been gnawed off. Mew sprang up and let out a loud, happy chirp.

"Mr. Metos!" Charlotte ran up to him. "Mew!" She picked up her cat gently and buried her face in her fur. "Oh, you poor, brave baby." She kissed the cat a couple of times and then turned her attention back to Mr. Metos. "Are you okay?"

He nodded, "Reasonably. I'm healing already." He motioned to his bloody abdomen, and Charlotte winced. "Hey, I got an Immortal liver out of the deal," he added grimly. "And you two?"

With rushed breath and overlapping voices,

Charlotte and Zee told their stories. Mr. Metos seemed particularly satisfied to hear of Philonecron's end.

"But won't he make trouble in the Upperworld?" Charlotte asked.

"I doubt it. Stripped as he is of his connections to the Underworld, I don't think his powers will last. He will wander about helplessly until he finds a group of Immortals to join and make petty trouble. Nothing to worry about. Energy schemes, mutual-fund bilking, insider trading, Department of Defense, that type of thing. And until he becomes accustomed to living up there, he'll be quite uncomfortable. Now . . . perhaps we should get out of here?"

"What about the shadows?" Zee said.

The shadows, who had stood at attention at the sound of Zee's voice, were lined up, waiting for their next command. Here, on the other side of the river, they looked small, like the children they had come from.

"We're taking them with us. I was able to merge the replicated shadows into their hosts."

"But there are more," Zee said. "A few in the lab."

Mr. Metos held up his hand. "I know, I know. A few of my trusty soldiers here got them. We have them all, and once they're up in the Upperworld, they will find their way to their humans. It's in their nature."

"But some of them are from England," Zee said.

"Yes. They'll come with us through the passageway. We will end up at the door at that hideous Mall. There are doors like that all over the world, but it is all the same door, if you get my meaning—the shadows will find their way. Now, if you children will help me up . . ."

Charlotte put down Mew for a moment and grabbed Mr. Metos's hands, and Zee moved behind him and lifted him from the back with his good arm. It was a long process, and Mr. Metos made little grunts as they helped him up.

"An A for both of you," he said with a pained smile. "Oof."

He moved as if to start off, but before they left, Charlotte had to ask him something. She looked at him shyly, chewing on her lip. "Mr. Metos . . . is there something we can do for the Dead?"

He shook his head and winced. Zee stayed behind, supporting him. "Awful, isn't it? I'd heard about it, but I'd never seen it before. This is just what I was telling you before. The gods do not care about mortals, not at all."

Charlotte thought about this for a moment. "Well, what about Persephone?"

"What about her?"

"And Orpheus. You know. Orpheus was in love with that girl—"

"Eurydice. Yes, Charlotte, I'm familiar with the story," he said drily. This was one of Charlotte's favorite myths—or used to be, before she found out it was real. Orpheus was a musician, and he fell madly in love with Eurydice, and then she died and was sent to the Underworld. But Orpheus was so heartbroken he went after her and pleaded with Hades for her return. Hades wasn't moved, but Persephone was. She begged Hades to make an exception, just that once. And he did— except he told Orpheus to walk out of the Underworld without looking back to see if Eurydice was following him, and just at the end he looked back. Eurydice was taken into the Underworld forever. She was still here, now, though Charlotte hadn't seen her. She would have liked to.

"Well," Charlotte said, "Persephone helped Orpheus. She convinced Hades to let Eurydice out."

"She was doing it for her own ends," said Mr. Metos curtly. "She was just causing trouble for Hades. No god or goddess cares about people. You don't see Persephone helping them now, do you?"

"I guess not," Charlotte said. They hadn't seen Persephone at all. Charlotte gathered she didn't like being around Hades very much. Charlotte could hardly blame her.

"I promise you this," Mr. Metos said. "I will make

sure the Promethians look into it. Perhaps there is something we can do for the Dead, maybe a way we can convince Hades to acknowledge them or at least to control the Harpies. I don't know what, but I will try. Now . . . can we get out of here? Speaking of Harpies, I'd really rather not see any more today."

Charlotte couldn't argue with that. With Zee supporting Mr. Metos and Charlotte carrying Mew, they prepared to set off, back through the Outer Banks, toward the passage to the Upperworld. Mr. Metos motioned toward the awaiting shadows. "Zachary, will you do the honors?"

Zee nodded and turned his head. "Shadows," he called, "follow me!"

Going up the passageway was twice as arduous as going down, but Zee and Charlotte barely noticed. They were going back home.

What a sight they must have made—the boy, the girl, the cat, the bleeding, groaning man, and the five-hundred-odd shadows—working their way up to the world of light.

They were glad of Charlotte's water and her cereal bars. (Good thing she hadn't told Charon about those!) Soon it grew too narrow for Zee to support Mr. Metos, and at a few words from Zee two of the shadows picked him up and carried him—much to Mr. Metos's consternation.

"I could get used to this," Zee whispered, nodding back to the shadows.

"Don't start getting a big head on me," Charlotte said.

They were largely quiet on their journey back—just about everything that was to be said had been said. All there was left to do was concentrate on home and the home-like things that would be waiting for them.

"Zee?" Charlotte whispered. "Do you think we'll wake up tomorrow and this will all have been a dream?"

"I don't know," Zee said, "but I wouldn't mind going to sleep to find out."

That sounded good to Charlotte.

She led the way this time, cradling Mew in her hands, her cousin following her, and Mr. Metos and the shadows behind them. Again Zee's watch provided the only light, but it did not matter so much this time. She knew her cousin was behind her and that they would keep each other safe.

And slowly, carefully, they made their way up, up, up—the air grew more and more comfortable, the smell of Harpy grew faint, the Underworld seemed a great distance behind them—and finally, eventually, Charlotte saw the light reflecting off a cool metallic wall. The door.

"We're here!" Charlotte breathed.

Zee sucked in his breath. "Think Hades left it unlocked?"

"Hope so," Charlotte said. "He promised."

Mr. Metos let out a small snort. But Charlotte reached out, grabbed the nondescript knob, and turned. The door opened.

Light. So much light. Charlotte, Zee, and Mr. Metos fell back a little into the tunnel, their eyes burning.

"Great," Charlotte said, "I'm a bat."

But slowly, gradually, they moved out of the tunnel, through the door, and into the world.

It was the same. The corridor was the same. The world was the same. The Mall was open—daylight streamed in from everywhere. At the end of the long, nondescript corridor Charlotte saw a pair of women pass by, and then another, and then another. They were all older women, wearing tracksuits and sneakers.

"Mall walkers!" whispered Charlotte.

"What?" asked Zee and Mr. Metos simultaneously.

"Never mind," said Charlotte.

It was morning in the Upperworld. Early. There was no telling how long they had been gone. They moved into the corridor, slowly adjusting to the light, while giddy mall walkers trotted past them.

Behind them the shadows came through the door.

Only a fourth of the number that had come up with them emerged—the others had gone through other doors elsewhere. Except they were all the same door. Or something like that; it didn't matter. The shadows would find their way.

And then suddenly the group of shadows took off, and great black flashes moved through the air and were gone before anyone could blink.

"There goes your army," Charlotte whispered to Zee.

"I'll live," Zee grinned. It was a beautiful grin that stretched all the way to his ears, revealing straight white teeth. It was the sort of grin that made you want to grin too.

If the mall walkers noticed the bleeding man supported by two sooty, filthy kids and one ratty-looking cat with a tuxedo-pants sling heading for the doors, they didn't say. Perhaps their minds were on other things. Perhaps they were concentrating hard on their mall walking. Perhaps they saw groups like that all the time in the Mall. We can never know. All we know is Charlotte, Zee, and Mr. Metos stepped outside the great glass automatic Mall doors, surveyed the mostly empty parking lots, the great tangle of roads and freeway exits, the cars honking and buzzing by, and together took a great breath in, savoring the air. Charlotte had never taken such a beautiful breath.

"My car is here," Mr. Metos said. "I'll drive you home. Then I'm going to take a nice long nap and wait for my liver to regenerate."

Home, Charlotte thought. Then something occurred to her. She gasped and turned to Zee, panic in her eyes.

"What are we going to tell Mom and Dad?" she whispered urgently.

Zee shook his head and grinned again. "I'm sure you'll think of something."

Grandmother Winter's Last Adventure

THE PASSAGE INTO DEATH WAS SO SIMPLE, LIKE THE end of a breath. All Grandmother Winter knew was that at one moment her body and her soul were intertwined, and the next they were not. The body became a shell, no longer a part of Dalitso Winter.

Interesting, she thought.

She could no longer see, really, or hear—not in the way we always think of seeing and hearing. Her eyes and her ears were dead, gone, but she found she still *knew* everything about the room—Zachary's head was bowed by her side, with tears running down his cheeks; her daughter was leaning in to wrap her arms around her body; her son-in-law reached in to embrace the whole family. Grandmother Winter was *aware* of everything—the strange, sharp smell of the air, the cotton sheets about her body, the taste of lemons in the room, and her beloved family, so close and impossibly far away.

She did not like seeing her loved ones like this, bent over with sorrow; everything in her wanted to cry out, to thrash and scream at the sight of it. But she knew that great grief came from great love, and that their grief was an honor to her. And she did love them so very much.

And Zachary. The taste of her last premonition would not leave her. Something was going to happen to her boy, something terrible. There was evil in the world, and it was going to come for him. She could not protect him, she could not warn him—she had not had the breath left. She could not say, "Find this man, he will help you"; all she could say, with her dying breath, was, "Metos," and hope that someday he would understand.

And now she was leaving them. For there was a presence beside her, something decidedly not human, something tall and thin and Immortal, and she could feel herself being drawn to him. He reached into her body—the shell that contained her—grabbed her soul and began to pull.

Like that, Grandmother Winter was out of her body, floating in the air, led by a messenger with winged feet. She scarcely had time to look about the room for one more glimpse of her family, her grandson, before he pulled her off. But she would be back. She had promised her grandson that she would be back, and Grandmother Winter always kept her promises.

Through the house the Messenger led her, out the door, and down the street. The world sped past. It was all wrong somehow, the light, the noise, the air. She did not belong here anymore.

She was a little surprised when they went into the bowling alley, but she didn't ask questions because the Messenger clearly wasn't answering them. They traveled through the bar, past the bowling lanes, through a wall, into a storage room filled with cracked bowling pins, and then through a nondescript door that read, NO ADMITTANCE.

Down they went, through wetness, through blackness, through coldness. It made Grandmother Winter slightly nervous, of course, that they were heading downward, but it did not seem prudent to panic.

And then suddenly there was light again. Well, not light exactly. But not darkness, either. They emerged from the tunnel and before her was grayness, a great, flickering grayness, like a fog lit by fire. The world was made of rock—a deep red rock that looked like nothing on Earth, craggy and cliffy and endless. They flew over a great expanse of rocky plain, and then the Messenger began to slow.

Below her was a great strip of light spreading out before the snakelike form of a river, which appeared to be steaming. No, not a strip of light, but rather lights, hundreds of lights. Bodies of light. Ah, she realized, they were the Dead. She was the Dead. They were all the same.

The Messenger dropped her off at the end of the line, slipped her a small coin, and flew off.

And there she stayed.

She was standing next to a form like hers, a creature of death and light, and behind her was the rocky terrain they had just come over. She could not see what lay ahead.

The being next to her spoke. "Hello. Long line, huh?"

Well, no, he hadn't spoken, not really, but his words appeared in her head. And she found, too, that she could not talk, per se, but she could project words to him.

"Quite," she agreed. "What is this place?"

"Greek Underworld," he shrugged. "Who knew?"

"Hmm," said Grandmother Winter. That was a surprise. "What are we waiting for?"

"To cross the Styx," he said.

"And what happens after that?"

"I don't know. . . ."

This did not seem the time for further questions. She would wait, she would cross, and then she would set about getting back to her grandson.

She spent her first weeks in the Underworld learning about the way of things. The best way to do that was to be quiet and listen, and that's what she did. She learned about the Immortals and the Dead; she learned about the City and the Plains, about Hades and his Administration, about the absent Queen. She learned there were the official rules and then the way things were really done. And that, of course, was what she was most interested in.

And she began to ask around. "I need something," she would say. "Where do you go when you need something?"

And she learned. She learned there was a guy who could get her some blood to drink. (Strangely, that sounded pretty good to Grandmother Winter, though not what she was looking for.) There was a guy who could sneak her into the City, a guy who could give her a brief power of taste and some wine to boot, a guy who could get her gold, a guy who could smuggle things from the Upperworld (lots of guys like that, actually)—but there was no one who could help her keep an eye on her grandson.

I made a promise to my grandson, she said. I promised I would watch over him. And I always keep my promises.

The City guy, the taste guy, the smuggling guy—none of them knew. This is beyond us, they said. But I can get you a great deal on some Harpy repellent.

Then she met the blood guy. And she told him, "I need something. I need something beyond the City, beyond gold, beyond blood."

"Beyond blood?" he asked carefully.

"Yes, beyond blood."

"You need the Witch," he said quietly.

"The Witch?"

Yes, the Witch. Grandmother Winter needed the Witch. The Witch was a great secret, almost a myth in the Underworld. Some thought she did not exist. The blood guy, though, he had seen her—or so he claimed. The Witch hid in the caves behind the City, wearing a great black cloak made out of night and shadow. She was almost as old as Earth itself, and she looked it—shriveled, wrinkled, haggard. The Witch had great power and was greatly feared. The Witch could grant wishes, impossible wishes, but she was angry and unpredictable. People went in there and they never came back. That was the price you paid for having an impossible wish.

"I will go," said Grandmother Winter.

"You might not come back," the blood man warned.

"I know," she said.

It took quite a while for Grandmother Winter to find the Witch. The blood man had told her to go to the caves beyond the City, but the caves were vast and confusing.

And then, after days of searching, she found a small cave with a small stone door marked with a Greek letter that she could not read. She knocked, and a raspy voice said, "Who has come?"

"My name is Dalitso Winter," Grandmother Winter responded in the soundless way of the Dead. "I have come to see the Witch."

"Enter."

The woman before her was small and bent over and completely wrapped in a black cloak with a black hood. Stark, white, bony hands reached out from black sleeves, strings of white hair escaped from the hood, and Grandmother Winter could just make out a face made entirely of wrinkles, with a long, crooked, Witch-like nose.

"Why have you disturbed me?" the Witch croaked.

"I have worked hard to find you, the great Witch who can grant impossible wishes. I have a grandson. I promised him I would watch over him."

"I see," said the Witch. She sat down at the stone table in front of her and looked up at Grandmother Winter. "Why should I help you?"

So Grandmother Winter told the Witch. She told her about Zachary, about how there was something all closed up, hard and tight inside of him. How the only time he seemed to expand, to live, was in the summers with her. How he was a boy with a good heart who did not know quite how to use it. How she had left him too early, how there was so much more help she wanted to give him. And how she had decided she would come back to him even before she had had a final vision, a portent of great danger.

The Witch nodded slowly, then said, "Here is what I can do for you," and she proceeded to explain.

Grandmother Winter listened carefully and nodded. "I understand. And I accept."

"Now"—the Witch pointed Grandmother Winter's attention to the stone table—"your grandson." The Witch waved her hands over the table, and an image of Zachary appeared. He was sitting in a chair in the living room of his house in London, staring vacantly into space. Grandmother Winter could have burst with the need to reach out to him, to put her hands on him. "But," the Witch continued, waving her hands over the image, "he will not be here for much longer." The picture shifted to reveal an empty chair. "He is going here, with this family. . . ." She waved her hands again, but Grandmother Winter did not need to look at the picture. She knew where they were sending him. It was a good choice.

"Now," the Witch continued, "I must tell you something very important." And she leaned in, taking off her hood.

Her face was just as you'd expect—a hag's face, old and wrinkled and broken, the nose looking as if it had lived one too many lives—but when the Witch shifted, Grandmother Winter saw something quite else. A flash, no more, an image under the surface, of a wholly different face, with great black curls, green eyes, olive skin, and a strange, sad smile.

In shock, Grandmother Winter blurted out, "Queen Persephone!"

The Witch took a step back. She shook her head. "How . . ." She looked around frantically. "You must not tell. If anyone found out—"

"You have my word!"

"You must not tell!" She grabbed Grandmother Winter's hands. "If I am to be down here, at least I can make it easier for others who must also be deprived of the Upperworld. But if the Immortals were to find out . . ."

Grandmother Winter said firmly, "I will not tell."

"All right," the Queen said. "I believe you." She leaned back and smiled. "Now, you must understand what will happen to you. You will not be Dalitso Winter anymore. If I turn you into a sparrow, you will become a sparrow. Dalitso's memories will become the sparrow's memories, as a sparrow would remember. You will not have human intelligence, but"—she raised her hand—"you will have *instinct*." She leaned in and added, "And in your case I believe that instinct will be remarkably strong." She gazed into Grandmother Winter's eyes intently. "If you make this choice, Dalitso Winter will cease to exist. Do you understand?"

"I do."

"Very well. Have you decided what kind of animal you wish to be?"

Grandmother Winter smiled her Grandmother Winter smile and said, "I should like to be a cat."

BESTIARY

Argus

An extremely large monster with a hundred eyes covering his body. He never closes more than half his eyes at once, making him an excellent guard—albeit kind of a creepy one.

Centaurs

Beings with the heads and torsos of men and the bodies of horses. A convivial and erudite lot. Probably best to not try to ride one, though.

Cerberus

The three-headed dog that guards the doors to Hades. Cerberus is said to have a mane made of thousands of small snakes, the paws of a lion, and the tail of a viper, but all that might have been exaggerated a wee bit for effect.

Cyclopes

Big, mean, cave-dwelling monsters with one eye and a taste for human flesh; excellent at metallurgy.

Empusa

A shape-shifting female demon with hair of flames, legs of bronze, and hooved feet; also, a vampire.

Erinyes

Three jet-black female demons with hands made of snakes, the heads of dogs, wings of bats, and really bad breath. They administer punishment in the Underworld.

Gorgons

Hideous female demons with serpents in place of hair, golden wings, stringy beards, and hands with claws. Best not to look them in the eye, unless, of course, you want to be turned into a statue.

Griffins

Beasts with the bodies of lions and the heads, legs, and butts of eagles. Not very nice.

Harpies

Massive creatures with the bodies of vultures and the faces of nasty old women. Mean and very, very stinky.

Hydra

A dragon-size serpent with nine heads. If you cut one head off, two grow back in its place. Better to just keep your distance.